ADVANCE PRAISE

The author carries us through the lifetime of a fascinating Jewish man who used his wonderful hands to survive. They also were filled with romance as he and his wife spent 6 decades together. The reader will look at his own hands and wonder out loud if they have been as energized as those of the hero. I, too, ask myself – how many special traits do my ten fingers possess? Robbins' book offers each of us our own personal answer.

David Geffen is an American-born historian, author and rabbi living in Jerusalem. His writing has appeared in such publications as The Jerusalem Post.

Author Roni Robbins weaves together a historic novel inspired by true events that is a page-turning credit to her literary talents. Her book *Hands of Gold* is a testament to her storytelling ability, a timeless treasure lost in the horrific tragedies of war, with a spirited main character who lived through one challenge after another. Robbins portrays the spirit of a man, though broken, who is memorable as he holds onto life, time and what truly matters most. An amazing book about resilience, worthy of your immediate attention.

Robyn Spizman is a media personality and an award-winning New York Times bestselling author who has written more than 50 books.

"Where are all your great miracles now?" the story begins, in the hoarse, wry, honest voice of the much-travelled, much-aggrieved Sam Fox, a Zelig of a fictional spinoff of the author's grandfather. An Eastern European immigrant, born at the start of the new century – "My birth was not the greatest timing, I know. But who was I to question such a thing?" – he managed to taste, and to suffer, much of what midcentury America had to offer, from the golden age of TV & radio to a mass shooting at a workplace. A natural-born survivor, skipping across borders, changing identities, harboring secrets, Sam always made time to relish moments of happiness, always displaying – even when on the run, even when grieving his loved ones – a tremendous love of life.

Melissa Fay Greene, a two-time National Book Award finalist, is the author of *Praying for Sheetrock* and *The Temple Bombing*.

Based on the lives of her immigrant forebears from Hungary and their American-born children, Roni Robbins has written an absorbing and richly detailed novel about the struggles and triumphs of people who made their way in the promised land of America during the last century. The novel traces the lives of the many members of the Fox family. The characters are vividly drawn and the novel contains many moving stories and episodes. One, in particular, that stands out in the mind of the reviewer involves the journey of Mo Fox to Europe in the wake of the Holocaust to retrieve a family heirloom that represents the title of the novel. Readers interested in learning much about the story of the Jewish immigrant experience in America will find Ms. Robbins' novel a richly rewarding experience.

Sheldon Neuringer is a retired history professor and published author of stories about history and Jewish life, including two novels about Jewish youths growing up in New York. He recently wrote a short story, *For the Love of Yiddish*.

HANDS OF GOLD

ONE MAN'S QUEST TO FIND THE SILVER LINING IN MISFORTUNE

RONI ROBBINS

ISBN 9789493231863 (ebook)

ISBN 9789493231856 (paperback)

ISBN 9789493231870 (hardcover)

Publisher: Amsterdam Publishers, The Netherlands

info@amsterdampublishers.com

Hands of Gold. One Man's Quest To Find The Silver Lining In Misfortune is part of the series New Jewish Fiction

2023 International Book Awards Winner, Fiction Multicultural

2022 American Fiction Awards Finalist, Family Saga

2009 Amazon Breakthrough Novel Award Contest Quarterfinalist, Historical Fiction

CONTENTS

PART 3

Behold, I send an angel before thee, to keep thee by the way, and to bring thee into the place that I have prepared. (Exodus 23:20)

AUTHOR'S NOTE

Although I have tried to be true to historical facts, this book is a work of fiction, and all characters and events described are works of the imagination. A few scenes and personalities may be loosely based on my ancestors' lives, but they have been radically altered to fit within the context of the story.

ACKNOWLEDGMENTS

This book is dedicated to my family, especially my grandparents and my uncle; may they rest in peace. I would like to thank my grandfather, first and foremost, for leaving his life story on cassette tapes, the very loose basis of this novel. Thanks to my aunt, for giving him the tapes and asking that they be made, and my mother, for passing them onto me, knowing how much I would appreciate them, and also, for carefully reviewing each page and offering encouragement.

My uncle, who died last year, deserves recognition for editing an early draft and answering my endless questions about family. Special thanks to two of my cousins, including Sophie's son for his family tree research, for filling in the missing pieces in the book.

My entire family should be recognized for their contributions, including my sister-in-law, who read the first draft. Thanks also to David Holzel, a former editor, for his guidance; Melanie Lasoff Levs, a journalism colleague and friend, for her professional editing services; A. Louise Staman, a published author of historical fiction, may she also rest in peace, who offered encouragement and suggestions for improvement; and Gin Shaw, for help with my genealogy research.

My husband, Ian, deserves much credit for supporting me in my decision to retire from my full-time journalism career for a while to focus on this dream. I have since returned to full-time journalism.

To my children, Seth and Lena, thanks for affording me the time to write while you napped or played or attended school.

───────────

When he died, my grandfather had four children, 11 grandchildren, and eight great-grandchildren. Seven more great-grandchildren have since been born, my children among them. My first-born, Seth, was named in my grandfather's memory. As a result, every day I am reminded of my Grandpa in a physical way, beyond the inspiration for this book.

His progeny include nurses, law enforcement, realtors, investors, salespeople, artists and even a rabbi. We all know that he's watching us proudly from heaven, hand-in-hand with his soulmate. As a testament, their joined tombstones have a simple statement at the bottom: "They live in each of us." They certainly live in my family. Perhaps they'll live in yours too.

1 THE LOOSE ENDS
DECEMBER 1990

Philadelphia

Where are all your great miracles now? Couldn't ya spare just one more? Would it be too much to ask? Really, would it kill ya? Okay, maybe not that last part, considering to whom I'm speaking and the predicament I'm in. The *chutzpah*, I know! Ackh! It is too late for courtesy with the Almighty, and I am too old and frustrated to pretend to care about the consequence.

My words and thoughts are unraveling before me as I sandwich Hannah's weathered hand between my own. She is a sliver of her once meaty frame. I alternatingly stroke and press her hand to my face and lips. This weak hand that once provided me strength, when the tables were turned, is now just a network of blue veins bulging from tissue paper skin. It is still the hand of a mother who might have used it to stroke the heads of our children or bake some sort of sweet *chazerei* for them. Oh, how I missed our one son in particular, the one who didn't live long enough to watch his own children become adults. No longer the caretaker, Hannah is at the mercy of time and circumstance, here, in the care of others.

The single fluorescent lamp above her bed forces our ghostly shadows to the wall behind her, and a machine resembling an accordion expands and deflates with Hannah's every strained wheeze. Along with this flopping sound, I listen to the music of the room hum around me. The faint buzz from the light and heater. The incessant bleep of the monitors, blinking on and off. The churning of leaves and other debris as arctic gusts of a Philly winter raged outside the window.

But here we are. Hannah is an electronic device receiving pulsating currents. Her power source: plastic tubes carrying clear fluids, medicine and nourishment, delaying the inevitable. And I refuse to accept it.

It was at this visit that she gasped out those prophetic words to me. "Meet me in heaven." She squeezed my hand, struggling to relay sensible thoughts. "Tie up loose ends." Another few strained breaths as I warn her to rest. Stubbornly defiant, she persists. "Say goodbye to our family, and then meet me in heaven." After 65 years of marriage, you do as you're told if you know what's good for you.

January 1991, Manor Crest Nursing Care, Philadelphia

In sickness and health. Could have done without so much of the sickness and a little more of the health. Would that have been so terrible? Back at the nursing home where Hannah and I have been living recently, the children come periodically to visit and take me to Hannah at General, where she is recuperating from a broken hip. The rest of the time, I mope around Manor Crest, this "home" for *alter cockers,* like myself, schlepping this decrepit body through its bright, urine-stenched hallways just to have something to do. I nearly always pass a room with its door ajar exposing the occupant in some stage of undress. Was this how I also appeared with layers of limp skin draped over a bowed frame like the branches of a weeping willow?

2

I continued trudging to what was Hannah's room. That is, her room before she fell a little over a week ago.

We hadn't shared a bedroom in quite some time now, what with our unsynchronized snoring habits. Even at our home in Philly we had separate beds. The family decided we were too fragile to stay there on our own anymore, especially Hannah. No one was able to help us as much as we needed it and no one volunteered to take us in. Who could blame them? They had their own busy lives and they didn't live nearby.

As much as we hated to admit, we needed to be here. But now I was away from Hannah and I couldn't stand it. Of course, whenever I asked to see her room at Manor Crest, to feel close to her, between visits to General, the attending nurse escorted me, unlocked the door, and let me in. I sat on the bed, inhaled Hannah's warm, comforting scent from her pillows, the patchwork quilt and the woolen blanket she knitted a lifetime ago.

Maybe it was the trace of potent menthol in the Noxzema that masked her face nightly. Perhaps it was my vague recollection of the White Shoulders she wore in healthier years that I longed to recapture in this now empty room. But I couldn't help to see her face in the mirror, combing her thick, gray hair or applying some pale pink lipstick. She'd have lumbered across this room with legs often swollen from poor circulation. I could hear her voice berating the housekeeping services here. "You can't trust anyone to do a decent job these days," she'd complain. "Not the way I like it." Then she'd reorganize and refold and remake and restore, shaking her head in disapproval and frustration as she labored. It was her way and I didn't question it.

I appreciated her strong will. She knew how she wanted it and the care with which she cleaned and prepared was not to be challenged by me or anyone else. Why bother? I let her bother herself with certain tasks, despite my concern that she was working herself up for nothing. To her, it was worth the effort.

We old guys don't live as long. It's a scientific fact. So I was a bit of a big *makher* and a novelty of sorts to the old women and the nurses who fawned over me. I needed the attention of women like a hole in the head, but at least I was aware of what was going on. Most of them here were *meshuga*, their minds gone. Thank God I had most of my faculties. I played cards with those who could manage. I read the daily paper, a Jewish book here or there, perhaps a gameshow on T.V. Still, it was a slow, gradual walk here. All of us just waiting as if for a dinner reservation.

Clearly, we had reached the end. I couldn't take care of her at home and the children knew that I wanted to be with her. So they moved us here. For a change, it wasn't my health as it had been so many years ago. All in all, I guess I wasn't doing too badly. Granted, I had nearly died several times in my life. At least I was alive now. Living... Ha! If you could even call it that.

What am I to do now? Surely, others have asked the same question at this stage.

My youngest, Eliza, had an idea that she shared with me during a recent visit. At 40, Eliza has long been kept close to us. She lives about an hour away and our care has fallen more on her than the others. But she doesn't seem to mind, even though she's a single mom on a limited income, as a poorly paid secretary for a real estate company. When she makes suggestions, we tend to listen because we know that she has our best interests at heart. "It might be a good therapy for you if you record something for the family to leave behind," she told me, searching for the right words. "So that we could still hear your voice, for when the time came, you know? It might help take your mind off the present, don't you think?" She handed me a new Panasonic tape recorder similar to the ones I used in the past to listen to cantorial concerts. How I love Jewish music.

4

But at this point, I can't fathom anything releasing me from these convulsive sob-till-I'm-sick episodes. I felt this sock-in-the-*kishkes* helplessness being separated from Hannah, not knowing what the future holds for us. Okay, so maybe it wasn't such a *cockamamie* idea. Isn't that what everyone wants anyway? To be remembered after they're gone, for making a difference? Like much else was happening in this good-for-nothin' wasteland. Wait for the next meal? With the dreck they feed us? Look for some *shmendricks* with half a brain to play checkers with? Then I'll have to listen to their senseless *kibitzing* and *kvetching*. So why not do this for the *kinderlach*? Might even play tricks on the nurses who come to check on me. They'll think I'm talking to myself.

Now where to begin with this taping for Eliza? I was a decent man, I suppose. Had a few adventures, more than my share of challenges. Loved and was loved. Worked hard for my family. Could have even been considered a hero for a short spell. That and a nickel might have bought some day-old bread at one time. But there was more. Certain details from our early lives that Hannah and I, together, finally unleashed from our guilt-ridden vaults and agreed, just days earlier at the hospital, that I should share with the children.

For years, I looked for opportunities to purge this ravaging tapeworm within me, but every time I got close, I lacked the nerve to continue. Hannah was much better at letting sleeping dogs lie. Of course, I had ceremoniously tossed my sins off riverbanks during the high holidays, breadcrumbs dissolving into fish food. That was never enough. This little recording project could just be what the doctor ordered. Might not even have to face accusing eyes this way. It was enough to confront Hannah's.

Still, there wasn't much time left, and the children deserved to know the truth. That is, what I remembered with the distortions that come from selective memory loss. So I pushed the recording buttons on the Panasonic and drew a deep breath.

PART 1

1 POLITICAL HOT POTATO
SEPTEMBER 1905

Hungary

Soon after the launch of a new century and the tail end of the Russo-Japanese War, my *shmutzy tukhes* chose to greet an ever-restless Europe. My birth was not at the greatest timing, I know. But who was I to question such a thing? Even if the intensifying drum roll of my opening number was overshadowed by the rat-a-tat-tats of gunfire, at least in the anxious minds of relatives preoccupied with war. Plus, I was yet another *moyl* to feed in an already crowded lineup of siblings, so my whole entrance into the world was more like a *déjà vu* than a cause for the kind of *kvelling* one might garner if they were, say, the first, second or even the third child. But the ninth?

If I had to hear another story about my untimely entrance, so help me. It seems some *nudniks* masquerading as family have nothing better to do than to remind you how tough things were back when they were young, as if by informing you, you'll somehow remember being so hungry you ate bugs or grass or something. I don't think I did, by the way. Apparently, the news of my birth was passed around the Jacovo shtetl, accompanied by the latest rumors of approaching violence caused by Russian defeats in the Far East.

"Did ya know Motke and Etta had another one?"

"Don't they think four is enough?"

"Four? What four? The first wife had four too before she died. May she rest in peace. Don't you remember?"

"Oh, and to bring another child into this world with the way everyone is fighting. *Vey iz mir.*" (Note: Don't forget the triple dose of fake spit to ward off the evil eye.)

I don't remember much of my early years. We had a big family, as I had mentioned. We worked together on the farm, eating the food we gathered, and we spent a lot of time praying. My father and older brothers taught me how to plant and pick vegetables and how to speak Yiddish and Hebrew. What we didn't sell, my mother and sisters cooked for us in our cramped home. We didn't have much, but we enjoyed our food and we thanked God for the blessings. I think I was happy being surrounded by family and food and Judaism.

But there was always this fear that bubbled around us. People were afraid and I felt that fear. It all stemmed from the constant wars. The Russians liked to fight, I think. They were back in 1914, when I was nine, after their embarrassing loss to the Japanese. This time, they were drawn into war by our very own neighbor assassins, the Serbs, fresh from slaughtering our country's heir to the throne, Franz Ferdinand. A shame, too, because he had promised to listen to grievances from peasants like us, and grant greater freedom to all ethnic minority groups, maybe even the Jews.

My family had grown accustomed to their hopes of profiting from farming and being treated equal to the goyim. Being dashed by the war, their country and their lives being thrown into turmoil, it wasn't fair that we had to work so hard and this fighting, we had nothing to do with, would get in the way.

In this case, Germany came to Austria-Hungary's defense against the Russians and Serbs and that's what kicked off the Great War, otherwise known as World War One or my personal favorite, the overly optimistic, War to End All Wars. Yeah, right. To think it all started in our backyard, well, not literally. In Jacovo, we may not have been directly impacted, but we certainly felt like we had taken some deep wallops to the *kishkes*. We farmers couldn't sell our vegetables because people were preoccupied by war. People stayed closer to home instead of traveling to the market and older boys were called off to fight. Our lives had been hard before, but with war, they were even more so.

I remember Hungarian school had already started in Jacovo at that time, but was interrupted abruptly. "By order of the Hungarian Ministry of Education, all the nation's schools will cease instruction, effective immediately." Our teacher, Mr. Varga, a very strict man with graying hair that stood up on his head like a toothbrush, read solemnly from a sheet of paper, his gold-rimmed glasses perched near the tip of his nose. "Our school is closed. You may go home now. God be with you." With that, he collected his books from his desk, secured them in his briefcase, and left the room without further explanation.

The stunned students stared at each other in dazed disbelief. We sat, bolted to our seats, immobile for a few minutes before we realized we were free. My greatest wish had been granted, although I never imagined it would really happen, and certainly not in this way. We were truly being sent home. There is a God. I didn't have to wait for others to respond. I grabbed my tattered wool coat, threadbare scarf and gloves, and charged into the meadow outside the school. Just a few months ago, this patch was dotted with violets, where now I plow through a carpet of damp leaves, some still making their slow descent from shivering oaks, elms and black poplar, as fall bows to winter's long, gray reign. As I looked back, the other students were streaming out behind me. Took them long enough to catch on, *shlemiels*. I didn't have many friends at school; only the Jewish ones we saw at *shul* or at events in the shtetl. With so many brothers and sisters, I really didn't need friends. They were my best friends.

Having more time on my hands before Hebrew school and after-school chores, my plan was to head out to see what I could catch. Approaching home, the familiar fumes of fried onions assaulted my nostrils. Mama was hunched over the stove like always, the *schmaltz* sputtering in the pan, as I entered the room. She spun around, startled. "*Gottenyu*, Shimshon. You scared me half to death." She removed the pan from the burner and sat down to regain composure. "*Vos is dos?* What is this? What happened? Why aren't you in school? Something wrong? You don't feel well, bubelah? Tell me. Oy, I don't have enough *tsuris*. You want this should be my last day on this earth, you coming upon me like that?"

"No more school, Mama. We were sent home. I'm sorry. I didn't mean to frighten you."

"You think I was born yesterday, Shimshon? You tell me this? When does school ever let out just like that? Always with the head in the clouds, *luftmesch*. How can you expect to get anywhere in life like that? You should be more like your brother, Shlomo, may God protect him."

Shlomo was 18 and working as a shoemaker in the closest city, sending home money, and trying to avoid having to serve. His separation from the family was a source of constant fear for my parents, although I sort of thought it might be neat to serve in the army.

As she pretended to spit on the floor, I seized my cue. She could go on for days like that, I'm convinced. Just wind her up and watch her spurt. "Mama, it's true. I promise I wouldn't make something like that up. I think it has something to do with the fighting you think I don't know about, but I do."

My younger sister and brothers, who were in different classes, returned home shortly afterwards with similar stories. "Most of the teachers had to report to the army or the navy, Mama. Some of the students were crying when they left the school. It was so very sad," my youngest sister, Mina, reported in great detail about the aftermath of the teachers' departure. My jubilation over the news was her disappointment. She loved school. Funny, about perspectives, how two people could see things so differently. But then again, she was only six, so her classes were super easy and mine were hard. It didn't matter. She had Mama's attention, like usual, being the baby of the family.

At this point, the neighbors came over to compare notes. They, too, were baffled by their children's versions of what had transpired and wanted to see if we had the same experience. Regardless of the situation, the elders decided that we still had to take care of our chores and go to Hebrew school. Our Jewish education stopped for nothing, so it seems. There weren't many Hebrew teachers around either, with the best of them off fighting. Those left behind for whatever medical reason or having connections in high places, knew practically *bupkes* about Judaism, but they tried to teach us anyway because enough parents felt like mine about our Jewish studies. It didn't matter to me. How much can you learn when you're doodling about bombing and gunfire and daydreaming about bloody enemy soldiers with their guts and heads blown to bits? In my doodles, I was the big-muscled soldier saving Jewish children, killing the bad guys through my amazing strength. My mind was on the battlefield, not in the books. And the teachers reminded me of that whenever they had the chance. A swift rap on the knuckles with a long stick kept aside their desks for such occasions usually did the trick, and it's probably what led to a nice case of arthritis later on. The least of my troubles, I can tell you.

Many of my siblings – 12 brothers and sisters – were still living at home with me. We learned from others in the town what was going on at the front. It even got a little closer when, for a few months in early 1915, the Russians waged an offensive in the Carpathian Mountains, standing guard in the distance. On very silent nights, I might have felt the faintest of vibrations from distant detonations. I might have seen flashes of mortar along the horizon. But then, again, what I felt and saw could have easily been a rumbling of thunder, a shooting star, my imagination playing tricks. If there was ever an emergency, though, we'd be ready. We certainly had enough drills in school, cowering under our desks in the fetal position, practicing how to file orderly to the shelter below the Hebrew school, should the need arise. It was stocked, mostly with pickled vegetables and bedding, so I certainly had hoped we didn't have to go there because who'd want to live off jars of sour green tomatoes. Not to mention sleeping on the cold cellar floor. But I guess it beats the alternative, the depictions in my classroom doodling.

While we were bracing for the worst, Shlomo, my oldest brother, was a five-hour train ride away in the big metropolis, Budapest, with its wide streets, tall buildings and streetcars. There, he could hide from the Austro-Hungarian army, which now occupied the entire area. Budapest had always been particularly tolerant of Jews and Shlomo had heard there were good jobs in the city. He went from shop to shop asking if anyone needed help. An aging cobbler was looking for a younger set of eyes to assist him. The pay was halfway decent and it beat struggling on the farm. People could live without vegetables, but not without good footwear. Shlomo actually became a sort of designer of men's shoes when not patching holes and repairing worn soles.

Papa wasn't as lucky to avoid the army. Evading duty was common – my brother, a case in point – so tighter security was necessary. Peasants, like my father, couldn't leave their families and didn't have anything to bribe their way out of service. They were required to help the town prepare for the possibility of the Russians coming. If the army needed you, they took you, with force, if necessary. As a conscripted private, Papa was led away with other men from the shtetl, flanked by armed soldiers in the morning and escorted back at night to ensure that he fulfilled his compulsory service to the government.

"They can make your life miserable, Etta," he told my mother a few days after we were released from school. "We have to cooperate or they'll start poking around about Shlomo or go after the others. Please Etta. Stop worrying. It'll be okay. I promise you." It did not ebb the flow of tears as we watched him being practically pulled from our safe haven to military peril.

Close to several borders, the area was a political hot potato. It changed hands so many times, from monarchy to communism, and later to democracy. Even had a Jewish ruler one time, Bela Kun. Interesting, considering what would happen to the Jews. With each subsequent war, foreign powers bit off a part of our former homeland. Jacovo was actually part of Slovakia when my older siblings were born there, Hungary when I came along, and Czechoslovakia in my teens. It's in the Ukraine now. But I digress.

Nothing is as it was. For starters, families aren't as dependent on each other as we were. The average family in Jacovo at that time had six to seven children, but there were a few families with ten to twelve members. We topped that with thirteen children – seven boys, six girls – from the two mothers. My father, Mordechai Fox, married my mother, Etta, after his first wife, Fanny, died during childbirth. (The child survived, by the way). The two women were sisters, so I guess you could say some of my siblings were also my cousins. How 'bout them apples? Don't hear about that every day, do ya?

It was a running joke in the family that has a track record for marrying among its own. Keep it all in the family, so to speak. I guess it's better than having to search far and wide for a spouse. It happened more than you'd think, back then, and it always kind of reminded me of the Bible story I learned as a child, of Jacob and his wives, having to marry the older sister before earning the younger.

Okay, my parents' love-triangle was a little different. My father and Fanny grew up in houses across from each other and were the same age, so they were friends before it developed into more. Of course, he came to love her younger sister, Etta, but it began mostly as a responsibility for the children than the kind of bond he had with Fanny. Still, thousands of years after Jacob, and my aunt's unfortunate passing, I'm here to testify that some traditions live on.

Mordechai and Etta had their own children, of which I, Shimshon Tzvi Fox, the best-looking of the bunch, I might add, was the fifth. When the two families united, though, I was pushed down the lineup to number nine. With so many siblings, one can understand how I might feel squished in the middle, knowing I had to be responsible for the younger ones, and yet, still trying to imitate my older brothers and sisters. Four of them had already left for America with the money they had earned and the connections they had made there. Hopefully they paved the way for me and the others to follow when they could send word it was safe and fund our travels. It was my ultimate goal, to get out of this frightful place. But it definitely didn't look possible at this moment.

2 FATED TO FARM

Even with brothers and sisters overseas, our home continually hummed with voices and activity. Mama surely had a difficult job, just keeping up with the cooking and laundry for the six of us left at home. Something has to give, she would say. It was the housework. While she was militant about our eating, behavior and clothing, the house wasn't always that clean. Of course, my older sisters tried to help, but they didn't always live up to her high expectations, so she ended up taking on most of the responsibility herself.

"If I had time to fix up this place..." she'd start. "How would anything else get done? Who would care for you? Who would mend your clothes? Who would cook your meals?" No one argued, she was overworked. Nonetheless, when one of us got sick, nearly everyone else did too because we lived in such a tight space and it wasn't always so clean, she had to nurse us. Nothing ever too serious. Thank God. Not then, anyway.

We didn't even own our home. We paid rent like most of our neighbors. The houses were mostly wood with some stone and cement or something that looked like brick, made from mud and straw. Just like in the classic Three Little Pigs fairy tale, although don't mention pigs around my family. Pigs aren't kosher.

In larger families, two to three people shared a single bed with up to eight in a room. I shared a bed with my brothers, mostly Hermie and Hershel. Some families kept their cows inside the house. Sure, we were *shvitzing* in the summer, but oh so awfully cozy when winter raged and ravaged outside. And when I say cold, I mean it, if you consider constant snow in temperatures hovering around freezing for days on end, cold. With only two rooms, there wasn't much to heat. There was an entrance hall, what one might call a foyer, and a living room, which doubled as a kitchen, bedroom or dining room. Dirt courtyards separated our home from the others, wide enough for two wagons to pass each other without touching. People drove in horse-and-wagons or rode bicycles.

Mostly everyone we knew were farmers. My father learned the trade from his father, *l'dor v'dor*, from generation to generation, except for Shlomo, sent away to Budapest and the older siblings who got away. It did, however, seem very unfair to me that my like-it-or-not destiny was pre-determined by family lineage and I had no escape at this point. What other choice did I have, considering my expected loyalty to my family and their attempts to keep up with the intense competition among Jewish farmers in Jacovo?

The area lent itself to farming, no doubt, it being a sort of valley with natural irrigation, courtesy of the Danube River, or Duna, as we called it, and offshoots spilling through the mountains, the Tisza being the largest to our west. On occasion, I was known to ditch my chores of tending the vegetables and milking the cows. The milking wasn't all that bad, I guess, and could become sort of a rhythm and I enjoyed making that kind of music. But if I found an opportunity, I'd sneak off from my siblings, strip half-naked to splash into the clear blue water known for its therapeutic qualities. Here, I'd float on my back, inhaling the cool mist, mingled with wet moss and dewy grass, and listen to the greenfinch's loud, rapid twitter. I knew to make it quick before my siblings tattled and Mama sent someone to fetch me for the dreaded verbal lashing on the evils of laziness (my brief bliss was worth the reprimand) or the farmers arrived, leading the animals there to graze in the shade of the adjoining forest. After his brief episode with the army, which ended when they realized he was too old to be of much use, Papa would be among those farmers. He started out working our neighbor's land while tending a little garden behind our home that grew over time to rival any of his competitors.

Ours was a big yard with plenty of trees, fruits and a proud assortment of vegetables. My father claimed to have the best method around for straight-as-rails string beans and cucumbers. He taught me everything I know. "Never let them grow on the ground," he'd instruct. He knew so much about vegetables. The vines of those vegetables would either be attached to long, thin sticks or to a fence. "See how everything hangs perfectly? There's nothing interfering with their growth, my son. This is the only way to do it. If the vines are lying on the ground and they hit a pebble, they push the pebble and bend and turn around it until they become round, thick and heavy and then what do you have? *Gornisht!*"

As soon as he deemed me strong enough – oh, how I longed to prove myself to him – he took me with him to the forest to gather the sticks he needed for the vegetables. I knew he did this with my older brothers and I was proud he was finally taking me.

"You think you can carry ten or 15, Shimshon?" I nodded, anxiously. "Sure, that will be good enough. They're light; they're thin. You can do that. But they have to be very long, as long as you can find them. Keep looking for the long, thin ones."

He chopped down small, young trees for the limbs and cleaned off the leaves. Then he made big bundles with maybe 50 sticks and figured I'd be able to carry a bundle of them instead. It must have been a six-mile walk from the forest to our town. On the way home, we greeted our neighbors. One older man whose grandson was my age, hobbled along with a cane, but stopped to point it at our bundle. "You must be growing beans again, Motke, *nu?*"

"Beans, potatoes, tomatoes, green peppers, yellow peppers, cucumbers..." He would have gone on further with his list of planting successes had he not been interrupted by the frantic hoots of a woman flagging us from a distance down the path. "Motke! Motke! Come quick, Motke!" She waved us toward her. "Your wife gave birth to a boy... Hurry Motke! Hurry!"

Since my aunt had died, birth arrived with the prospect of death. My father dropped his bundle.

"Just leave it all. We'll get it later," he yelled. His face went white. You could hear the anxiety. My heart began pumping harder. He tossed his pile in the back of a nearby house and I did the same and we raced toward home.

When I got there, moments after him, gasping for breath, I found my mother as peaceful as I've ever seen her. Only hours before she was ripe with child, her typical angry self, but now she was sedate. "Mama, you okay? Mama. Are you alive? Is the baby okay?"

"Shimshon, bubelah, everything's fine. Calm down. Meet your brother, Mori."

I eyed the puffy mass. Looked like a hairless baby monkey to me, same as the others I'd seen newly delivered with everyone making a fuss over. Okay, it's a miracle, I get it. But I only cared that Mama was all right. For the number of times I wished her harm for her nagging and then asked God's forgiveness moments afterwards, I was plagued by guilt that my inner evil would merit her demise. Not this time. *Whoa... close.*

The entire neighborhood knows about a birth within hours, trickling through with cakes, *schnapps*, the *gantse megillah*, to celebrate Jews and gentiles alike. With about 2,000 families, our town may have been a bit larger than others in the area. The Jews only made up about five percent or 100 families in Jacovo. Still, we were generally very friendly with the goyim, greeting them by name and sharing in each other's *simchas*. Maybe our town was different that way. We certainly heard of the violence against Jews in other parts of Europe and even Hungary, although we really had no idea what had occurred. As Jews, we were used to unfair treatment. "This too would pass", my parents would say.

As history would prove, our freedom had a short life. But at this time, in this place, the goyim let us be and saw us as part of their community, as they should. They had their place of worship and we had ours. So *nu*? What could be so bad?

3 ONE'S FAIR SHARE

Family life continued to be the center of the Jewish world, mine included. All my mother's brothers and sisters had at least five children, and we all lived within ten miles of each other, not like today with everyone scattered so far away... Oy, the sadness this brings.

One Shabbos, an aunt who lived on the outskirts of town invited me to dinner. My brother, Hershel, had to accompany me there on horseback on Friday afternoon and then take my horse home. I knew they were poor, but my brother said not as poor as us. Everything we had come from like the farm, was made from scratch, or could be bought or bartered for next to nothing. I guess we were among the poorest because of our big family. Maybe that's why I kept to myself, so that I wouldn't have to feel bad about what my classmates had and I didn't.

I arrived in time to attend *shul* and later to return to a home filled with the sweet warm smell of fresh-baked *challah* and cake, mingled with the acrid stench of onions and garlic, and my stomach moaned with anticipation. We sat down to soup along with chicken and gefilte fish. I'd call them meager servings, very, very small portions, like everyone at the table – all ten of us – had a ration. "That's what we have and that's what you eat," is how my mother would put it.

I wasn't usually a big eater, but everything tasted so luscious, worlds apart from the way my mother prepared the same dishes. The kugel, my ration of the slither-down-your-tongue, buttery smooth noodle casserole, is what I recall the most. It was so wonderful that I forgot where I was. There's another piece just sitting there on a plate in the center of the table, taunting me. What do you think I do? I take it, I didn't ask questions. My aunt was getting more dishes. When she returned, she blew up. "Who ate that last piece of kugel?" My cousins were quiet. No one tried to defend me, as bad as my siblings and classmates might be. Some of my cousins were around my age and went to school with me.

"I did," I mumbled, my head hung in regret.

The table was quiet, my cousins looking at their own plates.

"Did you not have *one* piece of kugel?" My aunt fumed.

"Yes," I confessed, timidly.

"You ate up someone else's piece of kugel?"

The rest of the meal everyone ate without conversation, only what was put on their plate, of course. My aunt was stingy with my dessert. I could see her giving more honey cake to her children than me for dessert.

I don't have to tell you the embarrassment when I left. Understandably, I never went back there to eat. I'd visit, but I never ate. Whether she remembered it or not, I don't know, but I certainly did. Every time I ate kugel after that, I'd savor every bite as if it was my last.

Nothing went to waste in our house. Some of us would hold our breath when chicken was served to see which of us would earn the favored *pupick*, the chicken's belly button. It was so chewy and thick. When it came to the last one to be served, he or she got a *feesela*, a foot, a *fleegl*, wing, *gogl*, neck – dreck you'd throw away today. Mama would alter who was the last to be served.

If anyone dared *kvetch* at our table, "You gave Papa so much," you'd receive a swift *zets* to the top of the head.

"Who do you think pays for the food you eat?" Mama said. Such was the school of hard knocks – practical education about living, working and supporting a family. And then there's the formal classroom kind. First, there was Hebrew school and a year or so later, we started learning Hungarian. Add Hebrew and Hungarian with Yiddish and you've got a lot of mixed-up babble in my home. Goes right along with the *meshuge* schedule I was keeping. Four or five o'clock in the morning, me and my siblings would get up and do chores: milk the cows, gather the eggs, feed the chickens, an hour later, go to Hebrew school, come home at 7:30 for a quick breakfast and off to Hungarian school by 8:30. Phew! It wears me out now just thinking about it.

At the top of Mama's long list of expectations was receiving a good education, considering she never had one. Girls just didn't go to school in her generation. (My sisters did.) She didn't even know how to read or write. If we didn't study enough, she'd scream at my father, as if it was his fault. "Make them learn, Motke. They are going to grow up like 'goys.'" By that, she didn't mean we would literally become gentiles, just not well-educated Jews.

I wasn't interested in learning in my youth, but I don't know of too many kids who were. My father took me to *cheder*, Hebrew school, small interior rooms in the synagogue with no windows and no air, and would hand me off to the rabbi saying, "Here is my son. Teach him. If he doesn't know something, keep him here all day and all night if you have to."

In case that wasn't enough pressure on the rabbi and me, my father would check up on us. Every Sunday, he came to Hebrew school and asked the rabbi, a jittery old man with little hair, a slumped frame, and bad breath, "How do you teach my son? He doesn't seem to know much more than last week."

"He doesn't want to learn!" said the rabbi, his voice breaking as he bellowed the words.

To that, my father pinched my ear and hung onto it while they both yelled at me. If I concentrate, I can still feel the pain in my lobe. It's not something you easily forget. Several ear torture sessions, along with knuckle smashing over the years, and you straighten out, pay more attention hoping not to be permanently deformed. In hindsight what it is, I wish I had learned more. Plus, I would have made Mama and Papa happier, I suppose. But who knew such things then, with all the chores and responsibilities of a big family on a farm. My siblings didn't seem to struggle as much. They did better in school than me, as a result. But I was tired and frustrated and angry, at what and who I don't exactly know, mostly my predicament. I could hardly think straight, not getting to sleep before midnight. It was understood that everyone had a job to do and was expected to pitch in. That's how we managed to scratch by, by the skin of our teeth.

The point is that back then we didn't have much. Our biggest extravagance might be traveling to Munkach, the closest big city about 15 kilometers, a little less than ten miles away. Munkach probably had more Jews than any other big city in Hungary at the time. There were enough Jews there to support a Yiddish theater with all of its popular musicals, comedies, satires and dramas. If there was a production we heard about, Papa worked overtime in the fields to pay for his children to see it, because he and Mama saw it as a way to expand our education. We loved these getaways and learned to love the theater, anything involving the arts, really. We traveled with a group of children our age – maybe 8 to 12 years old – escorted by one of the fathers or older brothers. I was just happy having the break from school and fieldwork for a change. I was sort of selfish that way, I guess, considering how much my parents sacrificed for me to have the experience.

There was also our safety in the big city to take into account. Mama was tenser than usual as she and Papa saw me off: "*Gey gezunt.*" Go in health, Mama practically moaned, through her tears, with my father instinctively offering a comforting embrace. She was always upset when any of us left. Maybe she thought we wouldn't return or would decide to stay in the city, which was certainly enticing. But I'd never let on to her about that. "He'll be fine, Etta," he would say. Then to me, he'd give me a bear hug so tight I sensed our ribs colliding. "We pray for your speedy and safe return, my son."

And I was off. Admittedly, I was a little nervous, too, as I watched their waves turn into blurs, their figures recede further and further into the distance, as the wagon headed for the station. On the train ride to the city, I saw vegetable fields give way to rows of towers and cobblestone streets and sidewalks, where workers rush and push and speak as fast and loudly as they move. A world apart from my sedated farm life, I was captivated by this whirlwind of adrenaline that raced through my veins as we navigated our way through the city. These trips, these small tests of independence, gave me the courage I would later need to venture from Jacovo.

4 REB HASKEL

I was destined to be a cantor. That's how Mama saw it. She didn't just want me to be exposed to the arts, literature, theater, music. I should attend *yeshiva*, where serious Jewish scholars study. Okay, maybe I had a pleasant voice. And Mama, for all her faults, encouraged me. She knew I wasn't going to be a serious Jewish student if there wasn't music involved.

As a family, we typically sang *zmiros*, songs from the Hebrew books, when returning from *shul* every Shabbos. We'd get rolling so fast sometimes, skipping and slurring our words, until they were hardly recognizable. The resulting fits of laughter undoubtedly would be ended with Mama's conclusion that we were all *meshuga*. "*Zol zein!* Enough *meshugas*."

"Send him to singing school," Mama pestered my father. "Let him learn to be a *chazzan*."

"Who needs a *chazzan*? Let him sing to the chickens, to the cows. They like it too. They'll listen."

But I knew they were proud of my musical abilities and it made me proud and I certainly enjoyed showing off to my siblings, who may have been smarter than me in school but knew they didn't have as nice a voice. They even told me so, a little jealously. I must have inherited my musical skills from my Zayde Haskel. My mother's parents died before I was born, but my father's were still alive then. Zayde Haskel was a small man, only 5-foot-6, but with a muscular build from hauling heavy crates of fruits and vegetables from the fields. His full gray beard made him appear so much like a rabbi that the townspeople called him Reb Haskel and even paid for his advice. While he wasn't pretending to be a rabbi, he spent most of his time studying in the synagogue.

We'd sit outside his home after dinner under an impressive birch at least once a week at that time, and he'd spread out his Bible or other Jewish books at our feet. I'm not exactly sure why he even brought them along, frankly, because he seemed to know their contents by heart as he instructed me on the prophets and their relationships with God, their tests of faith. At certain points, I couldn't tell if they were stories he had heard or even made up to impart some lesson about trust or courage, hope or survival. Either way, I enjoyed these discussions.

Aside from his magical stories, he sang me lullabies at night when I was supposed to be asleep, even if he didn't know that's what they were. I'd listen to his deep voice gently stroking the air like the bow of a violin across its strings.

In the kitchen, Bubbie set a pitcher of tea in front of him every night announcing it was ready and he sat there after everyone went to bed, singing, learning, studying. In between the songs, I could hear him pour a *glezel tay,* the spoon clanging against the side of the cup as he stirred in his honey. He'd blow, sip and return the cup to its saucer with another clink. The singing would resume, his voice resounding against the walls. I fell asleep with those melodies. They're ingrained so deep in this no-good brain of mine now, that sometimes, when I forget where I am, I dare to think I'm young again in the care of my Bubbie and Zayde. It's got to be this damn dementia the nurses talk about when they don't think anyone's listening. *Some of us still have working hearing aids, ya know!* Whatever ya call it, it gives you this *déjà vu* feeling. I've been here before. I've done this before. Like when I accompanied Zayde to *shul*, he'd let me play with the thin weaved fringes hanging from the edges of his prayer shawl as he and the men around us bobbed with their mumbled prayers. I'd swirl the soft fringes around my fingers and he'd hand me a peppermint or other candy, undisturbed by my subsequent challenge to muffle the removal of its paper wrapping in an otherwise tranquil sanctuary. Glancing at me, between prayers, he'd wink or wrap his tallis-draped arm around my shoulder. It was as if no one else existed, just him and me. I don't think he spent time like this with my siblings or cousins. If he did, I didn't know about it. In my mind, I was the special one.

One bright spot in old age is there's more time for studies and less expectation that you'll contribute anything. For Papa, there was no such reprieve. Townspeople called him a *soykher*, a shrewd businessman, a wheeler and dealer with brains and chutzpah. As I got a few years older, maybe I was eleven then, he bought horses, cattle, and chicken, drove the animals to the market, and made a profit. And that's how we survived. We needed clothes; we had a big family. In the spring and sometimes, the summer, he went to town to buy oxen and other livestock. My mother didn't think I was old enough for the trip.

"You can't take him. He's too young." She always seemed to treat me like I was too young. I was the fourth youngest, but there was a large distance between me and my older siblings – five years to my next older sister, Sasha, and 11 years to my next older brother, Saul, so I guess that made sense to her. Not to me.

"It's time for him to go, to learn some responsibility, to be a man," he argued. When my father made up his mind, she didn't even try to reason with him. With his conspicuous red hair, he literally had a hot head, my mother liked to point out. In my mind, his muscular body could rival that of the cattle he bought and sold. Even those mammoth, white Hungarian ones with their fierce white horns. He usually hired someone to help him drive two or three pairs of oxen. But this time, he just didn't want to lose the profit.

"Shimshon, you stay in the front and lead them and I'll be in back to drive them." I was so glad for this time, again, to prove myself to my father and my family. It was a new adventure. I always enjoyed spending time with my father, learning from him how to be a man.

Papa taught me some useful business principles that day, namely, coaxing is better than pulling an uncooperative creature, although if you twist their tail, they're more likely to respond. And walking too close to risky situations will leave you reeling. He looped a rope around the necks of the pair of oxen we were taking to market. "They'll pick you up on their horns and you won't know what hit you." To be sure, I stayed at least six feet in front of them.

It was Sunday. We drove them 16 kilometers. It took us six hours to get to the city, almost the entire day. Where do you stay overnight in a city when you've got two big oxen to care for? You certainly can't go to a hotel. The only place we could go was directly to the city market, where there were stables you can rent for the night, and they'll sell you feed for your animals. Humans have to get their own, so Papa left me to watch the oxen – and he brought us back a modest vegetable stew from a small inn. We put our coats down on the floor, spread a bed of hay near the cattle, and that's where we slept, or tried to.

Still alive and kicking, although groggy the next morning, we joined the assembled livestock sellers trying to convince shoppers why their animals were superior to those in the next booth. We probably had like a dozen buyers – butchers, other farmers, even horn collectors – none of whom wanted to give us the price. Papa wasn't a bargaining man. "You don't give me the price; you don't get the cattle. Simple as that."

The passing hours softened his stance. About 2 o'clock, Papa had held out as long as he could. Good thing too, 'cause I was getting nervous we'd lose the deal. I just stood by and took it all in, watching my father in action. It was all very exciting.

Papa was prepared to settle for less when a farmer made his way to where my father was dickering with his best offer. "They're exactly what I need. I've been looking for just such a pair to plow my fields for months."

"See son. Hold out, and the right one will come along. Patience. Nothing good ever comes from acting too rashly." It was a great lesson I would long remember.

Feeling like the rich must feel, we bought some basics – sugar, flour, salt – and then practically skipped around shops before settling on a little *tchotchke,* a music box, for everyone in the family to share. Then we headed home. How we planned to walk all the way with all those items, who knew? But, again, the good Lord delivers. A Jewish man in a wagon offered us a ride. The thing is, his wagon was drawn by a horse that looked like it was ready to keel over, but the man assured us that he was strong as an ox. The horse, that is.

"Funny you should mention oxen," Papa said as he hoisted me onto the raised seat aside the man. "Would you believe..."

Two young men came from nowhere and started hitting the horse with a long stick. We didn't even have time to react before they ran away as quickly as they had appeared. The horse jumped and got loose from the wagon and ran away, leaving all three of us stranded in the grounded wagon. We weren't hurt, but we had to walk the rest of the way while the man who had offered us a ride scampered off to find his runaway horse, rejecting our pleas to help him.

My father didn't say anything about the incident on our walk, but when we got home, he told my mother and she appeared to understand what it all meant. *I didn't. What did these strangers have against that horse? Were they just having fun, or did they have something against us or the nice man who gave us a ride?*

Mama was frantic, hugging and kissing us, crying and raving about how lucky we were. My father assured her that we were fine, and when it seemed she had exhausted herself with her own anxiety, she calmed down. Her attention shifted to our packages and a militant interrogation ensued into why we bought frivolities when we needed food and clothing.

"She needs something to *ferdray* about," my father would tell us. "Let it be. This too will pass."

The next day, Papa went to the police. He told an officer what had happened. "You go home; we'll take care of it." The officer chuckled, whispered something under his breath, something about Jews, and then returned to his paperwork. My father must have heard it too, because he was incensed. "*When* will you take care of it?"

"As soon as I finish up these other cases I'm working on. It's okay. Go home."

"No. No. *I'm* going to take care of it."

Hearing my father's raised voice, some of the other officers assured Papa his story would be checked. He agreed to leave it alone, but in the meantime, he asked around about our attackers. They were brothers who worked in town in their father's meat market. They weren't Jewish.

Papa broke into their house and ruined it, at least that's what I heard. He smashed some items and damaged their wagon, all while threatening, "You are not going to touch anybody any more. You keep your distance from now on or you'll be sorry!"

Whether he found them in the house or not, I don't know. Their parents apparently weren't around at the time. He was just trying to protect me, he said. I was on the wagon and he was afraid that I could have been hurt if the horse had flipped the wagon over. He couldn't let them get away with it.

"They could have killed you," my mother ranted when she heard what he had done. "They could have rounded up 20 people to go after you for what you did. Ever thought about that?"

We heard that the police questioned the boys' family, but no one came for Papa. I assumed it was because he was that respected. It's the way things were in our town; you defend your own. We saw those people many times, but they never bothered us again. Still, they had this creepy way of smirking at us, as if they knew something we didn't.

5 MAN OF THE HOUSE

It takes a special skill to be able to read the land like my Papa did, to know if a crop would be profitable or not. He taught me how to reap what you need to feed a family and earn a living from the rest. Besides the chickens we killed each weekend for ourselves, we had 50 to 80 making eggs we could sell. The same goes for the cows, with their milk and meat. With any meal, there were fresh vegetables from the garden. My favorites involved cabbage: stuffed cabbage, cabbage soup and sliced beef tongue with cabbage.

Makes my mouth water just thinking about it. Not that I can have any such delicacies like that now. Even then, they only came when the good Lord shined on us, or maybe it was Mother Nature. One of them, for sure. Our whole existence, as farmers, depended on the weather, and as anyone in that profession can tell you, that's risky business. It certainly was my 13th year.

One morning, my father got up like he usually did at two o'clock, started his day in the fields, and returned to wake my mother: "Etta, something has happened... Everything is frozen. It's all just lying down. Again, we won't have much food this year." We had done without much food before, but he was getting older and it was harder for him to work long hours, especially when the weather didn't cooperate. For some reason, this time it seemed he literally made himself sick with worry. Mama's fears all these years were realized, I guess. He was never ill a day in his life. Never saw a doctor, or so he boasted. When someone had a headache, he'd make light of it, "It'll go away. Eat something, then work harder and you won't even remember what was bothering you." That was his solution for most ailments. "A full stomach and a busy mind. You won't worry about your *tsuris*. Now get out there and work, and quit *kvetching!*"

Only a few days later, we first noticed that he wasn't himself. I came home for lunch and instead of a hot meal, I found Papa sprawled on the floor. There were candles burning around him. My mother and sisters were wailing. I watched the candles burn and flicker and the shadows that the flame and the people cast on the walls in the sunset.

It's truly unbelievable that Shlomo visited him the same day he died and was there when it happened. Fate. I really believe in that. I'm sure Papa was comforted to see him, to know he would take care of us. "You're in charge now. Thank you, God." Looking at the ceiling, he raised his palms, shaking them, I'm guessing toward heaven or that light you hear about coming for the dead. With that, Papa closed his eyes and left us.

The doctor we called to examine him labeled it influenza and directed us to take precautions to prevent its spread. Who knew of such things? Some of us had been sick before, but never something so sudden and forceful; never something Mama couldn't heal with chicken soup and cold compresses. A bad cold? That's what Papa died from. Did he realize how sick he was? Did he wait until he sensed somehow that Shlomo would be back, like death gives you some extraordinary powers to foresee what others can't? I guess 68 was a ripe old age back then. He certainly told us that he lived a good life often enough. How many people get to experience love, not once, but twice? Two families, many children. *Naches.*

It was only weeks before my bar mitzvah and already I was being treated like a man. I had to drop out of school to help support the family. If there was a silver lining, it'd be that I didn't like school anyway, so no skin off my hide, so to speak. Under the circumstances, it wasn't right to gloat.

Shlomo was staying put now, repairing shoes and making new ones in Jacovo. My mother, the younger ones and me initially pitched in, not making shoes, but buying supplies and handling simple repairs. We worked from 5 in the morning to around 10 at night. My mother, as you might have surmised, is not easily pleased. She never liked the business, and she let us know it. "The hours are too long and these kids are going to get hurt with all these sharp tools all over the place." We had to make a living and we realized how unforgiving farming was, so she had no choice but to look the other way.

My bar mitzvah arrived with probably as much fanfare as my untimely birth. In this case, who can really celebrate without Papa? Maybe there were 30 people there at our *shul*, tops, some of whom made the trip again to Munkach so soon after the funeral. Everyone was dressed a bit nicer, or at least cleaner, nothing torn. I wore the same suit my older brothers had worn for their bar mitzvahs. I completed my parts, leading the service as taught. In my discussion, I mentioned how my father inspired me to be a better man. What else was I going to say? It didn't take much for the handkerchiefs to make an appearance again.

Afterwards, we served Mama's homemade cakes and some of the men had schnapps, as is the custom, although not with their usual merriment. I can't tell you how many guests addressed me with something to the tune of "Your father would have been so proud," as they shook my hand, patted my back or kissed my cheek. There were too many tears at what was supposed to be a festive event.

It was almost too much for me to bear, being a key family provider. I wanted out, to be on my own. Still, I didn't really have an alternate plan for how to accomplish that. Shlomo ruled the roost, and wouldn't stand for any defiance. "The family needs your help in the cobbler shop and that's where you belong."

I wasn't the only one at odds with Shlomo. He couldn't get along with my mother, either, and they were constantly bickering about who was in charge. As the eldest, Shlomo could be counted on to support the family, financially anyway, with grand plans for how to expand the business. "I can't do it without everyone pitching in," he would say. He made a convincing argument. Even I couldn't shake the images of what my future could hold. Maybe it was one of royalty, lapping up goblets of wine as servants presented endless platters of steamy delights.

So, I caved in for the time being. Okay, it's nice to know a trade other than farming. I learned to put nails in the soles and heels, to polish work boots and fancier shoes. Some guy came along with a *shmutzy* pair of boots; I had to clean them before passing them onto Shlomo for repair.

Meanwhile, Sophie, my older sister, was gaining her independence. For the longest time, she had helped us in the shop and assisted Mina and Mama with the cooking, the baking, shopping and laundry. When another family asked her to clean their home and care for their children, she was allowed to go, to provide another source of income. In 1921, when I was 16, she left with them for America. She was already like the seventh in our family there. How I longed to join her, to escape. It was no secret, either, that I was dissatisfied and restless, once more.

Our numbers were dwindling. We were four brothers and Mina now. After several years in the shoemaking trade, Shlomo sold the business and at my mother's urging, fulfilled my father's wishes by becoming a farmer once again. On every street in Jacovo there were three to ten families. Each one had cows and they wanted to sell their milk. We bought their milk, collecting it ourselves to ensure that it was kosher.

If the farmer doesn't wash his hands before milking, it's not kosher, so you either watch the milking or do it yourself. There was another family that dealt in the non-kosher variety, gathering milk cans from yards and spilling those into larger containers.

We'd fill 50 and 100-liter cans, put them on our wagon or, in the winter, our sleigh, and take them to Munkach. Every Sunday we used part of our earnings to pay the people who sold us the milk, and the rest was profit. That's how we made quite a bit. At least it seemed like a lot at the time.

My younger brother, Herman, took care of the milk business while Shlomo branched out to selling other dairy products, along with eggs and then potatoes. The latter soon became our primary business. When we got up around 4 o'clock, the townspeople were already readying their horses and wagons with their first loads of potatoes. They'd bring their sacks to our yard and we'd pay based on the weight. One mountain of potatoes was so high that if I climbed it, I could see the whole town from the top.

With a yard full of potato sacks, we loaded the hundred wagons we'd bought for the purpose. The procession of horses and wagons stretched through the town for about two miles on the way to the train station. Shlomo accompanied the first wagon while I followed up the rear on the last wagon. Our commotion attracted a crowd and before long the streets were lined with townspeople watching us go by as if we were a circus parade.

Soldiers and police had to be called to maintain order. One impeccably dressed officer came up to me and wagged his finger, pointing to the animal droppings. "Boy, you Jews are making some mess out of our town, between the horse manure and the wheel marks. You think you can just waltz through here like you own the place? Somebody ought to teach you Jews a lesson or two."

I just shrugged my shoulders – caught off-guard by his unfounded hostility – and continued walking. Shlomo had hired a few men to clean up after us, so there must have been some misunderstanding. As I looked back, the officer was still eyeing me until he was diverted by the crowd of onlookers. I'd tell Shlomo later. He'd know what to do.

Once we arrived at the station, Shlomo and I had to wait for about three hours until the trains were ready for us to transfer the sacks yet again. Shlomo told me not to worry about the earlier incident. "That *shmendrick*. He's *farblonjet*, out of his brain. He should grow like an onion with his head in the ground. Don't worry, forget it. I've taken care of everything."

It was midnight before we were paid. Shlomo had arranged with this man to sell our potatoes in other cities. First, we had to pay the farmers for the potatoes and then everyone who helped us – the carriers, the loaders – and those who sold us the trucks, carts and horses. Here, too, we earned quite a pretty penny. So we were faring considerably well in comparison to others, and they let us know that they noticed. I couldn't hear what most of the neighbors were saying, whispering among themselves upon seeing us, but I picked up part of a conversation. "Look, these boys are really going places. When their father was alive – may he rest in peace – all he did was buy and sell horses and cattle. Now see how his sons prosper."

6 LOVELY LEORA

By 1924 we had accumulated enough to build a larger house. The true head of the household, Mama, made all the big decisions on the house: where to buy materials, who to hire and how everything would be built. We were there to supervise the workers, under Shlomo's direction, of course. He had been going out with a girl from another town, Rachel, and after a few months they got married. Again, he asked for our help. He wanted to share the home with us and, to pay for the construction. We had to work every day except Saturday when we were selling potatoes. No rest for the weary amidst the constant bickering between Shlomo and my mother, now with another family member, Rachel, in the mix.

If it wasn't for Rachel's disagreeable disposition, I might have actually been jealous of Shlomo. Rachel was a striking woman, a natural blonde. Although religious Jewish women covered their hair with a *shaytel,* wig or kerchief, if the wig moved a little, one could see a few wisps of the silky blond above her forehead. She had gray eyes, full lips and stood above most women at 5-foot-8. Her height, alone, made her intimidating. But she also kvetched about having to share.

"I want us to have our own space, to start our own family. I didn't marry your family, Shlomo. I can't handle it anymore. We need our privacy. So many people living in our brand-new house. It's not right. It's not fair. You work the hardest. Can't we find another place for them?"

"I promised Papa," was his only reply, head bowed in defeat.

Her house? What *narrischkeit*! We *all* built that house!

The situation was uncomfortable for us all, particularly my mother, who never felt Rachel was right for Shlomo. When Rachel was out of earshot, Mama would say that she was not an educated girl. She came from a poorer town, a poorer family. The women were constantly fighting about whose house it was and about Shlomo's decisions. Whenever I threatened to leave, Mama begged me to stay. "Don't leave me with these two. I'll go insane." She'd grab my arm for effect. "She's going to convince Shlomo to put us out; I just know it. Then, who will help us? You're the next in line. It's your responsibility. If only your poor father was alive..." She faded off in tears.

Sure, I felt bad. But, even without me, I knew everyone would be all right because Shlomo would never abandon his family. Plus, we had Herman and the others, who were getting old enough to pitch in more too. There was nothing anyone could say to stop me. My mind was made up. Mama knew it. "You are going to do it anyway, so what's the use of me getting in the middle?"

I was almost 17 when Mama changed her tune and began promoting America as an option for me. In another year, I would have to go into the Czech Army. Having grown up during wartime, my general opinion was that the Czechs could have their wars but I wanted no part of the bloodshed, the prestige of wearing the military uniform, or the power that comes from altering history.

What had this country ever done for me that I should be so loyal in return, to fight for more land or more power? I was still just a farm hand, subject to the wills of nature. That was to be my lot in life, to follow in my father's shadow. No hope for something better like there seemed to be on the other side of the ocean. I definitely held out for that hope. I certainly didn't see my future being tied up in the land, which was so unpredictable. One day, feast, the next, famine, as they say.

My family knew it wasn't right that, at the start of the new century, land reforms forced peasants like us to pay the state for the land we worked. We just weren't willing to risk life and limb to fight for justice, certainly not for the 14 months to two years of service required.

There was also a fear that Jews wouldn't be treated fairly in the army, that they'd be on permanent latrine duty or something like that because it was a well-known fact, even if we felt relatively safe in our *shtetl*, that not everyone liked the Jews.

For my mother, the issue of evasion was larger than me risking my neck. She was most preoccupied with the thought of me eating non-kosher food. America might be the same, but she decided it would provide safety, and it was worth the sacrifice of our sacred traditions for that. Anyway, I started becoming interested in America after a few of my older siblings settled there. They wrote to us about this place across the Atlantic Ocean that I could only envision, based on their letters, was utopia, where fortunes were made by other immigrants and opportunities existed to "make it big," whatever that meant. Many people in the Old Country had the same dream, to leave this primitive and restrained rural life, enjoy the comforts of an enlightened democracy, and see the world on the way. I was just one of the naive ones, meshuga enough to believe it could be achieved relatively easily.

America. The name itself always sounded like A-miracle to me. Three of my 12 siblings left in succession from 1911 to 1914. My father took each to the train station and sent them off to meet other relatives in the United States. Now and then, they'd send home a few dollars to help us out. In 1921, a year after my sister, Sophie, left, she wrote we should also come to America. There were many more opportunities than in Czechoslovakia and fewer run-ins with the *goyim*. She was responsible for bringing together those already there. They pooled their earnings and sent us enough to cover the trip, along with immigration papers to complete. My mother wasn't coming along. "How can I go? I'm too old. You go for me. Go, Sophie will take care of you."

Shlomo resisted, at first. He had the new house, after all. Just in case, though, he made up papers for him and Rachel, but never followed up. It had been eight months and none of us had heard anything about our requests. I knew why my papers were held up: the army had their eye on me, no doubt. If we made waves now, it would surely alert them further. That doesn't mean I gave up praying the papers would arrive any day as time went on, though, that didn't seem likely. Despite Mama's best efforts, she couldn't help tapping into the money my sisters and brothers had sent for the trip just to keep us fed until we had no choice but to appeal to the ones overseas for more.

At this point, Shlomo became a real thorn in my side, constantly challenging my motives. "Why do you want to leave? Let's find a girl for you and you'll get married and you can build a house on the lot beside ours and we'll live together, we'll work together and we'll be happy." Like the army issue would just disappear? He must have been convinced that marriage would save me somehow or just take my mind off my travel plans because he made it his personal mission to find me a wife.

A *shadchen,* a matchmaker, he went to the next town to seek my *bashert.* Truly, I didn't need his help. I was going with a lot of girls of 16, 17 or 18 years old, but there was one girl I especially cared for,

Leora. She was sweet and gentle, a bit shy and introverted. But she was quite smart and I enjoyed listening to her make up stories about life outside of Czechoslovakia – wars and soldiers and beaches and deserts. We talked about things that happened to us and adventures we predicted were yet to come. I shared with her what I hoped it would be like in America once I got there. Like others here, I had become the victim of brainwashing from American films into thinking it was utopia. My sisters and brothers did little to change that vision with their descriptions of the lives of the rich and the prosperity they saw there. On the other hand, there were also the dismal stories about immigrants being taken for all that they had. Strangers who took advantage of the newcomers, robbed or beat them, left them for dead in this new country. But those tales were not as popular as the successful immigrant stories.

"What are you thinking about?" Leora asked as we laid on her bed, staring at the ceiling. There were always water stains from previous leaks, and strands of dust swaying in the corners.

"Streets paved with gold." I spread my hands out as if they were sliding across the ceiling.

"What is it like to walk on streets paved with gold? Is it slippery? Can you carve off some and take it home and be set for life?"

"Probably not, because then it wouldn't be gold anymore, but scraped up, damaged and we would have heard about that."

"Yes, surely so." She gave my shoulder a playful shove. I nearly fell off the bed, and we giggled as she caught my arm and pulled me close again. The tension was unmistakable. I felt it surging. *Did she feel some nearly painful sensation down there too? Continue the conversation and refocus, Shimshon,* I told myself. "Do you think maybe it's all made up," he teased, "just a story to entice travelers to visit and see for themselves? It's not possible to pave streets with gold, is it? Wouldn't that be too costly? And what if people did try to take some, would they have to pave it all over again? Or are you allowed to take some and that's why everyone makes money there?"

"Only one way to find out, you know," Leora said before changing the subject.

Was she encouraging me to leave her? Ah Leora, who listened to my ranting and never once indicated she wanted to follow me to the ends of the earth to discover if the gold was really there. Maybe if I would have stayed, if I weren't preparing to leave, she might have wanted me. But she knew I was going to leave, to discover some of the places we spoke about. She had sisters and brothers in America, too. But she could never leave her parents, she often reminded me. Anyway, it didn't work out. When I broached the subject of marriage, she protested. "What's the use? You want to go away. How can I stop you? How would I live with myself if I did? I can't go. I just can't, but you should go and never look back. Go to America and if you still feel that way about me and if I return the feeling, I can come to America and we can get married there."

7 COLD FEET

If ever there was a reason to run, it was after an incident that occurred during the High Holidays of 1924. As God was deciding the fate of all Jews, mine became crystal clear. Shlomo and Rachel went to his in-laws for Rosh Hashanah and Yom Kippur, the Jewish New Year. While they were visiting, I went to look for my *tallis* so I could go to *shul*, and I realized that it was in their bedroom. The door was locked and I got so frustrated, I broke the door down. When Shlomo and Rachel returned, she went berserk, ranting and raving how I broke "their" door down. Several siblings and I had helped build that house for all of us to live.

"I built this house and nobody is going to lock the door in my house," I roared.

She wasn't finished with her verbal gunfire. I retreated to the barn; and after puffing furiously on two cigarettes, I was still fuming. Returning to the house, I found Rachel and pushed her to the floor. As I watched her slump over and fall, I ran out before Shlomo could return the volley. I don't know what came over me. It was the first time my temper got the better of me and while not the last, I never hurt another woman again.

To make matters worse, Rachel was pregnant at the time. What kind of an animal am I, right? But how was I to know? I was already on my way to the United States when they found out. By then, I had packed up my stuff before anyone was up, and left. If I had stayed, I would have surely been in a fistfight with my brother that day. There was no turning back. Taking whatever I had – an old pair of pants, an extra pair of socks, the clothes on my back, and a little snatched food – I disappeared. Nobody knew, not even my mother. I never said goodbye to her, a decision that remained on my conscience. Really, how could I leave her? I didn't even leave a note. I meant to go back. When I came to America, I planned to become a citizen and make a lot of money. I'd return and bring my family overseas if any chose to follow.

I went as far as Prague, the capital of Czechoslovakia. It was about 170 miles northwest and took me about ten days. Occasionally I hitched a ride on the back of a passing wagon. But mostly, I walked, taking periodic stops to rest or eat and relying on my limited knowledge of several languages to communicate with these strangers. My family only spoke Yiddish, which is pretty close to German, and a little Hungarian. But I also picked up some Czech, Slovakian, German, and Russian from listening to the gentiles in our town. When the little food and water I brought from home ran out, I used whatever bits of the appropriate language I could string together to beg help from homes I encountered. Shelter, too, if the family was particularly accommodating. Otherwise, I slept in the fields or barns, any abandoned structures I could find. Sometimes the weather was bad, bitterly cold or raining. After sloshing through mud, I'd have to find fresh water – a stream or a well – in which to bathe, wash my clothes and wait for them to air dry. Although I had some spare clothes and shoes, hauling wet laundry weighed me down too much and you can change your clothes just so much before it all becomes soiled or smelly. My boots, made by my brother for heavy farm work, held up the best. By the time I reached my destination, though, they would need patching, too.

Accustomed to being on my feet all day in the fields, I had developed strong leg muscles. Apparently, it wasn't the same kind of muscles used for walking great distances. And I had to constantly come up with new ways to talk myself out of the pain I felt in my limbs and my sore, blistered and swollen feet. Singing loudly sometimes worked. There was rarely anyone around to complain. Otherwise, I'd convince myself there was something more wondrous over the hill or just at the horizon and once I got there I could rest, clean and dry my shoes and socks again. Then, once I got to that spot, I'd push myself one more time, to see the next site. When there was daylight, I felt guilty taking a break. Again, life on the farm. No rest for the weary as long as the sun is shining.

The scenery kept me going. With the Carpathian Mountains on the far horizon, I passed open pastures, dense pine forests, barren mountain ridges and rough alpine peaks. Secluded valleys revealed farms of corn and potatoes. Occasionally, I'd see a wild boar or deer. From the depth of one gorge, I looked up to see gigantic pinnacles and grassy ridges. Then there were the majestic Tatras, where glacial valleys gave way to high passes, small lakes and expansive crests saddled by towering summits enveloped in mist. The trees were pine or fir. Even though I could not see much at night and might have feared some of the unfamiliar sounds, I preferred the peaceful country to the lively cities. Gas lamps lit dusty cobblestone streets. Alleys smelled of damp stone, clogged drains, and rotten fruit. Just like in the rural areas, there was no electricity or indoor plumbing where I stayed and you had to gather your own well water. But I didn't mind as long as I kept moving toward America.

In Prague, I stopped to find out how to get to America, what to do and what not to do. I didn't know anything about how to travel or how to go from country to country, from Czechoslovakia to Germany, to ports and ships and how to get across the ocean. I asked nearly everyone I met that looked friendly and knowledgeable. Many claimed to have relatives and friends who had done it and told them how it's done.

Another six months and I would be 18. Instead of raising a red flag about my army service, I requested permission just to visit, to tour Czechoslovakia. The answer: As long as you are back on your 18th birthday. I got the pass. But after seven weeks in Prague, I simply ran out of money and lost my nerve to continue. No matter what you do, where you go, it costs. You bribe here, bribe there.

While away, I wrote to my mother to assure her that I was okay. Because she couldn't write herself, she made somebody else do it, Herman or Mina, that I should come home and that things would be different when I returned.

I *so* wanted to be a strong man, to answer to nobody. I guess, when it comes down to it, I'm no more than a child who pretends to run away and even hides for a while before realizing home isn't so bad after all. Yes, I was a coward. My mother's appeal got to me and I pledged I would return to her, if only for final goodbyes before the army came for me.

It wasn't as difficult to walk back. I knew where I was going, where to seek help, where to rest at night. It didn't even take as long – a week instead of ten days. A nomad, of sorts, I had learned to determine which berries were tastier to eat along the way, where to find drinking water, which paths were more exhausting than others. I felt like a world traveler, set on venturing out again when I found the means.

Mama didn't say anything. She didn't even ask, "Where were you? How are you?" She just smiled. Not exactly the reaction I expected. Letting her awkward silence sink in a few hours, she was waiting for the chance to pounce. "You ran around? You had a good time?" Oh, she let me know what she thought about it. She wasn't happy, to say the least. You see, my mother, while accepting I would probably go, secretly knew if I left, I'd be back. She must have doubted my ability to make it on my own. My indecisiveness proved her right. When I left, she went to the city, to Munkach, to see the chief rabbi. Rabbi Aaron Pinchus, one of a long line of Hasidic rebbes with huge Zionist followings. She had given donations to his synagogue and to the rabbi – you never know when you need a rabbi's divine connection to the Almighty – and so he knew her name. After informing him what had happened, he assured her, "Don't worry, he'll come back." I did come back and the rabbi was right. I never doubted my mother again that rabbis talk directly to God.

This is when I learned about Rachel's pregnancy and how my pushing her hadn't harmed the baby. What had I done? It was hard enough to face them all again without this information. "It's not to be discussed, you hear me," my mother warned. "If you get Rachel upset, it'll be dangerous for the baby's health. She's under strict orders from the doctor to remain calm."

We all basically ignored each other. Eye contact was fatal, more so with Shlomo than Rachel. The resentment that could be expressed with facial expressions alone. It was clear that I should never have come home.

Leora had moved on too. Fickle as teens are – I had only been gone a few months, after all – she found herself a new boyfriend, whom she said made her happy and didn't have any plans to leave her or their country. I couldn't compete with that. There was no room for me in a world that accepted that this life was as good as it's going to get right here, right now.

8 BUBBIE'S GOLD WATCH

"I'm going to Munkach tomorrow," I told my good friend, Avrum, one morning. I had been home several weeks now, enough time to devise a better plan. "I've got to deliver milk. Can you come with me? You can bring home my family's horse, the wagon and the milk cans." Milk collection was my chore to help the family. That day I collected for the whole week. It was a lot: 2,000 koruny or about $70. I kept it and I gave the boy the horse and told him to take it home. He agreed to do it.

Everything fell into place. That was before I made one of my biggest mistakes, among those that plague me to this day. This one involved my Bubbie. I had visited her the day before I left and told her that I was leaving and going to try to go to America. "You said that last time and you came back, *ainekel*," she said, fixing me a chopped liver sandwich and some freshly brewed tea.

"That was different, Bubbie. I now know what I need to do to get there. I was just testing the waters before. I didn't know what I was doing. Besides, I ran out of money." I blew on the hot tea, tested it on my lips before taking a cautious sip.

"And now *bubelah?* What's different?"

"I figured it out, Bubbie. I know what to do."

She didn't press me further. It must have sunk in that I was serious this time because she started to cry. "It's so far away, Shimshon, are you sure?" She grabbed my hand and touched it to her heart, moaning, as if in pain.

I swallowed a bite of the liver, the onion flavor lingering on my tongue, and wiped my lips on the back of my hand, before responding. "Yes, Bubbie, yes, I'm sure this time."

She knew of my difficulty with the family because I'd tell her the stories about my mother, Shlomo and Rachel. "I can't watch them fighting all the time, tooth and nail for everything." Bubbie agreed that I needed to get away and was old enough to do that, but so far away and my family needing me to help out? "*Ainekel,* you're not going to stay too long, are you?"

"No, Bubbie." It seemed to allay her fears and she stopped sobbing. Now that I think of it, maybe she believed I'd be back again.

Bubbie was already 90 then. My Zayde had died several years earlier, a little before my father. Bubbie didn't stay in their house much longer after that. She moved closer to another son. He was a shoemaker in addition to being a singer and cantor. He had quite a voice. If he were in this country, he would have made millions of dollars with his voice. But over there, everybody sang. For such an old lady, she was doing pretty well. She had her own teeth. As far as I know, she didn't have trouble with her eyes. Actually, I don't know whether she could see or not. Regardless, she didn't wear glasses. She was still getting around, although she didn't walk much. Still, she didn't complain about anything. Whenever I visited, she'd give me something, a little gift, a chocolate or cookie. She'd whip me up a full breakfast or lunch even if I said I had already eaten. I'd see her on weekdays and holidays. It only took an hour to run across the field to see her. I went to my uncle too. They liked to see company. Even my younger brother, Herman, ran with me sometimes to see them.

"*Gay gezunt.*" She wished me the best of luck. Then she gave me something. She went to a drawer of an antique pine dresser and picked out a gold watch that I had seen her wear on special occasions. It was a reminder of earlier days when my Zayde had accumulated a small nest egg from neighbors who insisted on paying for his religious advice. Engraved on the back of its modest gold face was a message from my grandfather, in small Hebrew letters, "*Ani L'Dodi V'Dodi Li*," and in Yiddish, roughly translated: "To my beloved, Dora, your beloved Haskel." Bubbie showed me the engraving as she had done whenever she wore it previously, displaying it in her hand as if selling it in the market, allowing me to observe it from all angles. "This is something you will remember me by," she said, now placing it in my hand and closing my fingers around it.

I thanked her and I put it in my pocket, patting the pocket many times to make sure it was still there as I walked home. I said goodbye and went away.

The next day, a Sunday, I went to Munkach. I was all packed. In a small sack, like the kind that might hold potatoes, I put some extra clothes, a picture of my family, and cigarettes. I put the bag in the wagon and set off. As I said, I was in charge of collections. I was supposed to send the profits home to pay for the milk we bought. I figured my family would be okay. They would understand, I was convinced. So I pocketed it, vowing to myself that I would pay it back when I got to America. I didn't trust Avrum with it. He might say I never gave it to him. Although he was a friend, I was still suspicious of him. He wasn't the most reliable person. I had heard that he once stole from his mother's dresser to buy cigarettes. Now it was *my* money and I couldn't risk it. Before we parted, Avrum asked, "Sam, why don't you leave me something for my troubles?"

"What can I leave you? I haven't got anything to leave you."

"I saw you have a little gold watch. I have a watch, let's exchange them." What did I know? His watch looked newer and shinier than mine. I figured it had to be more valuable than Bubbie's old, scratched up one. I gave it to him. I just wanted to go and this was my chance. He was bigger than me and I feared what would happen if I resisted. And he *did* help me get this far. So we swapped.

Turns out Avrum also sold the horse and tried unsuccessfully to sell the wagon. When he couldn't sell the wagon, he left an anonymous note telling Shlomo where to find it. Given a second chance, I would gladly relive that day and behave differently. I didn't know how valuable the watch was when I gave it to Avrum. It must have been 50 or 60 years old at the time. And that was it. Only many, many years later did I truly understand what I did, that I should have guarded it with my life in memory of my sweet Bubbie.

9 BEWARE THE POLICE
DECEMBER 1924

Germany

With milk money in hand, I was off, for good this time, I vowed. And I meant it. How could I live with myself if I turned around yet again? No, I would be successful this time. I just *had* to be. Following the path I had now plowed twice, I returned to Prague within a week, visited the same people I did before and made arrangements to go to Germany. I paid those I needed to pay. Making my way across Czechoslovakia, Austria and into Germany – exactly the same distance as the first leg of my trip to Prague – required hiking, begging rides on the back of vegetable trucks, depending on the kindness of villagers for shelter. To do that, I used whatever bits of their language I could piece together to make some kind of sense. It was a strenuous journey. Often, I walked as long as I could and when I needed to rest, I did so under trees or in bushes, depending on my extra clothes for warmth and my sack for cushioning.

Now I have seen cities before when I was traveling. But Berlin was mystical. The modern architecture. The political ranting in the street as baton-wielding officers readied to quell uprisings. The jazz tunes emanating from classy joints called cabarets where immodestly dressed performers and dancers strutted on stage. I spent three days just exploring, admiring the shops, the parks, and the houses of worship.

From the time I was very young, my mother had taught me that whenever I needed help, I could count on my own people to be there for me. "Jews take care of their own," she would say. I just didn't have reason to remember her words until now. It hit me. That's how I would get to America.

It wasn't difficult to spot the Jews. Their clothes and confidence gave them away. On Shabbos, the men wore black tuxes with cylinder hats. They arrived at *shul* in white, gold-trimmed carriages drawn by large, white horses, and directed by chauffeurs in shiny-buttoned uniforms. These were the Reformers, and apparently, they had money. While dazzling on the outside, I would find their services much tamer than what I was accustomed to. Where I'm from, congregants holler their prayers so that nobody hears what the other says. Here, every word is clear.

So, I'm in *shul* and I notice a familiar face. Small world. You can travel around the globe and reunite with someone you knew from a previous life. Reuven and I attended school together in Jacovo, although he was a bit older than me. He was a drifter now, passing through Berlin with no set destination in mind, only that he would know it when he got there. I didn't realize he would actually be so much of a bad influence and distraction.

Reuven and I agreed to go in together on food and a hotel room. That was all the assistance I needed for now, I thought. While showing me a few more sites he had discovered, I guess I convinced him to stick with me until America, where he also had a family. Together we left Berlin and headed toward Hamburg, nearly 190 miles away, catching a ride along the way on a horse and buggy. Fourteen exhausting hours later, we arrived in Hamburg and looked for lodging. It was

December of 1924 and frigid. We had to find a place to stay that didn't cost too much because the money was running out fast. I guess we could have been beggars, but I was too afraid of the police and what they could do to me if they discovered my identity. They would send me back home for evading the army. It was better not to draw any attention to myself. Luckily, we found a boarding house for a very modest fee. It was quite crowded. Everybody wanted to be in Hamburg this time of the year.

They call Christmas in Germany *Weihnachten*. It lasts like the entire month of December with big parties and endless spreads of sumptuous dishes. Through Reuven, I learned how to stand outside in the best second-hand-store glad rags small change can buy and wait for tipsy guests to mistake us for acquaintances, escorting us inside with their arm around our shoulders as if we had been invited all along.

There is only so long you can avoid reality. We were totally broke now and desperate to find work. That's when Reuven left me. He had contacted his family in America, told them about his new plans, and they arranged for his passage there, at which point he left me to pay his bills. The *chutzpah*, I know. A couple of months later, I received an envelope with a $5 bill inside. I had never seen American money before. It was crisp and green with a picture of a very dignified man in the center who I imagined must have been pretty special. The green paper lasted me a week. I knew I had to make more if I wanted to follow my friend to America. I wrote to my family there. They sent me $5 here, another $5 later. It helped, but I couldn't go on too long like that.

In the meantime, I had to report to the police to get my passport renewed to say I'm like a visitor for six months. I had to be careful, not even to use my real name when I thought necessary because I was already 18 years old and they were looking for me in Czechoslovakia, in my town, because I had dodged the army. The police came to our house and asked my mother where I was, and she covered for me, as any mother would do, "I don't know. He went away. He's not here. Haven't heard from him in months. Can't even write to his poor Mama. *Farshtinkener*, he is, to leave us like this. His Papa, may he rest in peace, he left me, too, with all these *kinderlach*." With her apron she wipes a few stray tears and the sweat beading on her forehead and pushes the officers toward the door. "Now get out! Can't you see I'm busy? *Gay Avek! Makh Shnel!*"

They did not stop there. They questioned other family members, too, and heard the same story; how I left without a note or forwarding address and how they hadn't heard from me since. And it was all true. I suppose the officers could have used force. It was to be expected. I'm sure they scared my family. The threat of punishment for hiding me was enough. "We'll be watching, don't you worry," an officer barked. "If he returns, rest assured, we'll be back for him."

Safe in Hamburg, and alone again, I resumed my job search. Reuven and the seduction of Berlin had distracted me, but I was back on track. The most natural thing for me to do would have been to use the skills I learned growing up, to be a shoemaker's assistant, an apprentice again. But I didn't want to work inside anymore. I didn't like being confined that way. And it wasn't my ambition to be a full-fledged shoemaker. So instead, I touted my farming background.

I located a *shul* and attended its Friday night services with a clear ulterior motive, my mother's advice echoing in my ears. The cantor was in the middle of the temple and the choir in the back with the organs. Maybe a couple of hundred people in attendance. I knew it's sort of a standard practice, after services, for congregants to greet newcomers and welcome them home for a Shabbos meal and a place to stay. It's part of our tradition, actually, welcoming the stranger. If my father brought somebody home from shul, my mother bickered, "You brought me home a poor man for Shabbos? I didn't prepare nothing." Well here, no sooner had services ended and someone approached me with the standard inquiry about my marital status – predictable matchmaking for unwed girls – my lineage, my hometown. "Certainly, you have to meet the Schwartzes." And so I did. It worked like a charm.

The Schwartz family graciously agreed to put me up and locate employment. Over dinner, they peppered me with questions: Did I have a girlfriend? How did I get here? Did I plan to stay long in Hamburg? I didn't want to tell them too much because I was still just on a visitors pass. They certainly didn't need to know my long-term objectives. I told them I needed a job and that I was going to look for one. Albert Schwartz was quick to offer assistance. "Tell you what. Come to *shul* tomorrow and I'll introduce you to Isadore Siegel. He'll know how to help."

I did as he advised. After services, we approached two older gentlemen, taking a pause from their conversation to enjoy some *schnapps*. "Have you seen Izzy?" They pointed to a tall man, a little over 6 feet, wearing a dapper, tweed suit, and wingtips. I took it from there. I introduced myself and told him who directed me, pointing at Albert, who was waving from a distance in acknowledgment.

"Hello, good Shabbos. Sure, sure. Albert's a mensch, Of course I know people. Why don't you join me for *oneg*? We eat. Then we talk. My Gussie, she'll fatten you up good. Come."

"If you wish."

"Of course. Let me grab my coat."

In addition to his wife, Izzy had two young sons. The food didn't disappoint: the soup, the chicken, the kugel. They blessed the wine. They sang songs. All very familiar, except they were Reformers and I came from a more observant family. Slightly different melodies and recipes, but still, the feeling of being among extended *mishpachah*.

After supper, Izzy and I went into what they called a sitting room. It had soft burgundy leather chairs and delicate glass lamps aside white porcelain bowls filled with wrapped toffee and multi-colored hard candies. Huge watercolors of girls in ball gowns, beach scenes and wildflowers were among those hanging on the wall, illuminated by brass sconces. I was in awe. Yet, I was also painfully aware that I didn't fit in here with my old clothes and plain talk. The maid brought in a tray with tea and all kinds of gooey little cakes, a few slices of marble cake, some chocolate parfaits, truffles and fruit-filled danish. After we finished sampling the delicacies, Izzy was ready for business. "So, you're looking for a job? What have you been doing until now?"

I told them about the sale of livestock and milk, the shoe making and repairing. "But mostly I've been a farmer and that's what I'm best at."

"And what exactly do you consider farming? Plowing, digging ditches?"

I described how we planted vegetables and bought and sold oxen and that I took care of horses.

"I think I may have a place for you, a farm, a very, very rich farm." We used to call them, in German, a *Grundbesitzer*. It means somebody with a lot of land and people working for him. I could hardly contain my excitement. He went over to an old oak writing desk and scribbled something and then handed the paper to me. It had his name on it. I was a little confused.

"When you get there, go to Freidric's Farm. It's kind of a posh place. Got to be a big *makher* to stay there. But go. Ask for Jacob Grumer and give him this note. He owes me a few favors," and mumbling with his hand to his lips, leaning closer, "keeping quiet about a bit of indiscretion, if you know what I mean," to which Izzy winked.

Jacob Grumer was the eldest of three brothers. The other brothers had since moved on, elsewhere in Europe, but Jacob stayed to tend the family farm and later turned it into a vacation spot for visitors seeking leisure activities in the countryside.

I took a train on Monday morning. When I got off, I asked a couple sitting on a station bench where Freidric's Farm was.

"Oh, it's about four miles. Do you have transportation?"

"No. I'll just walk. What's a few more miles when you've already walked thousands?"

They eyed me suspiciously, but just as quickly returned to their conversation as I walked off.

At the center of town, I found this Villenkolonie, a colony of large villas with a lake running right beside them. I crossed a bridge and I was there. A few people were milling around at the foot of one of the buildings and I inquired, "Herr Grumer? Herr Jacob Grumer?"

I was told he'd be back later if I wanted to wait. In the meantime, I entered the largest villa. I had to walk up about 30 marble steps just to get in. There must have been a thousand people inside. Rich red carpets, cut glass sculptures and brilliant chandeliers. I had never seen anything like it. If I could work here, I'd be set for life, I thought.

After about an hour of touring the place, I asked at the front desk and was told again that if I wanted to wait, he'd be back late at night. "Late at night? How can I talk to him late at night? If he comes back, he may not even want to talk to me." There was no response, just a shrug. *Who am I?* A stranger. I waited outside and somehow the villa staff knew I was out there. They sent somebody out at lunchtime, about 1 o'clock. They called me in saying that I should come in and eat lunch. I went in. I was directed to the servant quarters downstairs. Upstairs, people were being served lunch by girls in white aprons, wearing white little hats. The workers from the farms, the fields, the stables and the yard were downstairs. They were all eating downstairs and they fed me and I ate a hearty lunch of stuffed cabbage with plenty of hard-crusted rolls for soaking up the sweet tomato sauce. After lunch, I went outside to wait again.

Suppertime, the same thing happened. I came at 6 o'clock and the villa staff called me in to eat supper. I welcomed the chance to be inside because it was getting cool at night, being springtime, the end of March. They didn't want me to sit outside because I would walk around and then come back to inquire whether Jacob Grumer had come back earlier. While waiting, I found out the Grumers were fine Jewish people. Three Polish Jewish brothers with an old mother.

"There's somebody here to see you." Jacob Grumer was alerted to my presence when he arrived.

"I have no time," he mumbled gruffly in German, giving me the quick once-over. I was only a few feet away from him. "I have no time and I'm tired." Before he could brush me off completely, I walked towards him and he tried to pretend like he didn't see me. He looked agitated.

I introduced myself anyway. "I've been told I could get a job here."

"Kumen morgn in da free," which translates to come back tomorrow morning. He spoke with a deep voice and the staccato rhythm of the language.

"I live in Hamburg and I had to take the train. I have to go back tomorrow."

He took a deep breath and conceded. "Okay. *Araynkumen.*"

I did as he instructed and followed him inside.

He interviewed me, asking me numerous questions. It was about 9 o'clock in the evening when we finished. "Come back and work on Monday," he said as we shook hands and prepared to part.

"Thank you. That's fine."

"How are you going to get to the train now?"

"I'm going to walk."

"Nein, kenst nakht vuckin," which meant you can't walk at night without knowing the language. He laughed and then ordered one of the drivers to harness a horse and take me to the train.

I waited with the promise that things were looking up for me.

10 DESIGNATED DRIVER

Monday morning, I got up at about 5 a.m. The train didn't leave for around two hours, so I grabbed some coffee and a sweet bun from the station café. Then I heard that the train was going to be late and I was supposed to be at work at 9. I wasn't going to make it in time, so I had to walk. It took me about an hour, maybe longer. I got there at a quarter to 10 and I went to see my boss, Joseph, explaining my delay. He was the oldest of Jacob's three sons. There was a Joseph, Leon and Philip. "When you come to work here, make sure you are on time. You're late," he scolded, which sounded even harsher in German. "I couldn't help it because of the train."

"You should have gotten up earlier. Now follow me," he said, curtly, leading me to the stables, where I would work and live. My job was to take care of the riding horses and offer carriage rides to the guests. They had four gorgeous breeds. When you put a saddle on them and mount, you may think that you are sitting atop a barn. At first there was another man to help me. He was retiring, training me to be his replacement before leaving.

It was a huge tract; must have had thousands of acres of land with about 200 milking cows. Every morning, two big wagonloads of milk were delivered to the city, just like back home. There were oxen with big, white horns and Clydesdales – huge, heavy horses. They worked in the fields, plowing, pulling heavy loads of potatoes. The similarities with my youth ended there, though, because this farm, if you can even call it that, was beyond what any Hungarian farmer could pray for.

At one point, I stayed in a room in the stable with the chauffeur. Even there, it was nicer than what we had in our houses in the Old Country. The stable rooms were spacious and clean with ample furnishings to make the stay comfortable. It was warm and, let's say, aromatic. If the stench became too unbearable, we just spent more time outdoors. Otherwise, it was quite satisfactory. I'd have stayed in worse accommodations, so I was overjoyed.

They called me *kutscher*, coachman. What a big *makher* I had become. In addition to the riding horses, there was a little one we harnessed to a two-wheeler to give rides. We sat inside an enclosure with a little door in the back. Most people who wanted to take a ride requested that little horse. He was fast as the devil. All anyone had to do was tell me a few minutes beforehand that I should be ready with a certain horse and wagon. One wagon had lights all around like a hearse and others were fancier with open tops.

I drove men and women, whoever came to visit, to the train or to the city. Once, even to a funeral. Ladies were dressed in their finest, feathers or scarves around their necks, the men in woolen jackets over elegant suits, and I sat in the front in a uniform with shiny buttons like the ones on the chauffeurs in Berlin.

It was thrilling. And my motivation never wavered. I was going to make enough so I could go to America. When I wrote to my family in America again, they told me they couldn't send me the $100 to $200 I needed. That's what it would cost to pay for the boat trip that takes you across the Atlantic. You had to work on board, but you paid the captain in case you might not come back with the ship. It took time to figure all of that out.

I recall winter's sting chilling the air, numbing my face, hands and ears, my toes feeling frozen even through my shoes and socks. Patches of snow lingered under trees and kept the ground moist and muddy, sometimes making it difficult for the horses and me to move quickly. By April, it was still a bit nippy, but buds on shrubs began to open tentatively to the imminent warmth. I worked from March through June. It was a lot of fun, though there was plenty of grueling physical labor. In the summer, there'd be 20 odd Polish families working in the fields every day.

Too bad I couldn't write home about my journey and job. My family would have been proud. Had the Czech or German police found a letter though, they would have caught me and sent me home to serve in the army. Whenever I met people from that area, as I undoubtedly did, I would ask them to tell my family that I was well. That's all the family really wanted to know. I made my messengers commit not to reveal my whereabouts for fear of discovery.

Mama wouldn't have approved of the company I was keeping. That was for sure. Philip was a gambler and the middle brother, Leon, a *shicker*. He'd go off and get drunk for two or three days at a time before returning. It was no wonder they had gone astray. Their father was in over his head with maintaining the extensive property. Their ailing mother probably couldn't control them either. She died in the summertime, around July or August, and for the second time in my life, I was part of a *shiva minyan*, the ten-man quorum needed for services during the seven-day mourning period. The other time was for my father.

Meanwhile, Philip continued gambling. Every Friday night, I'd escort him as part of my job. I'm not proud of it, but it paid. We would hook the little horse to the little wagon and go to Hamburg, to a pub, about

25 miles away. In the front, men were drinking. In the back, gambling. When we got there at 10 o'clock at night, he'd give me his orders. "At 2 o'clock, come into the room so we can go home." At the designated time, my job as fire extinguisher was to try to rouse the spendthrift from his chair. He'd argue for a few more minutes and I'd have to return repeatedly as if scolding a wayward child: *"Ya, gain tzu hoiza."*

I don't know what he lost, but he was half-drunk and when he decided to leave, he'd pick up a bunch of bills and coins from the table and put it in his pocket. When I got him home, he couldn't even undress; he was so plastered. I had to take the lush all the way to his room, upstairs in the villa. There must have been about 30 bedrooms and I couldn't even recall which one was his.

Once in a room, while putting his clothes away, I thought, *If I wasn't so damn levelheaded, I could have become a millionaire by just taking half of his earnings when he got home.* He never knew how much he won or lost, so he would have never known I took anything. But I never touched a penny. At night, he gave me money to hold for him and he didn't remember the next day when I gave it back. He'd ask, *"Iz duss meyn, ya?"* You'd think I was one of those *schnooks* the way I returned every dime. Anyway, I looked out for him and he gave me tips for doing it, with which I used to eat and drink.

One Friday night in September, I told him that I'd like to see a show. He allowed it. On the way, I passed chestnut trees with their fluttering sun-tinted leaves. I stopped to taste the glossy brown nut inside its soft green shell. The meadows around me were draped in crimson rhododendron. There were two shows, one from 6 to 9 and the other from 9 to 12. I told him that I was going to the 9 o'clock show.

Leaving him to gamble, I went off to see the Strongest Man in the World. His name was Karlbach, a very powerful man. He bent steel, taking a long rod and twisting it around his arm like he was putting on *tefillin*. His assistants laid three heavy stones on a board on top of him. Then they took away the stones and three big horses walked over him. When I got back to Philip, I took him home. I was told he lost a lot. He never spoke about his losses.

Over the next month or so it became known that the Grumers could no longer handle the place. It was too much for them. With Philip and Leon gambling and boozing away the profits, they went bankrupt. By the time fall arrived, I heard the property would be auctioned. They gave me notice around the middle of November that I was no longer needed and should move on by the end of the month. That's how it was. I had spent a nice couple of months there, but it was over. They paid me off and I went back to Hamburg, complete with a lesson in how recklessness can sabotage a business.

11 JUMPING SHIP

With some savings now, I had no reason to delay. Onto America. The owner of the boarding house in which I was staying, Muriel Vogel, knew of my plans. She made it a point to know everybody's business. "We'll try to arrange it. We'll talk to people and we'll get you there." She gave me the addresses of other boys she had helped go there before me. When she wrote them and said that I was interested in going there, they wrote me back about where they stayed, where they were living, what to do and what not to do.

Muriel's husband worked in the shipyards, loading and unloading the ships that came in. He knew people, and one night he came home and told his wife that I should go to see this captain. He would take me across the ocean. He agreed to see me in five or six days. The ship was going to the sea on December 10 or December 15. I don't recollect the day. I paid $100.

Either not being honorable or not understanding our under-the-table arrangement, the captain signed me up as a regular ship worker, requiring I return with the ship to Europe. There would be several stops along the way before reaching the destination, Boston, USA. It was my best shot. I took all my clothes and a few possessions: a single family photo, a comb, toothbrush, washcloth and a piece of mirror I had found.

Once on board I was sent down to the bulkhead where I had to shovel coal from one big bin to another so that the guys who throw the coal into the stove to power the ship had the coal ready. It was hard labor. I had to shovel 20 or 30 tons of coal a day and pass it to the fireman. That first leg took me 30 days. We stopped in England to pick up some supplies. The workers loaded it and then rested. It set off again and then didn't stop until St. John's, Newfoundland. From Canada, it was to go to Boston. But in St. John's, after 29 days on board everybody was allowed to get off the ship for about six hours. You've got to get off the ship in the morning and be back at nighttime.

I got up in the morning, got dressed and went into the captain's office to get paid. I was supposed to get $1 a day. So, I was owed $29. Instead, he gave me $15. He was to pay me the rest at the end of the line. You are not allowed to take anything with you when you get off the ship, nothing because if you take something there's the suspicion you might not come back. You just wear what you have and resolve to leave the rest. But I was cold already. This was January. I packed on more layers: two pairs of underwear, two shirts, a couple of sweaters. I must have weighed a ton getting off the ship. I put all the things I could fit under my coat. I know I looked bulky and lumpy even for having so many layers. I was so hot, I was sweating and shuffling more than walking.

There was another young man I became friendly with. He didn't like the captain. When we got off the ship, he said to me, "I'm not going back to that ship." I didn't dare tell him I had the same idea, but maybe he suspected. Still, I ate lunch with him, pretending everything was normal and he was the only one being dishonorable. He shared his escape plan and I listened, still without letting on I was taking notes in my head. "It's easier to get to America from Canada," he said. "People were known to slip across the border all the time. Boston's ports are much more secure, so it's best to get off here."

I feigned disapproval at this point. "What if you get caught?"

"Ah, I'm a sneaky little devil. I'll find a way. What's the worst that could happen to me? They'll bring me back to the ship. The captain will double my workload and dock my pay, make my life unbearable. No big deal. Like I said, I won't get caught, so I'm not worried."

I had more to risk than that. I was a wanted man in Europe.

After lunch, we went our separate ways. I watched him leave before changing my course. As far as he was concerned, I was going back to the ship. What did he care anyway? He was looking out for himself.

In the winter it gets dark early. I knew I needed to find a hotel room, but I also had to find out when and where the train goes. So, I went to a place I trusted, where I had sought direction many times before: *shul.* It wasn't too difficult to determine that a nicely dressed group of people walking in a certain direction on Friday night was heading to *shul.* I followed them. Like the synagogues in Germany, people stood by the door after services on Friday night and asked if anyone is homeless or wants to go for supper. One of the men approached me, a stranger in the midst. I told him I had no place to stay. He said, "Come with me," in Yiddish, and he took me home for supper. His name was Lazar Holstein. His home was very modest, with minimal furniture. "Please, take off your coat. Make yourself at home here," he said, attempting to help me.

Seeing how heavily clothed I was, Lazar became intrigued, curious. He stared at my clothing and then at my face, inquisitively, waiting for me to explain. I wormed away from him and sat down to a plateful of a sweet and sour fish I'd never had before. It was warm and filling. "It's very good, thank you," I said, making eye contact with Lazar's wife. "Thank you for your hospitality. You are very kind."

Lazar couldn't stand it anymore, watching me eat and hardly taking a bite himself, as he waited for his opportunity. "So now that you've eaten, tell us about yourself? Where do you come from? How long are you here for?"

I told him the whole story about trying to get to America, minus a few details about my agreement to work round-trip on the ship.

"But you're in Canada," he said, taking a mouthful of fish.

"So, I'm in Canada. It's easier to go to America from Canada than from Europe, don't you think?"

"Can't argue with you there," he laughed. After dinner he led me down the hall. "Get a good night's sleep here, and I'll see about helping you tomorrow if that's what you want to do."

He gave me a room, if you can call it that. I was just in a section of the hallway, partitioned off by a few trunks. Their son used the cot there when he came to visit periodically and the couple didn't disturb it.

Lazar called that night, and confirmed the ship I had been on was headed to Boston. I don't know why he doubted me, but he definitely thought I was a passenger, not a worker. When I awoke the next morning, he asked, "Why don't you go with the ship to Boston?"

"It's too late. I had to be back to the ship by 9 o'clock and I'm not there." I wasn't going back and he didn't pursue it further.

"So, you go to Montreal and from there you'll go to New York. It's no big deal," he advised. It was decided. First, we went to *shul*. We came back and we had lunch. In the afternoon, he found out when the train left for Montreal and put me on it.

"How much do I owe you?"

"Nothing." I didn't pay him, just goodbye and profuse thank-yous.

PART 2

12 REAL HOTSY-TOTSY
JANUARY 1925

Montreal

It had taken all night by train for me to arrive in Montreal, Canada. It was early Sunday morning. And I was one step closer to the US. Still, I was in America; North America, that is. I had an address and I went to the place Lazar told me about. When I got there and knocked on the door, a couple came to the door. "Who are you?" a woman inquired warily. I told them that I was Lazar Holstein's friend and that he told me to ask for Zeb Levine. "Oh, he's not here anymore. He went to New York."

"Do you have a room for me? I really need a place to stay. You can't imagine how far I've come and I'm extremely exhausted. Please..." She cracked the door ever so slightly to reveal a man sitting over a newspaper smoking a pipe. "Yeah. We'll find a place," the woman said, now softening. As luck would have it, Stu and Selma Lewis were sheltering a few other nomads in a sort of boarding house for the poor and homeless. They put me in a room with four other men. The Lewises had a verbal agreement with those who stayed there that they pay for room and board as they could. "Life has been good to us," Stu told me, as I settled in with the others. "Surely what goes around comes around, so to speak. Blessings will be returned to us tenfold, my boy. Besides, I inherited a bit from my uncle, so I'm set. Plus, I have my pension." He told me how he had been the top supervisor of a machine shop that repaired broken down railway cars. The room he brought me to had about five beds. Some of the men snored, but I quickly learned the best way to a sound sleep was to get on their rhythm with my breaths. The Lewises were quite soft-spoken. I had trouble hearing them at first. Their wrinkled faces and graying hair put them in their mid-sixties, I figured. Very comfortable in their role of helping others, they seemed to live vicariously through our lives. They also had many friends to do favors for them in their neighborhood.

The day after I arrived, they had already found me a job. They asked friends and sure enough, I had work. A boy who was supposed to go to school – he must have been around 11 or 12 – took me on the trolley car to my job. The only trades I knew were farming and a little bit about shoemaking that I learned from the Old Country from my older brother. It wasn't my favorite type of work, but beggars can't be choosy.

I reported to a place where they were making and repairing shoes. There was another fella that was repairing shoes and my job was to help him. For that, I received a whopping $4 a week. It all went toward my room and board. Whenever I asked for help, my sister and brothers sent me money, so I always had enough to get by. Not quite enough to go to America, though, which was frustrating.

By March, it was getting warmer. I didn't want to stay there too long. To smuggle me over the border from Canada to the United States, I was told, was going to cost $100 to $200. Would you believe that's the same as I paid coming across from Czechoslovakia to Germany? Must have been some kind of standard smuggling rate. I'm being facetious. I knew it would take a lot to reach utopia. How can you put a price on paradise? It would be worth the cost, I knew it.

Later I would learn that it would have been very easy to just walk across the border. There was so much forest and uninhabited land between Canada and the US that immigrants were slipping across the border all the time without repercussions. I had actually been swindled, probably like so many naive immigrants before and after me, poor saps.

I stayed in that boarding house for about three months. There, I met Menachem Kaminsky who came to play cards with the goyim. We chatted a few times about his children, who were about my age. One day he asked, "Why don't you come live with me? Why do you have to live here with four or five people in the same room? You can sleep in my room." Well, I went to see it, and moved in with him.

Menachem had two sons and two daughters who were living elsewhere. The younger daughter was going to school. The older daughter was working. She was about 19 or 20. Maybe he had ideas about making a match between his daughter and me, but I didn't think about settling down then. There really wasn't time for girls, or so I thought.

Soon after arriving in Montreal, I began working in a cobbler shop as an apprentice, falling back on my skills from the Old Country. One Friday afternoon, my boss approached me as I was finishing a pair of old work boots. "Sunday night my wife and I are going for dinner," Marvin Miller began, speaking over my nail pounding with the arrogance of a man who presumed to know what was best for everyone. "Would you like to join us, Samuel?" He stopped for a moment to survey my handiwork with just an approving shake of the head, and then continued. "You should meet some friends of ours. They are very nice. It would be good for you to get out and get to know different kinds of people, not just the ones you associate with at work."

"I'll think about it," I said, curtly, buffing the worn leather shoe.

He wouldn't give up needling me. Almost like clockwork each week, he'd hand me my paycheck on Friday and ask about my plans for the weekend. "I don't want to be too nosy, but wouldn't you like to meet some new people, a nice lady perhaps? I've got one and there's nothing like it to kill the lonely nights. Maybe you'd like to settle down, have some little ones. You seem so lost here, if I might say so. You're in this comfortable cocoon as I see it. All work and no play, you know the saying."

Again and again, I'd shrug him off, and distract him with some question about a certain repair job I was doing. He was right, I knew. It's just too hard to get to know strangers. I'd had enough of that just making it to North America. After what must have been his fifth inquiry into my weekend's social calendar, I conceded, less than enthusiastically, to visit some friends of his. At the same time, I was thinking: *Fakhtik! Enough! Just get off my back yenta! Beat it! Scram!* If he had been anyone other than my boss, I would have given him a piece of my mind.

He gave me an address and I took the trolley car the following Sunday night to the Stein home, a large apartment on Clark Street. There I met Yossi Stein and his wife, Leah. They had this little baby, maybe around two, who hugged my legs, circling me like a cat as I walked. I was so afraid my first impression on this family would be of me crushing their child, landing on top of her and having to peel myself away from a bloodied toddler. Yossi, I learned, was a furrier, so the family dressed well and warmly, with the finest coats, along with other fur adornments on shoes, blankets, wraps and sweaters. There was even fur on places you didn't expect to see fur, like bed covers, lamps and picture frames. I'll admit they were odd birds in their love and display of fur. It gave me the heebie-jeebies. I, for one, don't mind eating meat, but would rather not think too hard about where it came from. The fur trade had been big business in Montreal since the city's inception and the Steins were apparently profiting from that history.

Despite their eccentricities, these were fine people who otherwise appeared normal enough. They enjoyed the theater, social events and entertaining guests. They contributed generously to their synagogue and community from the profits they made not only in the fur business, but real estate too. One of their investments was the apartment building in which they lived.

Their own four-bedroom unit was decorated with antiques and artwork. Walking around the living room, I noticed thick, stuffed chairs and sofas that looked so inviting. I dare not sit, though, for fear that I might doze, maybe even in the midst of conversation. A full week of work had taken its toll and I was exhausted. To avoid drowsiness, I kept moving around.

A large portrait of several generations of the family was anchored above the fireplace. Fresh flowers in a blue glass vase graced the mantle. Another wall was filled with photos of family members, mostly children. I met many of them that evening. Aside from the baby, there were a few older children. One was a darling, exuberant child with flaming red hair, who also clung to me, asking me more than once to put her on my shoulders. "These children are quite affectionate, aren't they?" I asked one gentleman in attendance.

"Just beware of that little one," the man, who introduced himself as the child's uncle, warned me, gesturing to the redhead. "Don't let her energy fool you. You need to treat her gingerly. She's had a heart defect from birth."

Expressing my concern, I respectfully backed away from the child. "I'll keep that in mind."

The home smelled of the baked goods set out for the guests. Leah was known for her practically sinful apple strudel, made with cinnamon, golden raisins and nuts. She was happy to tell anyone who asked how she labored over the crust for hours to get it just right, kneading the dough, tossing it on the kitchen table time and time again until it was pliable enough to be rolled out, stretched and formed before the other ingredients were added. From where I stood, I could see several people admiring the dessert, seemingly discussing the pastry's merits and anticipating every sugary mouthful they would savor later. They remained glued to the table as they beat their gums, mostly about apple picking in the Old Country, which I overheard as I inched closer to the crowd. Many were sipping wine or cocktails or holding plates of *forshpeiz*: a *bisl* chopped liver, gefilte fish, herring, lox. "We spent all day picking apples from the orchard during the fall harvest period," Leah told the group, wiping her hands on her apron and then untying it from around her waist. Others chimed in about their memories of picking apples and other fruit, even speaking over each other until I couldn't tell if it had become a debate or a competition over technique and selection.

Losing interest, I returned to the children and involved them in a game I learned from my grandfather. A small speck of paper, coin or other small item exchanged between the palms of your hands and you've got an instant magic act known for generations of Jewish families to break the ice with kids. My grandfather played it with me as a child and I always liked it. "Keep your eye on it," I advised them, shuffling the paper from hand to hand. "Don't blink or you'll miss it". They were intrigued, as if I was performing magic. The way they smiled and whooped and jockeyed for a better position around my hands. They each had their theories for how the trick was done. "It's just a matter of paying attention," I offered. "I know, I know," from one. "I think it's that one," from another, pointing at the chosen hand.

So, I'm rotating a tiny ball of paper from hand to hand and the kids are tapping which hand it's in when I noticed her out of the corner of my eye, observing from a distance. The girl. I call her a girl. She was young. I guessed around my age, say 20, 21, but she was definitely built like a woman. Handsome too. My mother would have said she was *zaftig*, with meat on her bones. I liked that, a girl with a healthy appetite – maybe in more ways than one. Other girls I had known definitely didn't fill out the chassis the way she did. She wore a dress that clung to every curve, extenuating full breasts and broad hips. She was a real hotsy-totsy. Absolutely a doll, in my opinion. I could have sworn I was having trouble breathing or at least I was breathing faster while admiring her; I'm not sure which. She was busy making the rounds, greeting relatives with kisses. When she glanced over at me, she smiled, and then a guest pulled her back into conversation, and she continued her rounds. Had she returned my glare I would have surely been caught gawking.

As she moved closer, I could tell she didn't wear much makeup, except a pale pink gloss on full lips, but her cheeks were extenuated as if with a dash of color. Her skin was so smooth and unblemished. Thick auburn curls were pulled back from her face and secured with a clip of tiny silk flowers at the back of her head. I scanned her figure once more down her curves to her hemline, revealing hearty calves, her ankles springing from double-strapped black, leather heels that did not look in the least bit comfortable. Then again, I didn't see how women wore those kinds of shoes anyway.

Apparently, Leah Stein noticed my attentions and grabbed her sister by the arm, excusing her from her rounds. Arm in arm, the two sisters approached. "This is Hannah," Leah said, smiling mischievously, nudging Hannah towards me. "She's visiting from New York. She's a seamstress there in the garment district." Our eyes met and she could hardly look at me without blushing – as I was – and smiling coyly.

All throughout dinner, we glanced at each other between mouthfuls of brisket and *lukshen kugel*. When we weren't talking to others at the table, we exchanged brief smiles. We were obviously flirting and it made me feel warm and a bit flushed. I had to loosen the top button on my shirt. She watched me as I did it, and then looked away before I could catch her eyes.

In the evening, after we finished supper, as I prepared to leave, Leah suggested to Hannah, "Why don't you see Sam out?" Hannah nodded, trying to conceal her fascination with this stranger. "I'll take you to the door," she said, very matter-of-factly, as the family bid their final farewells to him and started on second servings of tea and cake. A few of her smaller cousins giggled as we left the room.

When we reached the door, she handed me my coat. Our fingertips touched and what must have been static from my coat gave off an electric shock. "Sorry," she said, a little embarrassed.

"No, I'm sorry," I countered. *Can static electricity be someone's fault?* Caught off-guard by the situation, I boldly asked if she would take a walk with me.

"I'll have to ask permission first," she said.

"I'll wait here."

"Just a minute." She ducked back into the living room and then emerged a few minutes later with her coat – fur-rimmed, of course. All smiles, she said, "They said I just have to make it quick."

We walked side by side the whole way to the station, where I met the trolley car. We could see our breath as we spoke, keeping our hands in our pockets for warmth. We talked about her relatives and how we each came to Canada from Europe – she from Romania and me from Czechoslovakia. The conversation was remarkably comfortable for two people who just met. Tending to be a bit shy anyway, I was a little nervous to start. She had what I can only describe as maternal warmth that quickly calmed me. When the trolley arrived, neither one of us wanted to part. Successfully convincing the driver to wait a few minutes – luckily there were no other passengers at the time – I quickly made plans with her to meet the following Saturday. Then she walked home by herself and I went home, replaying every moment we had just spent together in my mind.

The following Saturday, I took her to the movies. To get there, we walked several blocks from her sister's home. She sported a ruffled orange dress, layered in chiffon, revealed from under the same coat she wore the other night. The dress came down to below her knees.

She wore the uncomfortable-looking heels I saw her in previously. She sure looked swell, all dolled up though. We walked slowly, mostly because I had been accused by former dates of walking too fast and dragging my company along like a stubborn pet.

When we got there, we stood in a short line before getting our tickets. Braving the chill, those assembled snuggled into coat hoods or readjusted scarves around mouths and ears until it was their turn to enter the warm theater.

It was a silent movie. A fellow by the name of Joe E. Brown was in it. A comedian and acrobat in addition to actor, he was a very funny guy with a big mouth. Nothing came out of it though. He was a boxer who understood astrology, which gangsters capitalized on to pick winning horse races. It may not have been the best picture to take a girl to, but she didn't seem to mind. Also in it were Marian Marsh, Fred Keating and Edgar Kennedy. I'll never forget that movie, not because of the film itself, but because of the influence it would have on my life in bigger terms.

The first date. A big spender, I sprung for a soda, popcorn and chocolate, quite a feast. We shared it all. It was a spectacular date. I didn't even try to put my arm around her in the movie, but we exchanged smiles. It made my cheeks flush every time and my head feverish with excitement. It was amazing that I was able to follow the movie while having these feelings. On the walk back to her sister's, we talked about the movie, our jobs and family. At her gate, I kissed her on the cheek, longing for lips, but settling for a gentlemanly peck. "I'd like to take you out again, if that's okay."

"That sounds nifty," she said, with a nervous excitement in her voice. *A little encouragement. That's all a man needs. Everything on the up and up. No mixed signals, no games.*

We agreed to another date the following Saturday night. I promised to call and we parted.

13 HANNAH AND LENNY

Hannah and I came from similar worlds. We were both Eastern European and lived in small Jewish villages with traditional Jewish upbringings. We came from places where you helped support your family while attending Hebrew school and studied Jewish traditions. You had your place: me in the fields or cobbler shop. She, in the home, learning to cook and sew and care for her younger siblings. She was one of six children growing up in Galicia, northeast Romania. Two of her siblings had already immigrated to Montreal when Hannah's father brought over his son, Sidney (Sid, for short) in 1920 to keep him out of the Romanian army. Ironically, the same reason my family wanted me to leave Czechoslovakia a few years later.

Quite close with her brother, Hannah begged to accompany them. What started as a temporary visit with siblings turned into an indefinite stay. By the time I arrived on the scene, Sid and Hannah were living in Canada, their father having returned to Romania. While he prepared to send for the rest of the family back home, he concluded instead, the new country wasn't Jewish enough for him. He knew his children belonged in America, already a melting pot, but he could see the changes it caused and some of them he didn't like. Everyone felt the need to work on Saturday, the Jewish Sabbath. That sort of practice didn't occur among Jews in the Old Country and the father just couldn't accept it. Hence, he returned to Europe. His wife gave him constant hell for leaving their two children in another country. The admonishment was always the same: "You and your high morals. Look where it's gotten you. We're all alone here and they are all alone there. This is not how it's supposed to be. What kind of a family are we now?" Little did she know her husband's decision actually saved their children's lives, just as my decision to leave saved mine. The couple died in the Holocaust like most of the family left in Europe.

Hannah had two other brothers, each with their own fascinating stories. One migrated to Montreal, then left his wife and six children for another woman, headed to Winnipeg, and was never heard from again. The other brother tried to come to America, but he had a disabled son and the government wouldn't let the child leave the country. After much deliberation, the family, fearing rising antisemitism in Europe, decided to leave the child in a well-respected German institution. Ironically, the same day Hannah's brother got his immigration papers, his daughter was born. Then, in a cruel twist of fate, he suffered a heart attack and died on the way home from the hospital to tell his children that first, they had a new sister, and second, they were all going to America. How's that for bum luck?

His wife fulfilled their dream, though, and brought their four healthy children to Montreal to start again. A relative later snuck the disabled child out of Germany when things got bad, and into Israel, where he could receive proper care. The Montreal family kept in touch through written correspondence with the boy's caretaker. Despite all the safekeeping, the child died of pneumonia a few months after the journey. More harsh misfortune.

Meanwhile in Montreal, Sid was working overtime in a textiles plant to support the family coming from abroad. Once he found steady work at the plant, he sent for his wife, Doris, and their six-month-old daughter to come by boat. Hannah and Doris grew up together in Romania. They were about the same age, while Sid was three years older. As he promised his father, he took Hannah under his wing and she stayed with the family. She knew she couldn't outstay her welcome; that Sid really couldn't afford another mouth to feed. Besides, she and Doris weren't getting along. A rivalry grew between the women because Doris did all the housework with three children to care for. She was 17 when she was married, and resented Hannah's carefree existence. Everyone lived in one room and in such confined space, tensions escalated. "You lounge around," Doris accused her sister-in-law, a slightly altered version of her typical tirade about Hannah. These outbursts usually followed a day in which Doris was either cleaning for guests or particularly exhausted from other household chores. "You can go out and parade around town and I'm stuck here cooking your meals. Why can't you get a job too and help us?"

A few more lectures on her sloth and Hannah got the hint. She found employment, except not in Montreal. She decided to go to the States, where she believed she could do better for herself. Sid obtained a temporary work permit for her and told her if it worked out, she should apply for US citizenship. It took her some 60 years to accomplish that goal.

Sid took her to the train station to send her on her way to New York, where she could stay with some distant cousins, the Golds. She became a seamstress, something she learned in Europe. There was a huge call for those talents in New York and a very popular immigrant job at the time. As a result of her dressmaking skills and her work in Manhattan's garment district, she was usually very fashionable. Dressed to kill, as they say. Her trademarks were the flowers or other hair adornment, a flapper headband, for instance, along with tight shoes or boots. Her stylish looks and seamstress background came in handy in her after-hours activities as well, such as singing in the Yiddish theaters of Second Avenue – another talent she had developed in Romania. By day, she'd craft dresses, and by night, she'd perform alongside major stars in the hopes of being discovered. Many of the theater troupe members were also from Romania and that made it easier for her to gain parts. She was also a welcomed addition to the cast because of her ability to make costumes.

She enjoyed the pageantry of the stage, the creative energy that sprung from the Yiddish folk legends she grew up with in Europe. Sometimes, the theme was serious and political, and another performance, comedic. Despite her best efforts, Hannah never ended up center stage. The closest she came to stardom was singing backup for the famed *chazzan*, Motel Alter, before he became the popular Yiddish Valentino.

Coming from a long line of cantors in Romania, Alter's gift was literally revealed as he sang in the toilet. He was cleaning them at the time as a custodian, the only work he could find as a new immigrant.

Hannah, like other women in the cast, carried a torch for Alter, who was several years her junior. She never verbalized her feelings and Alter only suspected the crush. He'd smile in passing at her, but she was too intimidated by his good looks to do more than blush. Like bees to honey, the admirers fluttered around and she wasn't one to compete for anyone's attention.

Only on rare occasions did he address her directly and then it was generally to show her where to stand or which notes to accent. "You have a lovely voice," he told her during one encounter, lifting her chin to indicate how to project better. Hannah practically swooned at the touch. He had noticed her after all. "And I'm hearing great things about the costumes you've made us. If you cooked too, I'd marry you on the spot." The crew laughed. He was flirting, she suspected, as he did with all the other girls, toying with her affection.

"Actually, I am pretty handy in the kitchen too," she retorted, not really knowing where her audacity came from. It was enough to set him in his place. A good ribbing from those who laughed at her and he moved onto more naive prey. From the New York theater to Hollywood's silver screen, Alter was destined for greatness.

One summer, she joined her family for a getaway in the Peekskills, where her aunt and uncle had a second home. Living in close quarters with her cousins, Hannah found herself drawn to one of them. Hannah flirted shamelessly with Lenny, and unaccustomed to such aggressiveness by women, he fell prey to her lures. Many men before had pursued Hannah, mostly through her theater work, and she had grown very confident about her full figure and fashion sense. As such, her family was concerned she might get into trouble with the wrong boy.

Lenny, at 18, was the youngest of three brothers and didn't have the occasion to know many women, especially none as bold as Hannah. The older brothers were busy with their plumbing business, so Hannah targeted Lenny, who was still in school and spent many hours at home studying. Lenny was tall and brawny. The Golds were big people anyway, so Lenny became so too, despite the fact that he didn't do as much physical labor as his brothers. Although they knew relations between cousins were taboo, they couldn't help themselves. Complications were inevitable. On several occasions, they snuck out late at night when the house was quiet and all were expected to be asleep. "Come with me," he said the first time, sneaking into her room after midnight. He led her by the hand into the hallway, and she succumbed willingly, eagerly. "Where are we going?"

"Shhhh," he said, holding a finger to her lips, maybe a little too long, for it stopped them both for a moment. He kissed her then, replacing his finger with his lips, still leading her toward the back door as they kissed.

"You trust me, right?" he whispered, when he came up for air.

"Yes," she said, tenderly, softly.

"Just follow me then. I know where we can go."

He took her to the family barn. It became their secret rendezvous. Despite a few close calls – thinking they had stirred a brother one time and his mother another – they learned their way around in the dark, where the squeaky floorboards were, how to open and close doors like professional burglars, and the like. During these clandestine meetings, they unleashed sensations neither had known before. Nearby, in other stalls, the horses and chickens rarely neighed or cackled. If they did, the noises of slightly agitated animals were not enough to alarm their owners.

Like many naive couples, the pair mistook love for lust and drunk with euphoria, they cemented their relationship in a private civil ceremony before the town justice. Lenny never finished school, instead falling into the plumbing business like his brothers to support his wife. The brothers took him under their wing, keeping the marriage secret from the family for as long as they could. To say his parents shunned the marriage would have been an understatement. When they found out, they forced the couple out of the house to find their own way. Neither Lenny nor Hannah had much. The ache they once had for each other faded with each battle over the need for money until the thrill of forbidden love was a distant memory.

They were only married maybe six months without producing any children. Hannah always told me it was a marriage of convenience. Marriage was a way to pool limited finances, she claimed. Regardless of the real reason, I'll never know the truth. The marriage was annulled; Hannah had the paperwork to show, because they never had Jewish witnesses at the spontaneous ceremony.

That was all before Hannah met me.

14 'I'M HERE, SAMUEL'

When I came home from our first date, I felt queasy. *That goofy sensation that comes with mutual affection was more powerful than I had thought was possible. What kind of giggle water was in my soda? Had we been to a speakeasy instead of a theater?* In truth, I thought it was all the food we ate or the butterflies of a first date. Wishful thinking. I was ill all week. On Saturday morning, my roommate, Menachem, woke me up. "You were talking all night, talking in your sleep." He put his hand on my head, "You must have a high fever." He called his doctor at home and the doctor told him to take me to Royal Victoria Hospital right away. When the cab arrived, he carried me to it, lying me down in the back. He continued to watch me from the front seat as I fell asleep on the cab's torn leather upholstery behind him.

I don't remember much about arriving at the hospital or my initial treatment. Menachem took me there and a medical team whisked me from the car onto a gurney and into a room. Everything was a haze. Doctors and nurses were leaning over me at various points, but they were just blurry figures. I could see their mouths moving. But just couldn't make out what they were saying and I didn't have the energy to try.

Coming from a deep fuzzy fog, I found this man I worked with at the shoe store visiting me. Elijah Schwartz was his name and he was a very kind man. He was on his second wife, having had two daughters from his first, who died years earlier. Elijah had introduced me once to his 17- year-old daughter and wanted me to take her out. Pretty girl. Short black hair pulled back around her ears and dark eyes. Nice features, small hips, curves just starting to blossom. But I shied away. I didn't want to date anyone at that time, especially someone who didn't speak Yiddish, because that's all I knew.

I put him off. Every time he broached the subject, I'd say, "Maybe next week. Maybe next week, I'll take her out." Delay tactics had become my specialty at the shop, one would think. They were always trying to get me fixed up with some Jane or another.

Now he was there at my hospital bed. Relentless, he tried again, "I'll send my daughter over to visit you."

"No. Don't!" I snapped. "I need to be alone." I didn't want to see her, but I didn't have the energy to explain. That was the last thing I said before blacking out again. My fever was quite high, and it took a few days until they found out what I had: scarlet fever, typhoid, or like a bubonic plague. A lot of people died from those in the Old Country after the First World War.

Initially, I was sick about ten days with fever about half that time, burning me up. To get it down, I had to lie on ice from top to bottom. Other than that, there was nothing the doctors could do except wait it out. Fluids were being pumped into my body. Bottles of liquid sustenance hung in clear bags, allowing life to course through my veins. It wasn't enough.

I went into a coma and was lying on a bed in the middle of the ward. They put me at the door, covering the bed so nobody could see me. If I had gone fast, they would've probably figured they could slip me out the door and not have to pull me through the whole ward and have people see me, point, gawk and whisper about another poor schmuck who died, penniless, and alone. Well, they didn't give two cents for my life.

I found out later that I was in a coma for three days and two nights and I was talking like a madman. When I came out of the coma, the nurses asked me, "Who's Hannah? You were calling for Hannah all the time." My temperature went up to 106 and they didn't think that I would pull through. But I kept hollering, "Hannah, Hannah, Hannah. Where's Hannah? Hannah where are you? I need you. I have nobody here. You have to come now."

She *did* come see me. My boss, Marvin Miller, the man who introduced us, told her where I was. I guess the nurses relayed my pleas for her. He put two and two together. "Remember that nice young man you had the date with? He's in the hospital."

Hannah stayed with her family a couple of blocks away from the hospital when she came to visit me. She was living in New York, but she came to Montreal every Friday night by train while I was sick and returned to New York on Sunday night. I don't know why, but she was there with me. All night long she heard me talking about her.

One Friday night, around 9 o'clock, the nurse was there to give me intravenous dinner. She told me Hannah held my hand, reassuring me, "Samuel, I'm here. I'm here, Samuel."

My memories of those last few moments in the coma were very clear. I was in an extremely dense forest with what seemed like billions of towering pine trees blocking out the sky. Walking between the trees, I repeated, again and again: "Hannah, where are you? Where are you?" It was very dark. I didn't know where I was going.

Then I heard the distant echo of a woman's voice: "I'm here. I'm here." I don't know what happened next. I just recall hearing what must have been God's voice, a deeper tenor, saying, "It's not time. Go to Hannah."

It was Sunday and there sat Hannah by the bed, holding my hand. I opened my eyes and the room was spinning. Then I saw her face. She was focused on our entwined hands and quite solemn. Then she looked at me and screamed. My eyes opened wider, dazed by the screaming and the unfamiliar surroundings. Within seconds, this frenzied woman – now familiar to me from my unconscious thoughts – was sprinting out of the room. She returned moments later, still screaming, with a nurse at her heels. "Oh, you're right, he opened his eyes," the nurse said, half screaming it too as she raced to the intercom to notify the nurses' station. "Call for a doctor. He opened his eyes."

The first thing I said to Hannah was, "You're here." That's all I recall. That's how I woke up. After three weeks, I had come out of it. I had been pretty far gone.

I had remained in the hospital close to seven weeks. During that time, my relatives from New York never came to visit. Menachem, my roommate, wrote them letters and they called, but nobody showed up to see me in person. Menachem was there for me, though. He brought me vegetable soup and roasted chicken. He took very good care of me. "When you're ready to come home, let me know," he said. "I'll come and take you. I'll get a cab and bring you home."

I should have taken him up on that offer. When the hospital signed me out, I decided to walk home rather than bother anyone for a ride. Besides, I wanted to be outside in the worst way. It nearly killed me because I had to cross some pretty steep hills in the middle of the city. I had to rest a few times on the side of the road. What should have been a 20-minute cab ride to get home, took four hours of walking. But I got there. Menachem greeted me at his door, banged my head with his hat and said, "You stupid jerk! In your condition, you could have died." He was right.

15 THE KISS

I saw my Hannah all the time now. She was my girl and I, her feller. Before I got sick, I hardly even knew her. Now I felt as if our lives were somehow irrevocably meshed. Funny how my illness sped us through the awkward dating process.

The only problem was she was living in New York, where she worked. On weekends, when she could manage it, Hannah took the train to Montreal to see me. It was going on like this for June, July and August. She came every two or three weeks. When we didn't see each other, she would write me about the day's events, who she visited, how she missed me and that she couldn't wait to be back in my arms. I wrote her back in kind.

I liked her, loved her even. What she saw in me, I don't know. I was a *pisher* with nothing to offer her. Others might not have given two cents for a *pisher* like me. I was a greenhorn while she was already in America a couple of years and was a year older than me.

While in Europe, I had occasions to date all kinds of girls and women: nice ones, smart ones, plain ones, pretentious ones. There were the take-your-breath-away beauties that kept you longing for more even though you knew they were wrong and dangerous. They inspired passion surges that lasted from a few moments to a day, a week, until the next one came along. I was certainly no newcomer in the mysteries and allures of the opposite sex.

But Hannah was different. She had some mystical, magical quality about her that drew me in. I felt at peace with her, safe, content. She was surely something to look at, but sweet too. Her auburn hair fell upon strong shoulders, hiding the delicate curve of her neck. Skin, that when I caressed it, gave me the sensation of slipping between warm cotton sheets after a rich, relaxing bubble bath. She had a natural glow, her face blushing without artificial hues. Hypnotic brown eyes between long eyelashes, real ones, not thickened by a type of ink that left blotches on other women I knew.

I towered her 5-foot-2 frame. I was a thin 6-foot-1 and might even be seen as lanky. Dapper, I was told, and I considered myself as such. My best feature would have to be my eyes, the kind of hazel green that sometimes looked blue. The hairline, a dark brown, was starting to recede a bit even at this point. Maybe to make up for the loss on my head, I was growing it elsewhere – a well-groomed mustache.

Hannah and I were a well-matched pair, I suppose. I never really thought about it much, only that we seemed to fit, and I felt comfortable and comforted by her presence. This must have been the Real McCoy. Her family didn't see the compatibility. They had qualms about me, especially her sister Leah, her brother, Judah, and his wife, Ruth. That, despite the fact that Leah really was the one who introduced us.

We all came from the Old Country, so it was like we were all family. But when I first met Hannah and then started dating her, Leah quickly changed her mind and concluded her sister going out with a greenhorn who had only been in America a few months wouldn't do.

During one visit, I overheard a conversation she and her husband were having in the kitchen. I just happened to pass the door at the right moment when other guests were occupied in a lively discussion on politics in the living room. I was on the way to the restroom when I stopped to listen. "Leah, leave it alone," Yossi whispered, his tone forceful. The door was open a crack and I could make out that he was helping her gather some dishes and trays of hot cabbage soup and brisket to serve.

"She can go out with an American boy or a Canadian boy that has something," Leah countered. "I should send her back to Romania. Papa would know what to do with her. She doesn't listen to me when I try to tell her what's best for her. She'll be on the poverty line with hungry children begging for spare change at this rate. What about that nice boy, Levy, she was dating? His father owns the drug store on the corner. If only that had worked out, she'd have a nice life."

"Let it go, Leah," Yossi said, still under his breath, but raising his voice a little more. He grabbed the potholders to carry the hot trays. "We've been through this before. You know how headstrong she can be. Don't go meddling or she'll stop coming here altogether."

"All right. Keep your voice down. Grab those glasses. Let's get everybody seated for dinner. This is not over yet by any means," she said, approaching the doorway with her hands full.

I shot away to the bathroom and then to the assembly, and never let on I had heard, but I was noticeably quiet for the rest of that evening and often whenever we'd visit. It was true. I didn't have anything. I couldn't even support myself. When I met her, I think I was making $12 a week at the cobbler shop. It cost me that much for room and board. Scraping by, I managed.

What did Hannah think? I asked her on the way home about her sister's verbal assault. "I don't care about money," she said, grabbing my hand as we walked toward the subway. "As long as we're together, we'll work it out. Others have survived on less."

"But do you know what it's like to not have two pennies to rub together? Do you really want to suffer so much?"

"We'll be fine. Don't worry so much."

Man, how I loved the rebel in her. She was willing to throw caution to the wind not knowing what hardships lay ahead. I swore from then on not to let her down. My lack of finances wasn't her family's only concern with me. They didn't like me because they thought Hannah paid too much attention to me and abandoned her family. She no longer took their children out to the park or to the matinee. Instead, she spent that time visiting me, and they were jealous of that.

We were together every weekend, all day, Saturday and Sunday. Although my illness brought us together faster than the norm, I still took my time making any impulsive moves. From walking and sitting side by side without contact, we progressed to holding hands. She didn't resist when our arms brushed while walking and so I capitalized on the chance to feel her soft skin against mine. We smiled and I knew the gesture was accepted, welcomed. Then, the magical first kiss.

We were in my apartment, looking through old photos of my family when I caught her eyes. Instead of looking away in embarrassment, like other times, we just stared at each other and smiled as if understanding something greater lay ahead. See, my Hannah had been married before and was no newcomer to passions of the heart. So, when I pulled her close and ventured to the next phase, she was a very willing participant.

The kiss. It was the kind that inches forward first by savoring each other's warm breath for several moments. Then contact, soft lips pressed together as the pulse quickens and the world drifts away and two people share this near-breathless, heart-pounding sensation. A hypnotic trance, a hallucination too fantastic to be believed. Funny how the mouth can give so much pleasure, from food to romance, from the delightfulness of fine chocolate to the moisture of a woman's lips and tongue. The floodgates to the heart lay open before us now. No more holding back.

"What's going through your mind?" I asked her after the encounter. Still embracing her, I pulled away enough for her to look into my eyes, her head back and mine leaning in for more.

"Nothing, everything, I don't know what to think, really."

"I do," I said, now cradling her hands in mine and holding them to my face, sweeping them across my lips, my cheeks. "We're in love. This is what it feels like... I'd like to kiss you again."

Still no protest. She nodded, eyes fixed on mine, invitingly.

At first, we slept in separate rooms. I offered her my bed and I slept in the living room on the sofa. It was the right thing to do, not to rush into passion too quickly, too irrationally. But after about a month of this societal brainwashing, when my roommate Menachem was visiting friends or relatives, as he so often did on Saturday nights and Sundays, we gave in to the seductive tensions that inevitably develop between the opposite sex in their twenties.

It was sensuous and pleasurable. Several encounters would occur over the weekend. At the beginning, it felt like we never left the bedroom. When we did, it was to take a walk in the park or window-shop or get something to eat at a delicatessen. Sometimes, we'd shop at the market and prepare a meal ourselves. We both enjoyed cooking; it was another shared passion, our experimenting and improvising on dishes Hannah learned from her mother in Romania. I was a willing student under her spell. She was a masterful chef. Sometimes, I'd surprise her with my own version of her recipes, trying to impress upon her that I had skills in the kitchen in addition to the bedroom.

"See how I've learned?" I teased. "See what you've created? Look at me. If the boys could see me now, huh?" I paraded around like a flapper, hiking up my apron as if a short skirt. We laughed until we ached and Hannah had to beg me to stop, clenching her side and gasping for air. As was the case all too often, the boundaries were blurred as a satiated stomach led to the fulfillment of other desires.

Each moment together we relished as if it was an experience that didn't come along very often. And then Sunday night would inevitably come, when Hannah had to go back to New York for work on Monday. We would stand at the doorway for half an hour every Sunday, Hannah with tears in her eyes as we kissed our last goodbyes, kisses that had to last for a week until our lips could touch again. For days, I could smell White Shoulders, her scent, in my apartment. It made me smile sinfully, wishing I could stay here all day and just breathe the fragrance instead of having to work.

Hannah and I had gotten to know each other very well in just a few months, and at the end of the summer, I decided to talk about coming to New York with her. That's when Hannah's family really got upset about the relationship. They knew that if I left Montreal and came to America, they would see Hannah even less than ever before because she wouldn't come back to Canada as often. Because of their constant harping on the issue, Hannah and I made it a point to visit them more often during our weekend rendezvous.

With time, they grew to like me. They realized I wasn't such a bad guy, that I wasn't trying to intentionally hurt them by stealing their Hannah away to spend time with me. Judah even helped me get to America. We talked to people and learned how to avoid trouble. At that time, if I were caught on the border, I would have been sent back to Czechoslovakia to serve in the Army. Of course, I didn't want that.

It didn't take long before I was ready to move closer to Hannah. As I shoved my sparse belongings into a satchel, my roommate, Menachem, pleaded with me to stay. "You can't go." He was shadowing me as I crammed the burlap bag. "What are you going to do there? You've got everything here. A good job, for starters. You'll have to start all over there."

He was certainly right, not that I expected it to be easy. When was it ever? "I appreciate all you've done for me. Truly, I do Menachem. I won't forget you. I have to be with Hannah now. She's my life. You must understand." Sure, Menachem had taken care of me when I was sick. I was indebted to him for that, and I told him so repeatedly, to no avail. He was already mourning my loss minus the torn lapel and black suit. How ironic, considering how close our relationship would bring me to subsequent peril.

By this point, I had saved nearly enough, and when I appealed to my family in New York, one of my brothers, Yohanan, sent me the rest. Immigration laws had become stricter since Hannah got her temporary work permit, with quotas for European arrivals like myself. Also, there wasn't as much need for my farming and shoemaking skills as for Hannah's tailoring experience in the fast-growing garment trade. Yohanan couldn't get me a permit.

Instead of pestering my American family again and waiting for a response, I resolved to enter the country the way I was led to believe was illegal. Why not? I had evaded the Czech Army this long and no one had come looking for me here. Couldn't I be equally as lucky to escape detection by Americans? I knew the risks when I left my country and I didn't come this far to turn back now.

Asking around, among people I met – certainly not the ones who could set me straight – I found a guy who smuggled trusting immigrants across the border. It was 45 miles from Montreal to the US border. We had to walk a mile, board a train, a bus, and cross a bridge at the exact moment when the supposed guards changed on the American and Canadian sides. Watching from a ridge beyond a supposed guardhouse using the smuggler's binoculars, my heart was beating a mile a minute.

It only intensified as we waited. Surely, I would have a heart attack anticipating what would happen if we were discovered. I could see my breath in the chill. But I couldn't feel the tips of my fingers or my ears. They were numb. I was numb. "Maybe we should go back," I cautioned. "This wasn't a good idea. We're going to freeze to death out here." He ignored me, shaking his head with a mocking grin.

Where's my chutzpah when I need it? What a putz, am I. Cockamamie idea anyway.

"Run!" The smuggler grabs my arm and negates reluctance. Funny how I didn't see any guards as we crossed. Where had they gone? Were they tracking us? I tried to glance, but it's difficult to do when you're being pulled along so vehemently by a faster runner. At the closest station we settled the deal, as agreed. He didn't stay long enough to see me buy my ticket and board the train.

16 SO, THIS IS PARADISE?
DECEMBER 1926

New York

I never saw the Adirondack Mountains, the Catskills, nor the massive lakes and waterfalls I had heard so much about. Wouldn't ya know, my bum luck, I had slept through it all. The jolt and screech of the train at the station told me we had reached New York. I wanted to shout a deafening "I've made it New York!" in the best English this greenhorn could muster. But I opted to restrain myself, lest it draw more attention than my disheveled ragamuffin get-up. As I stepped off the platform, I noted how closely packed the buildings, how *shmutzy* the streets were with blackened snow and fetid water. A mass of pedestrians pressed by me, and I was jostled several times without apology, practically pushed along by their frenetic pace. Heads were hung, scarves pulled around faces to fight the merciless wind.

So here I was in the United States of America, the date: December 12, 1926. I was 21 and ready for another adventure. But first I wanted to know: What makes this place so golden? The *goldeneh medinah*, golden land, as it's called back home. America. Where the cobblestones are made of pure gold. I surely didn't see any gold streets, let alone cobblestones. Only gray, uneven pavement. Oh, and *shmutz* and grime. This is what I risked my neck for? This is why I worked so hard, for so long? There must be more. I was determined to find what it was.

I headed toward the only people I knew would take me in. There were four brothers and four sisters in America, so I had my pick. Okay, so I know I said I wanted to be on my own, away from family. First, I'd need a leg up in this new place. Who knew I would come to depend on them so much in my life.

At my mother's suggestion before I left Europe, I chose my sister, Sophie. She was five years older than me, but the only one I knew as a child. I had written to her while in Montreal and she had agreed to put me up.

It was Friday night. I got off at Grand Central Station and took a taxi to her apartment in Brooklyn. Exiting the car, I looked up to the third floor, where she lived, and saw in the window the candles were lit for Shabbos. I straightened my coat, my trousers, and stood erect. *Deep breaths, Shimshon.* Following my own advice, I stood there for a few nostril drills before pressing the button alongside the name Goldman on the apartment directory.

"Who is it?" A female voice boomed from the silver-plated speaker on the wall. "It's Samuel," and as quickly as it registered, I corrected, "I mean Shimshon." They wouldn't have known me by my newfound English equivalent. "I'm here, downstairs."

"Shimshon, really?" You could hear an assemblage of octaves as my name echoed around the room beyond the speaker, and then the female one returned, a little more enthusiastically, "Yes, yes, come up. Come up Shimshon. Third floor, 312."

A buzzer sounded. I made my way up the two flights of stairs and knocked on the door. I practically fell through it as Sophie yanked it open, a number of semi-familiar faces enveloping us. She grabbed me to her with such force our ribs collided. Someone tousled my hair, a few bellowed my name and a child jumped around me in anticipation. Their eagerness quickly faded though when Sophie discovered the still-lit cigarette in my right hand. I was continuing to hug her, but she remained limp in my embrace. She pulled away and growled, "Your cigarette! It's Shabbos, Shimshon. We still observe that here, you know."

"Sorry…" I dashed away. Back down the stairs, skipping some for speed, and threw it to the ground outside while still holding the door open and I squashed it with an outstretched foot. Back up to start again. "It's out. Sorry again for that," I said as Sophie reappeared at the door and I entered the apartment, a waft of sweet-pungent European fare now alerting my senses. It pervaded the hallway outside, but I hadn't been sure from which door it seeped. End of mystery.

I found my older sister, Miriam, and my brothers-in-law, nieces and nephews polishing off a chicken dinner, eyes averted from me. It wasn't exactly the warm reception I received earlier. The act of Shabbos defiance apparently was too much for Sophie and the others to bear. *Was she so arrogant when we were younger? Did she inherit that from Mama? Were all the Fox women like this? I guess so.* Rachel, too, shook her head in disapproval. The men and children didn't seem as hardened, stealing glances and smiles when the sisters weren't looking.

Profuse apologies didn't do the trick. The downcast eyes and frosty dispositions of my sisters let me know I had ruined the Shabbos mood. Sympathetic to my cause, Sophie's husband, Daniel, gave me a knowing wink as he came over and led me to the table. "Have a seat," he said, ignoring the cold stare from his wife and gesturing to help myself to food. "Join us." I couldn't resist. I plowed through a plate of the chicken and boiled potatoes, barely noticing that others around me were eating in silence. Miriam abruptly cleared her throat.

"Shimshon, how is the family back home?" She scooped more of the salty potatoes for her husband and me.

"They're well," I slowed my chewing. "You know Mama still fighting all the time with Shlomo. He's always bossing us all around, coming up with all these ideas on how to make money. You heard Rachel was pregnant, I'm sure." The heads nodded. I paused to shove more chicken into my mouth.

"So, tell us how you got here." Daniel changed the subject. I gulped, nearly choking.

Here we go. Rather than sharing the truth – I had snuck across the border and didn't have a visa or any immigration papers – I claimed to have a temporary work permit like Hannah's. That satisfied them. *If they knew the truth, I thought they would have kicked me out, fearing I'd put them all at risk, for sheltering an illegal alien. If they only knew I was also on the lam, wanted in Czechoslovakia for evading the draft. Maybe they suspected that too. Still, no need to worry them further.*

The chilly air around me began to thaw as I shared with my newfound siblings stories of our youth, laughing about my difficulty pulling stubborn oxen, our brother Shlomo's temper and my experiences riding horses in Germany.

For me, it became a lovely reunion. Not sure I can even call it that, seeing as I never even met my sister, Miriam, before now. Family pictures were the only way I knew what she looked like. She had come to America when I was very young. Her eldest son was only a few years my junior.

The two sisters lived in the same apartment building, on the same floor, across the hall from one another. Can't get any closer than that now, can ya? Sophie married Daniel Goldman and Miriam married his father, Milton, after her first husband died. So, they were one big happy family or the merger of two, already common practice among my *mishpachah,* if you remember.

After a lecture on Shabbos observance – how they were not like other Jews who assimilated and abandoned their Old World traditions – they laid down the house rules; what was expected of me while I stayed with Sophie and Daniel. Next, finances. They were struggling to make ends meet and I would be an additional drain. *No beating around the bush there.*

"I have no money," I fired back before knowing what hit any of us. *Oh, so now I've got chutzpah.* "You have to help me until I can find a job." Obviously, they didn't take too kindly to that.

"You'll have to find a job, Shimshon, we can't just support you without you contributing something," Daniel said, harshly. "Didn't the work permit come with a job?"

I fudged. "Actually, it didn't. It's a general work permit that allows me to work anywhere. Can you help me find a job?"

He agreed and in short time he had called in a few favors and found me a job right away. No one ever asked to see my work permit. I came Friday night, and Monday morning I went to work. Only in America can you find work so quick without anyone even checking to make sure you're on the level. I knew I'd love this country.

The job didn't turn out great. Basically, what I did was help the truck driver who traveled between butcher shops collect fat and waste from chickens and beef to make soap. *What a disgusting use for schmaltz. In the Old Country, we'd use the same fat in tasty dishes that would feed an entire family. Besides, I came all the way from Europe for this? To assist a waste collector?*

We had to lift heavy iron cans filled with 200 pounds of fat onto the trucks and take them to this Long Island soap factory. We trucked all over New Jersey and downtown New York. I came to know all the routes and learned on the job about some of the lesser-known back roads, cultures and mannerisms within the melting pot. Starting work at 5 in the morning meant I got home early enough in the afternoon to take in a movie with Hannah or spend time with my nephews and nieces. Still, I looked for what I was supposed to find in America: gold. *I'd take silver at this point.* Maybe others had it better, but not me.

I didn't get paid until the end of the week. And aside for a few dollars my sisters gave me to get started, I was struggling. They made it clear they weren't going to give me any more handouts and that I would have to pay my way. So, after work one day during my first week, I went straight to New York's Federation of Jewish Philanthropies, where I was told I could get some help. The Federation, which handled fund-raising and services for the Jewish community, gave me a few more dollars and some *schmattes,* not much nicer than the ones I had on. The first thing I did when I got paid was shop for new clothes.

I went downtown to buy a pair of trousers, a sweater and a pair of boots. It was January and I needed warm clothes. When I returned to the apartment sporting my spiffy duds, Sophie ribbed me, "Look, the greenhorn. He didn't even pay his rent. Only here a week and he's already spent his first paycheck." *I had to get out of here.* I slammed down on a table the remaining money we had agreed upon as rent and stormed off.

My sisters, too, became jealous of my relationship with Hannah. Here I came from Europe and instead of trying to become a millionaire, like the rest of them, I spent all on a girlfriend. If I had so much, why couldn't I send more to my mother and family in Europe? I did send home some of my paycheck each week to Europe, just like they had done. It didn't bother me that they harped on how much I spent on my girlfriend. What bothered me was how they treated her. To them, she was ostentatious, brash. She spoke her mind, she was lively and confident, and she sported stylish, conceivably immodest attire. Certainly, she didn't fit the mold of the demure woman they envisioned for me. Regardless of their opinion, I had fallen in love with her. Maybe it shouldn't have bothered me that they gave her the cold shoulder, but it did.

17　DEATH BY TROLLEY

Whenever I had a day off, I ran to Hannah. Actually, I took the train. On those occasions, I didn't even return to Brooklyn. I slept in Manhattan with Hannah. A little heat to the fire. Pre-marital bliss. That had to rub my sisters the wrong way, but Hannah had already been married and didn't see the need to wait. She was no longer a virgin. I certainly didn't mind her self-assuredness under the sheets. I'm a man. I make no apologies. We had something special and I felt it was right. She might have left me if I wanted to wait. I couldn't take that risk.

I resolved to make changes as soon as possible to close the distance that kept me from Hannah. After six months on the trucking job, I quit. The work was wearing me out. I continued to see Hannah every weekend while I looked for a new job. She had moved to the Bronx, by this time, 180th and Garfield. It was much further from Brooklyn than Manhattan. The first time I took her home, I got on the train and was supposed to get off at Fulton Street, so when I heard the name announced, I got off. It's Fulton Street in Manhattan. It took me an extra three hours to get back to my sister's. It was worth it to have spent time with Hannah.

After nearly two years together, it was time to make the arrangement permanent. I had never met anyone like her before and I didn't want to try. I was content; fulfilled even without having a job.

One day, I was leaving her apartment. She was just standing at the door when she cried. "It's so dull without you here. When will you return?"

"Maybe we don't have to be separated so much," I said, dropping to the expected knee-to-floor pose with Hannah towering over me. "I have no job. I don't have much to offer. You know that. But I don't want to live with my sister anymore." My voice was faltering with uncertainty. "I'm going to move out anyway." *Seemed a logical reason to marry, nu?*

I didn't even have a ring ready for the occasion or any piece of jewelry. This is when my Bubbie's gold watch would have been appropriate, had I not traded it like a *meshugener* before coming to this country. I had heard somewhere that watches were sometimes given upon engagement instead of rings. Alas, I had nothing, only the promise to buy her the simple gold band, as is customary, for the wedding ceremony. Sympathetic to my plight, and overjoyed by the prospects of a married life, she said yes.

The date was set for several months later, June 26, 1927. By then, we figured that I could find a job and rustle together enough for the wedding. To be closer to me, Hannah moved from the Bronx back to Manhattan. It had just gotten too difficult for me to travel from her home to my sister's, arriving just in time to search for a job. Several factories, I learned, hired extra workers when the regulars didn't show for their early shifts.

Several months before the wedding, she informed me. "Are you kidding? I've hardly had time to adjust to the thought of being called a husband and now I'm going to be called daddy, too?"

I didn't know which emotion was stronger, elation or fear. *How am I supposed to support another person when I'm not doing so well just scrounging enough for the two of us? Just a lot to swallow at one time. Maybe too much, too soon, too fast.*

"I'm going to have a baby!" I screeched, my voice breaking as the tears streamed. "Me. A father. A real family, just like I had in the Old Country. Thank you, Hannah. Thank you."

The family was invited to the wedding. Hannah wasn't showing yet, so we didn't have to say anything about the baby. No need to cause a fuss. One thing at a time. There'd be plenty of chances later for the questions and gossip. Let them talk. We would be married by then.

A rabbi who lived nearby conducted the ceremony at our request. He put up a *chuppah*. My sisters, Nettie, Sophie and Miriam were there. Hannah's sister, Leah, was there, along with their brothers, Sid and Judah.

I rented a tux with a white bowtie, the first time I ever wore one of those. Hannah, appropriately, designed her gown after seeing a similar one in a dress shop window. It was not the typical floor-length kind, but a sleeveless, drop-waist number, as she described it, that fell below her knees. It was all white lace and satin, very smart and elegant. A long sheer train fell from a wide headband rimmed with tiny silk flowers covering most of her hair, accentuating her eyes and lips. And I noticed again, like so many times before, how purely lovely she was, holding a bouquet of crimson roses and looking like a portrait of a movie star.

This was to be my wife and I was proud of my choice, not in the least bit fearful of what lay ahead for us or what it was like to be a married man. I embraced it as I embraced her that day. How comforting to know I'd have Hannah all for myself from here on out. She was mine, not like a possession, but as a companion, a friend that was always there, a supporter and confidant. I was no longer alone and wandering. I was home.

That was it. A few confirmations that we were pledged to stay together and would respect each other, a glass stomp, the flinging of flowers, and we were married. Mrs. Moskowitz took a week's vacation, gave us her house and went to her daughter's. Our honeymoon. It was gloriously decadent. And practically sinful, taking from each other's bodies so much pleasure as we did, as if no other couple had ever experienced such bliss before. During this week, devoid of other commitments, we could explore and experiment over and over until all we could do was sink back into sheets somewhat drenched in our sweet sweat and wait for the next opportunity for our bodies to crave it again. We rarely had the chance to experience each other like that again, but we were happy and in love nevertheless.

Mrs. Moskowitz, a neighbor, invited us to live with her a bit and we took her up on the offer. I became a motorman on a Manhattan trolley. Other jobs I tried didn't suit me. I had the chance to be a fireman or a policeman. A Jewish boy shouldn't be a policeman, wearing guns, I was told all my life. Two of my grandsons would choose that path though, so apparently times change.

I became a motorman after a neighbor convinced me of its merits. "Anyone can drive a trolley. No big deal. You just have to get a good night's sleep so you can hit on all sixes. Watch everyone racing from all directions and make sure no one gets a free ride. When it's crowded, it's easy to miss a few hoods hanging on the back. We don't take any baloney. No wooden nickels, as they say. If they don't have the dough, they walk. Just let them know you're the Big Cheese on board and they know they can't double-cross you."

It sounded easy, the way this man described it. The company was hiring and would provide the training. A couple of weeks of classes and I was on board. Between 1926 and 1930, I worked at a job I truly liked. It might seem monotonous traveling the same route every day. The best part was comparing personality types and witnessing lots of *mishugium*, craziness. You learn a lot about people's lives, some volunteering more information than others, especially the regulars who you come to recognize by name and face.

At that time, people had it rough, but I had work. I wasn't blind to what was going on around me. People were on the streets, begging. They had been tossed out of their homes with all their possessions littering the streets.

Being a motorman turned out to be an exciting job, but one that required a lot of concentration to avoid distractions. There was so much going on around you. You had to be *so* careful when stopping and taking off. The occasional jumpers were the biggest problem, either as you were taking off or before you had reached your destination. Sometimes people got hurt. I was never found at fault, even when someone died.

A man jumped in front of the trolley. He wasn't looking. I had just started up again after my last stop and there he was. Maybe he was trying to jump on. I can't be sure. I tried to toot the horn, but he came out of nowhere. He didn't stand a chance. I ran over him before I could stop. The passengers and I heard the bump and I immediately stopped short, sending some of them flying out of their seats. "What was that?" someone yelled. "I think it was a dog," another suggested.

"Is everyone okay?" I asked, securing the trolley before rising from my seat to check out the scene. Having been trained in emergency procedures, I tried to remain calm as my heart raced.

No one on the trolley had more than bruises and small cuts. A nurse riding to work jumped into action, searching through her bag for bandages to patch up an elderly man, whose glasses had broken and cut into his forehead. "Everyone please remain on the trolley as I check this out," I said, then rushing out.

When crowds of passersby started to form around the front of the trolley, the passengers joined them. Order was futile. I was too distraught to care. All the training in the world couldn't prepare me for seeing a mangled, bloody body under my vehicle. The poor man. He couldn't have been more than 20 years old.

It was a horrible scene. He was caught under the trolley, on the track. The police station was nearby and someone who saw the scene ran to get help. My bosses came too.

"I didn't see him," was all I could say when questioned by police and my supervisors. "I don't know where he came from." The trolley passengers didn't know any more than I did. A dreadful accident, that is all. Some covered their mouths and shook their heads in disbelief, shock and empathy, gawking at the gory corpse before rushing off to find another trolley.

I'm sure the passengers had a hard time erasing the images from their minds. You can imagine I didn't recover easily either. Had I been able to seek comfort from Hannah, it might have been different, but that's the last thing I could do, at this point, what with her health and the baby's at risk. So, I suffered in lonely silence, keeping the details to myself.

Like other incidents in my trolley history, an investigation ensued and I was exonerated. After the dust settled, I inquired about the man's family and discovered that he left behind a wife and two young children. The trolley company helped them out a bit and I sent them what little I could, all anonymously. I would never be able to bring myself to approach them directly. I lived with the guilt. The memory haunts me. It would haunt anyone. I killed a man. You never forget or forgive yourself.

18 LITTLE 'WHITEY'

Not long after our wedding, Hannah and I moved into the same apartment building as Yohanan at 12th Street and Second Avenue. We rented three rooms, bought second-hand furniture and set up our home. The toilet was down the hall and we shared it with another family. When you needed a bath, you filled the washtub in the kitchen and sponged yourself off.

As Hannah grew, she let me feel the baby kick, hiccup, and I often remained glued to that position awaiting updates, imagining a *feesela* against my cheek, or a *tukhes*, as the baby contorted inside her. "Got enough room in there *bubelah*?" I'd ask occasionally, my lips practically brushing her stomach as I spoke, my hands secure on her hips. "We've got big plans for you *tateleh*. Can't wait to meet you. Oh, we are going to have fun, you and me."

It was such a wondrous time, predicting whether it'd be a boy or a girl, planning our future and the things we would do and see and show this child. Things we may not have done ourselves but believed the baby would like to experience like the amusement rides at Coney Island or the Bronx Zoo.

In 1928, when our first child, Moshe, was born, I wasn't there. Nobody could get hold of me to tell me Hannah had given birth. When I came home from work, neighbors relayed how they took her to the hospital to have the baby. I was 24 years old, and I was a father to a baby boy. "Little whitey," my family would call him because of his light blond hair. We preferred the English Morris, Mo, for short.

I thought then about the father I killed and the family he left behind, what he must have felt holding his child for the first time. How he would never hold another. How his wife was left alone and I was here with Hannah enjoying this new stage of our lives.

Our world had changed overnight. Even my relationship with Hannah was different. *Is it common to call your wife 'Mama'?* I suppose I'm not the first, but I often forgot to use her real name. When we were alone, she had to remind me. To me, she was no longer just my wife. She had a more important job as the mother of my child.

Hannah had stopped working. We were living off my wages now. I came home with about $30 a week, which was a lot at the time, and that was after sending a few to the deceased man's family. I was working extremely long hours to support both families. It was enough to buy new furniture: a sofa, loveseat, and a mahogany dresser. We replaced the second-hand dreck we started with.

We had arrived, as they say. Finally, I understood what America was all about. Working hard to succeed.

My family didn't agree. "How do you spend $500 for a set of furniture? People are starving outside and you're basking in the lap of luxury? You should be ashamed of yourselves." Why should that bother anyone? *Fardrai zich dem kop!* Go drive yourself crazy! That's what happens when you live so close to family. They're in your business all the time.

In 1929, after the big stock market crash in New York, it was bad in this country. I'd watch people stand in the street, begging for a nickel, a penny, selling apples. People didn't even have enough to help the person that didn't have a job. They had to support their families and there were no jobs to be had. I – thank God – had a job and I brought in pay every week. It wasn't a hell of a lot, but it was at least steady.

More babies soon came. Hannah was pregnant again. We figured we probably would have a few. Why not? It was nice to have siblings. We had another boy, Hershel, named after my grandfather, Haskel.

With four of us in the same apartment we had occupied for close to three years, we had become cramped for space. Extended families often moved in together, unable to pay the rent any other way, as we would later experience. The trend freed up available apartments and for now, we could make it on our own.

Nothing is sacred through the family grapevine, though. My sister, Nettie, heard we wanted to move and stepped up. She came to visit us and offered her house on Utica Avenue in Brooklyn, close to where I had lived when I first came to New York. The other side of the family apparently needed to add its two cents. "Don't you dare move back to Brooklyn," Hannah's sister, Sophie, warned. "You are going to have trouble." You'd think we were old enough to make my own decisions by now. No such luck. We didn't listen to anybody.

It was a two-bedroom with a coal stove in the kitchen for baking and cooking. The rent was the same as we were paying before. So, we moved back to Brooklyn. Hershel was about a year old and Mo was two.

Sophie must have actually known something we didn't. Nettie wasn't a good landlord. The first of the month, like clockwork, she came to collect the rent. She wanted us to pay the gas and electricity too. We realized we needed extra income and despite my protest – there really wasn't a way around it – Hannah had to go back to work. She found a job as a waitress in a small diner and a young girl down the block, Celia, came to take care of the babies during the day in the apartment.

I worked nights and Hannah days. I'd leave at 2 in the afternoon and not arrive home until 3 or 4 early the next morning. Hannah left a few hours later. It was very hard on our relationship.

When my sister, Nettie, came to collect the rent, she peeked into the pots on the stove that Celia had prepared for our dinner, the babysitter reported.

On the fifth month, we couldn't make the rent. "I'll pay you next week when I get paid or Sam will pay you in a few days," Hannah pleaded. We expected Nettie would have a heart, ya know, us being family and all. But she wouldn't have it. She went to the utility companies and told them to shut the gas and electricity. "You didn't pay for the gas. I'm not going to give you free gas and electricity. Either you pay it or you don't get it." Hannah was furious. "I can't live here another day," Hannah wailed, tears cascading down her cheeks. "Can't we please look for another apartment?"

And with that painstaking experience behind us, we were out from the watchful eye of family. We were back in New York with a more reasonable landlord, and it was worth paying a little more for the arrangement. For $35 a month, we got four rooms – two bedrooms, a bathroom, kitchen – on the fourth floor of an old apartment building at Sixth and Avenue B, a five-minute walk to my job and a five-to ten-minute bus or trolley ride for Hannah, who was still working with a new babysitter for the *kinderlach*.

With both of us working, we were able to set aside enough to complete our home, without anyone to tell us differently. We got another bed so the boys didn't have to share. A lamp here. A table there. One of the items that stayed with us for many years, while the children were young, was a three-by-four caricature of three storks carrying bundles through a milky sky. It seemed a fitting artwork for us, considering we came from big families and were growing ours too at this point. Also beat explaining to the children about the birds and the bees. Much easier to point and say, "The stork brought you." That satisfied them, at least while they were young enough to hang on our every word.

This was also around the time we bought a full-sized console radio, basically a collection of wires and bulbs enclosed in a fine mahogany cabinet with fancy dials on the front. Whenever I had the night off, we'd settle in the living room after dinner to listen to the *Lone Ranger*. There was also a later version of the outlaw, hero-villain story, the *Green Hornet* with his sidekick, Cato, remaining loyal when it was adapted for television and movies.

As a young man in Hungary, I never envisioned having indoor plumbing, let alone the ability to listen to a small box emitting sound and music. Progress is really something.

Seems, though, no matter how far we came, we took two steps back in terms of autonomy. Family always found us, despite our best efforts to succeed on our own terms. This time, though, we weren't the ones asking for help. We were in a position to offer it.

Hannah's brother, Sid, followed us from Canada to the United States in 1934 when he couldn't afford to pay for high school in Montreal for his oldest daughter, Molly.

Sid had a tailor shop in Montreal. The family lived in the back of the store and made suits to order. No one could pay for such excesses, so Sid lost money. With what he had left, he came in search of a job.

We took them in for a short while, repaying Hannah's debt to them for housing her years earlier. We were living on Prospect Avenue in the Bronx at the time. Perhaps due to my restless nature, we didn't stay in one place too long and moved quite often while the children were young.

Hannah tried to put aside her past disagreements with Doris, Sid's wife. With Sid, Doris, and their three kids, we were nine in our small two-bedroom apartment. In such tight quarters, conflicts were inevitable. Sid lost his patience more often than the rest of us. Once he flew off the handle when he caught Mo throwing water on Hershel.

The boys were sitting on the fire escape outside our second-floor apartment with a bucket of water between them. Hershel was screaming as his older brother splashed water first on Hershel's shoes, then his clothes, and then dumped the bucket over Hershel's head. Hearing the commotion, Sid came down with his yardstick and smacked Mo repeatedly across the *tukhes*.

You would have assumed from the shrieking that Sid was trying to kill Mo. Neighbors came running from all directions thinking Sid was beating Mo up. "Leave the boy alone," came shouts from upstairs' windows as the crowd rushed to Mo's aid. The thought of him taking a stick to the children that were not his own. I didn't see it, but others told me what had happened, and I had a few choice words for Sid. He and his family packed up and moved out after that incident.

Good turn of events for him later on, though. He went on to do well for himself, first as a model, and later a men's window dresser at Crawfords Clothes.

With Sid and family out of our hair, the extra room freed up by their departure was soon filled with animals. We always had a cat and every cat replaced with another by the same name, Kitty. Ironically, considering the sworn animosity between cats and birds, we also housed an aging yellow canary and a parakeet named Petey for a while. Over the years I taught Petey a few annoying phrases like "Go home!", followed by the name of whomever my children were dating at the time, especially when the date dropped them off late after a night out.

The *ruckhus* was my assurance that the children were home safe. From a sound sleep, I'd try to quiet the parakeet, *"Genug shoin!*

Enough already!" I'd intervene, so the rest of the family could return to sleep and give the lovebirds a chance to say their goodbyes.

At other times, the parakeet flew around the house and landed on my outstretched finger, walked on my shoulders, or looked for things in my shirt pocket. He'd also pick food from between my lips or harmlessly peck me on the cheek. The canary got loose sometimes, especially when we cleaned the birdcage. The cat would chase the canary around the room, and it became more of a game than a blood-thirsty pursuit.

One day when the window was open and Kitty was on the windowsill, a sparrow landed on the fire escape and the cat jumped for it. Well, she missed and fell two stories. Mo went to retrieve her, but she was badly injured. We got another kitten named Kitty, of course.

19 60 DAYS

In 1931, I started coughing uncontrollably, the result I assumed of too much smoking. Everyone was smoking then. What did we really know about the dangers?

I always enjoyed my smokes. The tranquil escape they provided. A moment of calm. Warm, soothing puffs amidst a busy day. Even just the accomplishment of rolling a successful batch of Bull Durham. The task, itself, making the smoking more pleasurable. Couldn't do without them. When Mo got older, I'd send him to get candy at the corner store and bring me back a bunch of Camels.

But the nasty cough persisted. It developed into something worse. I didn't feel too well, so I went to the company doctor. He examined me. "It's just a cold," he said and sent me on my way.

Another couple of weeks. Still, I was not better. I went to another doctor. He took some tests, some X-rays. Low and behold they found the problem was with one of my lungs. I had something like a break in the lung. The doctor warned me, "You've got to relax. You can't hustle too much. If you cough or overextend yourself by doing heavy work, you could break it and hemorrhage. I'm serious. Watch out." A bit taller than me, he held onto my shoulder as he spoke, his intimidating eyes fixed on mine to stress the urgency, as if he knew my type. The type that just won't listen to medical advice.

"It would be a good idea for you to go to the country for a little while, take a long vacation, stop working for a couple of months." That certainly wasn't what I wanted to hear. Who has time for a vacation? The more I thought about it, the more I became convinced there was only one place we could go: Canada. It might be more peaceful than New York. We had family there; and I'd heard it was an easier life.

Hannah and I talked and we decided I should return to Canada for an extended vacation. Hannah wanted to stay in New York with the boys. She was still working and didn't want to leave her job. We needed the money. My doctor agreed it was a good choice.

I appealed to the trolley-car company, where I had been working for about four years now. They allowed me to take 59 days' vacation. After that, I could come back, work for a day and apply for another 59 days of leave. But I had to report back by the 59th day. What can you do in 59 days, where can you go? We wrote to Hannah's family in Canada – her sister, Leah, and brother, Judah – about the idea. They had long since resolved to accept me as part of the family despite my shortcomings. Family was family, after all. "Come on, stay here with us for one month, two months and we'll see," Judah wrote back. "You'll find a job, maybe you'll stay here."

All this time I was not even a citizen. The trolley company had to give me papers to show I had a job. You've got to be employed because Canada didn't want to let in too many Americans. They knew Americans struggling to make ends meet came to their cities to find work.

When I got to Canada, I looked for a job. I couldn't just lounge around all day, living off the good graces of Judah and his family. My doctor might not approve, but I had to do something, as long as it wasn't too strenuous. Again, like so many times before, the question arose: What can I do? Small world, but I met some of the same people I met when I lived there six years ago. Marvin Miller, the man who practically led me to my wife, traded in his cobbler shop for a fruit stand. He offered me a job in a heartbeat as soon as he heard about my situation.

"What do I have to do?"

"You stay in the store while I go to the market each day." Simple enough.

Another man hauled boxes of fruit from the truck to the store when Marvin returned with a new batch. So, I didn't have to do heavy work. I was a cashier. The pay was enough to bring Hannah to me.

I wrote to her and asked her to join me. It was a healthier environment than New York, and I could breathe much easier, away from the city's heavy smog and traffic. "Let's give up the home in New York and live in Montreal. It's so much nicer here. I'll leave my job and you can leave yours and we'll start over again in the same place we met. Those were good times, weren't they, Hannah...? It's crazy, I know. We're still young. We can do it. Whatcha think?"

Hannah had to say goodbye to the life she knew, which was hard for her. On the one hand, she welcomed the opportunity to spend time with her family in Montreal, but on the other hand, she had a nice, comfortable apartment in New York. We knew it would be better for me. Not knowing what the future held, she sold off our hard-earned furniture for about one-tenth of what we paid for it.

Hannah was able to get work, too, as a seamstress in a tailor shop. So, she was happy. We were moving, finding a little apartment in a private home: two small bedrooms and a tiny kitchen. We rented it for the month,.

If I would have felt better, we could've really made a go of it there. It wasn't to be. I had active tuberculosis. Apparently, it was a pretty common illness among us Jewish immigrants. The disease can eat away at your lungs to the point you suffocate. Until then, you cough. The thing was, I didn't know until I finally sucked it up and went to the doctor. When the doctor explained it to me what the disease was and how serious it was, I had to make plans accordingly.

We didn't want to let Hannah's family know what was going on because she didn't want to depend on them for help. Here I was, already close to my 59 days of leave from the trolley company, and I informed Hannah, "I'm going back to New York. I'm going to go to the company doctor and see what can be done."

I needed ongoing treatment and the company would probably pay for that; at least I was going to see if they would. The next day, a Sunday, I went to the bus for a ticket and I left Hannah and the children in Canada. What happened in New York was my downfall. I planned to take an express train from Montreal and, at the last minute, I changed my mind, thinking it would be easier to take a bus. Monday afternoon was my 59th day and I was supposed to report to work to avoid losing my job.

I happened to get on a local bus, which traveled to every town and every city, but not to New York. The express bus would have gotten me there directly. By the time my bus came to New York, it took me more than 17 hours. It was late Monday afternoon when I arrived in New York and I couldn't even report to my office because it was closed.

Maybe I could get away with it. I'll go in the next day, the 60th day. At 8 a.m., I tried to report to work but I had already been taken off the worker list.

The supervisors wouldn't listen. I went to one boss, the big boss, touting my clean record. He reluctantly agreed to give me back the job. But I lost seniority, which was one of the greatest things that you can have in a place like that. And I lost my route because I was the last to pick one and all the routes were taken. My route used to be downtown, Avenue A and 14th Street because we lived downtown.

Now I had to travel all the way to the station at 59th Street and 9th Avenue.

Without my seniority, I had to get up one morning at 4 a.m., and another morning at 6 a.m. Also, I was an extra man, a relief worker. If someone took a day off, I got a day's work. Otherwise, I didn't work. I could never tell what time I would work or if I would work at all. At 4 a.m., I'd wake up. An hour later, when I arrived, there was no work. I would wait until 8 a.m. and if I still wasn't needed, I came home. No work, no pay.

Hannah had returned to New York and we had set up an apartment yet again. This wasn't the kind of life she wanted, by any means, dragging herself and the boys back and forth between New York and Montreal, uprooting them and replanting them every so often. Just because I had been a vagabond in my youth didn't mean my family had to be too. It was time to stop pulling up stakes, for the sake of my family's sanity and my own health. I promised Hannah we were home to stay. No more jumping around.

I remained an extra at the trolley company until I worked there long enough to earn a steady run, a steady choice of routes. From then on, I made it a point never to be late for anything, to leave early to avoid any mishaps.

Meanwhile, my health was going from bad to worse. I was losing weight. I didn't sleep. I couldn't eat. And the doctors warned me, yet again, "If you don't take a break, if you don't watch out, you're going to land in a hospital, or you'll land in a sanatorium for tuberculosis."

How did I get tuberculosis? Turned out Menachem, my old roommate from Montreal, had it. He was constantly coughing and spitting, but I had no idea he was so ill, and I don't think he even knew it until after I had already left.

My resistance had been pretty low when we lived together, especially after I came out of the hospital that first time. Supposedly, you catch the disease from crowded, dirty conditions. As bachelors, we weren't exactly the cleanest guys, I'll concede.

That was then. Now I was 26 years old and in New York. I had two little babies. And TB was a very, very contagious disease. I had to keep away from them. I even had to have separate dishes so they could be boiled clean.

The children didn't know what happened. We used to play around in bed with them. They'd come in when we woke and we'd tickle them. I'd wrestle with them. They wrestled each other. We used to have a lot of fun. But no more. Otherwise, they might be taken away from us and put into foster homes as if I was an unfit parent by purposely spreading the disease.

Mo was already close to four, Hershel, nearly three. They needed somebody to fool around with. How do you explain, "Papa is sick and can't play with you the same way until he's better."

"Why Papa? Will you be better?"

And usually one would ask, "Are you going to die Papa?"

Then, they'd cry, and Hannah would cry too. "Papa is *not* going to die, *tatelach*. Papa is strong, remember?" Then I'd distract them by pretending to come after them like a bull, and they'd run off giggling again. Surely, they missed the physical contact, the kisses, the hugs, and I did too.

In mid-1931, we had an unexpected surprise. Hannah was pregnant once again. She waited so long to tell me that we couldn't have done anything about it if we wanted to. It couldn't have come at a worse time, being sick, not working steadily and all.

It's said that God works in mysterious ways. If we were going to have a child, we prayed it would be a girl to bring a new element to our family. While God afflicted me, he answered our prayers when it came to our little girl, Deborah, born March 9, 1932.

It was a snowy morning, I recall, when I found out. I was so excited I spent all day calling the family in Canada and the family in New York. We didn't have a phone in the house, so I had to use a phone in a store down the block, trudging through the snow to get there.

When I went to see Hannah in the hospital, they wouldn't let me in because of the TB. But I had to see my baby, and no one was going to stop me from looking. I needed a peek, at least, even if it was from a distance. As I climbed up the fire escapes, searching for the right room, I felt like a rebellious boyfriend trying to see my girl, fearing the wrath of an overprotective father.

When I found Hannah's room, quite winded from unsuccessful attempts, I took a moment to catch my breath and take in the scene: Hannah with the baby cradled at her side, both sleeping peacefully. Two angelic figures wrapped in white sheets and blankets. I delayed waking them, knocking softly on the window, startling the baby a bit, but not enough to wake her, and leaving Hannah a bit stunned to discover the knocking was not at her door, but at the window. When she regained her bearings and realized what I was doing, I motioned to her to hold the baby up to the window for me to see. Such a precious face, pure and sweet. Her eyes were closed; she didn't even know she had a father yet. Hannah held the baby's hands close to the window for me to touch her, albeit through glass. A wisp of fine, brown hair could be seen from under a pink, cotton cap on her head. "Looks just like you," Hannah said through the glass.

I could barely hear her. "What?"

I watched Hannah's mouth this time. "She looks like you. She's got your nose and your chin." Hannah said, tears welling in her eyes. "I think we should name her Deborah after the judge in the Bible and your grandmother, Dora." She had to repeat it all a few times, slowly, so I could make out her words. My baby girl, named after my dear Bubbie, may she rest in peace.

"Fine with me," I mouthed back, nearly choking on the words, my mixed emotions of joy and regret. "Suits her fine," I shouted through the glass. "God judged us worthy and we got our girl. I love you." She must have heard that last part because she repeated it back.

Just then there was a knock at the door and I quickly vanished. "Just a minute," I heard Hannah say. I made my way back down the fire escape without any incidents. I saw my baby girl and I was at peace.

After that, I knew I had to see my boys. Hannah had put Mo and Hershel in a neighborhood nursery before taking a cab to the hospital to deliver Deborah. The two boys opened a door to a cabinet in the bottom of a counter and wouldn't let anyone pass the open door. They wouldn't take food. The nursery workers and I spent close to an hour trying to coax them out of their fort. Mo and Hershel were always getting in trouble like that.

Mo, being older, was often the ringleader. His first brush with the law came when he got lost in Montreal while our family was visiting relatives. He just opened the front door and slipped out. We were too busy to keep track of every child, thinking they were all playing together in another room. A policeman saw him crying because he was lost in Mount Royal Park. He was about three or four years old. The officer picked Mo up and put him on his horse. A woman in the park with another friend said, "The kid on the mounted policeman's horse there looks like Hannah's son." She walked over and told the officer, "I think I know his mother."

"Who's his mother?"

"Hannah."

"What's her last name?"

"I don't know Hannah's last name. But it's Hannah's son." The officer looked over at Mo and asked, "Is your mother Hannah?"

"I don't know. Her name is 'Mother.'"

The officer and woman chuckled. Turned out the woman was right. When the officer took Mo home to the address the woman had provided, sure enough he found Hannah.

When Mo was about six years old, he crawled into a cab in front of our Manhattan apartment while the driver was out eating lunch. Mo took a nap in the back. When the driver got back into the cab, he drove down 42nd Street to see if he could pick up a fare. He found one, but when the passengers headed for the back seat, they discovered the child sleeping there and wouldn't get in. "Is this your child?" they asked, alarmed.

The driver turned around in astonishment. "No, it's not my child. What do you take me for, a fool? How could I give you a ride if I knew a child was in there?" As he drove away, trying to decide what to do with the child, and while in contact with his dispatch office, he realized he actually knew this boy from the neighborhood and took him home. He charged us $1 for the lost fare.

Hannah had been frantic. The police station wasn't far from our home and Hannah was there several times a month. There was a standing joke in the family that whenever Mo was gone, Hannah would open the door to the police station, and they would automatically broadcast our son's description.

Mo was six or seven when he and Hershel got drunk for the first time. Hannah had made *vishnik*, brandy with sour cherries. Hannah fermented this mixture of cherries, sugar and water in a big crock on the fire escape. We went somewhere and left them home with a babysitter. When she was preoccupied with Deborah, they got into the *vishnik*. They didn't particularly like the liquid, but they ate like a dozen cherries each from the mixture. The cherries were very sweet. They got drunk. Somehow or another, they left the icebox door open. Kitty, the cat, got in and took out a chicken Hannah had cooked for dinner and ate the whole thing. All we found were bones.

When we came home, we found Mo and Hershel under the bed sound asleep, drunk as skunks. We pulled them out, and they couldn't stand straight. Without anything else prepared for dinner that night, we had mashed potatoes and spinach. The kids liked it though.

In the summer, when he was older, Mo could be found either at Yankee Stadium or the Bronx Zoo. We only lived about six miles from the zoo. Mo would hitch rides on the back of trolley cars, even on mine. I'd see him in my side view mirror and although I was a little concerned for his safety, I let him do it, hoping he wouldn't get caught and no one would know he was my son. Nobody ever suspected.

Why would I knowingly allow this behavior? Because I wanted him to learn to take risks, just as I did in my youth. He reminded me of myself at a time when I was also bold, fearless and independent.

Like many younger siblings, Hershel was his brother's shadow. Mo would take Hershel to Yankee Stadium with him. They stood outside near a security guard and tried to look pitiful. After the game started and nobody else was buying tickets, the officer would say, "Okay, you kids, go on in." That's how they got in every game.

Other times they would jump on freight cars to ride to the East River to go swimming. If they were really hungry, they ate broken ice cream cones and bananas found on the train. They didn't worry about the illnesses they could catch from such behavior.

Whenever I had a day off, the boys and I went somewhere. We'd walk across the Triborough Bridge, have a soda and walk back. Or we'd go to St. Mary's Park. Each of the trips were at least a week apart. We walked up Prospect Avenue, where we lived now, or down Westchester. Our favorite pastime was looking in store windows, and once in a while, for a treat, we'd stop at the delicatessen for a *knish*.

During one of our more memorable walks, we watched a man striding backwards on the bridge. Intrigued, the children and I discussed. We devised several theories. I expressed the one I liked the most. "Some people want to see where they are going and some want to see where they've been. Don't look back. Remember what is back there but look ahead." While they might not have fully grasped my meaning, they did find it fascinating. The glass half-full or half-empty theory; how we view the world, understanding our differences. One of the many moral lessons I hoped to pass along.

The children went to school from 8 a.m. to 3 p.m., followed by an hour four times a week of Hebrew school, Monday to Thursday. We went to synagogue every Saturday morning from 9 a.m. to 12 p.m., followed by the 10-cent movie theater. I would give Mo and Hershel money for the movie and a nickel for candy.

On Sunday, the children went again to Hebrew school for three hours. Once Mo and Hershel played hooky from Hebrew school and the rabbi, noticing the absence, came to the house to find out if they were sick. The boys had just finished telling me that *shul* was all right. After a long lecture on the need for Hebrew school, I still gave them a quarter for the movies. They stayed there all afternoon. I was a young boy once too and I remembered well the constrictions of education. What's wrong with letting them be boys? Admittedly, I had become a bit of a pushover with my own family.

They were good kids and I just didn't feel the need to reprimand them harshly. I raised my voice on occasion and I lectured when needed. They knew who was in charge and they learned to trust rather than fear. Other than that, I kept quiet and let them enjoy life.

Hannah was the disciplinarian. Her punishment was usually swift and painful. One time Mo told her to "shut-up," and quick as a wink, she got a broom and hit him across the *tukhes* with it. "That's not how you speak to your mama. I know I taught you better than that. Next time you'll think twice before you say something like that again," she

132

scolded between swats. She had a mighty swing and he, healthy lungs. He never spoke back to her again, though he still got a *gut zetz*, good smack, or if she was particularly angry, the often-threatened *delangen,* spanking, if he didn't play by her rules. Like when Hannah found out through a charge on her bill that Mo had gone to the bakery one day and put a donut on our account.

Every parent has his or her own way of disciplining. I knew Hannah spent more time with the children than I did so I let her do what she believed was best.

20 DAY OLD BREAD

We already had boys – and we loved them – but we were never as happy as we were when we had that little baby girl. Having a baby girl at home was something special. She was precious, a dainty little kewpie doll.

Deborah, was about six months old when my TB worsened. I hemorrhaged and had to go to Bellevue Hospital. It wasn't far away from our house.

The prognosis was terminal.

"He hasn't got a chance," the doctor told Hannah. "He's not going to come out alive." Hannah was inconsolable. He had to give her some pills to calm her. "It's going to be up to you to tell him, unless you want me to do it."

"You better do it," she told the doctor, still distraught.

"With this disease you don't survive," the doctor explained, gently, spouting out all kinds of medical mumbo-jumbo I didn't understand.

I was stubborn. Big surprise. "Are you sure? I feel fine now. I know I've been sick before, but I always bounce back. Besides, I'm too young to die and my grandparents lived a long time."

"That strong attitude of yours will help," was his only reply.

I had different plans than going down without a fight. It was my nature. Maybe God had different plans for me too. I figured maybe I'd stay in the hospital a few weeks, a month, and go home. Meanwhile at home, the children had to be examined too and they had to be given shots so that they didn't catch the disease. Once it's an active germ, you've got to be very careful and that's what I had.

After school or in the afternoon on days there was no school, the children had to take a nap and have their cod liver oil. That stuff was seen as the cure all for anything that might ail you. We gave the kids a teaspoon every day to ensure good health, followed by a hard candy, to take away the fish flavor. Doctors also checked them every six months to make sure none fell victim to TB too.

I was at Bellevue Hospital for about a month when they sent me to Montefore Hospital, a little further away. There was no choice. Montefore, at that time, was thought a better hospital than most. First of all, it was Jewish. Second, it had fine doctors. The only thing is they didn't know how to heal that lung of mine. They tried different things, putting air in the lung, expanding it, shrinking it. Nothing worked. For some people it did, but not for me. There was no real cure. Their solution was nothing but bed rest. I had to stay in bed all the time, which was boring and draining.

When I went to Montefore, the only family that came to visit me was Yohanan and his wife, Sylvia. My family from Brooklyn very seldom came.

Hannah certainly didn't have an easy time. Her sister would ask her, "Why don't you leave him? What do you need a sick man for? What good is he to you now?"

Three children and no money coming in, what do you do? Couldn't depend on the family. If they had a way to help, they didn't let us know. Maybe they had too much going on in their own lives to care.

What do you do, then? You go on what was called home relief, today's welfare. The city pays the rent and sends a cheque for food and clothing. There was no other alternative. I got a couple of dollars from the company. But we made quite a few mistakes that cost us. For one, Hannah didn't report how ill I was in time and we lost some of our home relief. Otherwise, they would have supported Hannah more. We were struggling for many, many years, as a result.

Around the same time I got sick, we entered the Great Depression and nobody had jobs. You couldn't always get money from home relief because there was very little available to help anyone. It was hard to make ends meet, but she made the best of it. She told me, "Many a time I went to sleep without supper. As long as the children had something to eat, it was okay. A glass of coffee, a glass of milk, a piece of bread."

Food was so precious that if the children didn't eat their oatmeal at breakfast, she'd serve it to them for lunch. Buying bargains in the market became her special talent. There was a bakery in the Bronx nearby she called the "Old Lady's" and she'd send the boys about once a month or so to buy day-old cakes and breads. They took a shopping bag, and filled up the bag. Two cupcakes that normally were a nickel were a penny if a day old. Ten cents' cakes cost them 2 cents and so on. There were all sorts of tricks to saving a few pennies and the family knew them all.

I was at Montefore for about two months. Then, the hospital strongly recommended – more like required – that I go to a sanatorium in the country, Bedford Hills, N.Y. That's where they sent guys like me. They only send patients there who are not too run down or too sick. Very sick people died in New York hospitals.

The sanatorium was like going on a needed vacation and staying at a country inn where the food was good and I didn't have to work. In my case, unemployment was a double-edged sword. My family needed me to work, and yet, if I did, I got sicker.

The forced relaxation served me well, despite the lost income. I started feeling a little better there. Every time the doctors examined me – once every two weeks – they said there was a lot of improvement. After a while, I was not on strict bed rest any more and started walking around a lot.

In the afternoon everybody had a two-hour nap from 1 to 3 p.m. If you don't nap, you could participate in activities like tinkering in the workshop, as I often did. I'd make little beaded bags, sewing the fabric of the bag and then stringing beads together for the bag's exterior.

I also accepted the position of mailman, delivering mail to all the patients once a day for five days. I made a few dollars off tips. Once a week we'd have an evening movie. I made extra selling ice cream during the movie. Anything I made I sent home to Hannah. Every Sunday, I could expect her to visit. It was a long trip, so an expensive taxi fare. She almost always came with the baby, Deborah.

I was supposed to be at the sanatorium for two years and it had already been about 16 months. If I progressed along and played my cards right, I might be well enough to leave in four months instead of eight. I hadn't counted on the hand I was dealt.

One afternoon, the sanatorium patients were sitting at a table in the dining room eating dinner. There was a teenage boy, maybe 17, newly assigned to sit across from me. He was a sloppy eater. There was nothing I could say because we were only there for half an hour, sitting and eating before we were to leave. He was put there and had to sit there or else I would have chased him away.

Apparently, I'm one of those outspoken guys who can't leave well enough alone. I blurted out, "You have to be so sloppy? You have to do what you're doing, eating like that, disgusting?" He wiped his mouth on a napkin and threw it in my plate. I got really mad, spun around the table, grabbed him by the collar and pulled him outside the dining room. Just couldn't risk the repercussions of hitting him in plain view. We had been sitting close to a hallway door and I believed I could make a quick exit before the dining staff could catch me. Sloppy Eater was caught off guard and was no match. I was older and apparently much stronger when provoked.

All the patients were watching and the dining staff ran after me. They didn't know what was happening. Sloppy Eater was trying to get away from me, but he couldn't. He was screaming for help by this time. When I got him in the hall, I let him have it. I smacked him around, pinning him against the wall as I struck.

He was a sick boy; I was supposed to be a sick boy, too. The staff got to me and pulled me off. I was taken back to my room by two husky orderlies and told that the matter would be reported and that I was sure to be punished. An hour later, I was called into the office along with the boy. I explained my role and he explained his to the sanatorium director and his assistant. They didn't make much *tzimmes*, fuss. "Wait outside. We'll let you know our decision," the director said to me sternly.

Fifteen minutes later, they called me in. "Go pack your clothes and go home." They threw me out. Nothing else I could do.

When I got home, Hannah was surprised to hear my story. We were left in a bind. She was getting help from home relief. A week, two weeks went by and the city learned about the incident. As a condition of home relief, I couldn't stay home. Also, a doctor hadn't discharged me, so I was considered a health threat. I had to go to another hospital, be cured, and receive discharge papers to show I was in the clear. The city found a spot for me at Sea View Hospital in Staten Island.

At the five-month mark, the doctor examined me through X-rays and other tests. He told me that I could go home; I just needed some additional rest to go back to work.

It was very good news. By this time, it was 1934 and Deborah was two years old. I missed her first two years of life, years of not being able to play with her or love her. Not to mention the two years of my sons' lives.

I wasn't cured, but it was determined I had an arrested case, and I was discharged. "As long as you're not working too hard. Take it easy for a couple of years, and you might have a chance."

Hannah had moved the family out of downtown again, 6th Street to the Bronx, while I was away. She couldn't afford to live downtown. As an added bonus, her landlord in the Bronx apartment gave her a month free rent. After a short while, they moved again, but always staying in the Bronx.

They moved around a lot because landlords would offer free rent to entice potentially good tenants to move into the building. With that kind of offer, you couldn't afford *not* to move. In addition to getting free food through home relief, Hannah shopped at the same store all the time until they got to know her and agreed to put things on a tab. They would wait until she received her monthly home relief check. When she received it, she paid everyone and found out how much she had left.

When I got home from the hospital, life was still difficult because I didn't work. Hannah had to work in a sewing factory that produced union workers uniforms and I had to stay home and take care of the children.

It wasn't what we wanted. It was hard to swallow, but we didn't have much choice. Hannah was a hard worker, ever since she came to Montreal and had to go to New York City to find a job.

Women really didn't work in those days. They went from their father's house to their husband's house, the man supporting the woman. But Hannah never had a choice. She had to be assertive and strong. Nothing stood in the way of providing for her family when I couldn't. Without hesitation, she assumed the responsibility.

Whenever Hannah came home, she greeted us by kissing the tops of all our heads. When she got to me, I'd often grab her close for a quick, playful peck. She'd pull away, modestly blushing with her standard "not in front of the children" line – they either shielding their eyes, offering a squeamish *ew* or *ick*, or try to mimic our actions – and I'd give her beefy *tukhes* a *patsh*, just for effect.

With an admonishing smile, she gained her composure and routinely distracted the children with a game we called *Check My Pockets*. Whenever she announced the game, they'd charge for the mysterious hidden treasure, all hands competing for the prize. "What is it Mama? Is it sweet or sour? Is it chocolate? I bet it's chocolate," they'd screech in delight. It was a joyous scene, all smiles and whoops and energy and laughter.

During the summer, the children were home. Mo and Hershel were in school by 1934. We didn't go away on any vacations, so I got involved in the neighborhood, the school, the shul, or in the Talmud Torah, where they went to Hebrew school.

When I needed help with the children or I didn't feel well, they'd go to the home of a neighbor, Mrs. Marinoff. She lived in an apartment on 158th Street. A heavyset woman, she had a big wart on her nose. You couldn't take your eyes off it.

Regardless, she was a very warm, cheerful person who didn't let the imperfection bother her. The children often ate lunch there. Their favorite was mashed potatoes and spinach, which she let them form into shapes. They'd eat from each side of the bowl and then plow a tunnel under what was left to form a bridge.

21 STREET SMARTS

Even without much, the kids found ways to entertain themselves. When we lived on Trinity Avenue, they used an indoor-gym the janitor had created to amuse his own son.

The janitor's name was Eddie Johnson. A 54-year-old black man, he was as brawny as a bull but as docile as a lamb. He went out of his way to be cordial, always greeting me politely with a "Good morning Mr. Fox" or "How are those boys of yours doing?"

He became a janitor after dropping out of school in the eighth grade to pursue boxing. He won a few medals in local and regional competitions, and he often showed the children those medals with pride. But he injured his right arm in a car accident, so he had to do what he could to make a living. Boxing was over for him. Without a formal education, he resigned himself to the menial work of housekeeping and maintenance because he could stay in the building for free. His son, Henry, was conceived out of wedlock with a girl who left one day and never returned.

Henry was around my age. He lived with his father and helped around the building sometimes too when he wasn't working in a car repair shop down the street. Mr. Johnson, as we called him, also had a Labrador named Prince. The dog was so big that Deborah could ride him. And she did.

"Giddy up Prince," she'd command, as she lightly kicked his sides like a racehorse. "Go faster horsey. Take me to the castle!" Poor dog. At least afterwards, he was rewarded with delicious candy. "Good boy Prince. You are such a good boy. Who is my good boy?" What dog could resist her affections?

The children played in the basement of the building, where Mr. Johnson, in his spare time, had created a sort of gym for his son to learn boxing. It was lined with old mattresses, the perfect environment for the boys to wrestle and the girls to practice gymnastics. On weekends, the teen-agers held dances in an adjacent room in the basement because it was private, and the concrete ceiling shielded upstairs residents from the music.

Sometimes, Hershel, and others their age watched secretly from a hole in the wall of another room while the older kids danced. After several dances, one of the parents objected to the idea of dances in the basement without chaperones. They made the kids have dances in their apartment on 158th Street between Trinity and Jackson streets.

Our kids were growing up too fast. They all had the spunk and mentality of life on the street, trying to fend for themselves.

With me in and out of hospitals and unable to support the family, Mo took it upon himself at the young age of seven, to help out. Hannah and I had talked about it and he must have overheard our sometimes-heated financial discussions. We initially objected. He was too young and it would interfere with his studies. But he agreed only to do menial tasks like bagging groceries and running errands. We said he could work on weekends and after school, provided he made time for completing his homework and that his grades didn't lag.

At first, he worked for Mr. Weiler, who owned the local grocery on the corner of 156th and Trinity Avenue. He folded the recyclable brown grocery bags shoppers returned in exchange for a nickel and delivered orders to women who couldn't carry all that they purchased.

Sunday mornings he went door-to-door, taking orders for morning rolls, milk, eggs and the like so people wouldn't have to make the trip to the grocery store themselves. He got a few cents tip for the service and Mr. Weiler gave him a quarter. Mo turned all of his earnings over to Hannah. He also worked for Mr. Cohen, who owned the fruit store, and did odd jobs. Again, all the money went to Hannah.

Mo worked for a time in a drug store as well. Inside, there were two telephone booths used by the neighborhood because no one had phones in their apartments. When the phone rang in the drug store, all the kids rushed to answer it. The first one there got to run to the recipient in adjacent apartments to inform the resident of the phone call. For this, the kids usually received a two or three cent tip.

Then there was the newspaper business. Saturday nights he waited for the newspaper truck to deliver the Sunday papers. He bought 15 to 25 papers and Mo and Hershel knocked on doors asking people if they wanted one, making about 2 cents a paper, which they split. His venture went belly up, though, when the candy storeowner complained to the newspaper vendor about papers being sold to kids on the street, taking away his business.

When Mo was in high school, he was among a group of students allowed to take classes in odd shifts, like 10:40 a.m. to 5 p.m., in exchange for working during school hours. Mo worked for a while at the laundry across the street from our apartment. He drove a horse and wagon delivering wet wash in a bundle to residents – for tips. Sometimes he had to tote the bundle on his shoulders up three or four flights of stairs.

Not everything Mo did sat well with me, such as his job at the little shul down the block. Mo convinced the Shabbos goy, the *shammes*, to give him a nickel for helping to shut off the lights after Shabbos services on Friday nights. The gentile man didn't really understand that Mo was a Jewish congregant, and Mo didn't try to enlighten him. One Shabbos, the whole family was there for services. The rabbi approached me during the Kiddush following services and asked if Mo was my son and was I aware he was being paid to shut off the lights. We weren't exactly observant, but I knew it was a task for a gentile, not a Jew. And that was the end of that. I wasn't going to have it and Mo knew he was in the wrong. He backed down and dropped the job.

Despite the financial hardships we endured, the kids survived and became tougher. Hershel was especially rugged, having learned his street smarts from Mo and other older boys. He wasn't afraid of anything or anyone. One day, Hershel was sitting on the curb playing marbles when a car stopped and the driver blew the horn for Hershel to move so he could park there. Hershel said, "I was here first. Go park somewhere else."

When he was in the 2nd grade, he got into an argument with his teacher about a certain pronged eating utensil. "It's a *guple*." Hershel told the teacher, who corrected, "It's a fork."

"I'm seven," Hershel responded, as if at that age he should have all the answers. "My mother told me it's a *guple* and it's a *guple*. You can tell me it's a fork from today 'til tomorrow, but it's a *guple*."

They called Hannah to school and said, "Your kid is discourteous to the teacher."

"Why do you say that?"

"We are trying to teach him that a fork is a fork. He keeps saying a word that we don't understand. He keeps saying *guple*."

"That's Yiddish for fork."

"Well, he's got to learn English."

"Yes, we understand."

When Hershel came home from school later, we discussed the incident. I said to him, "Look, if the teacher says it's a fork, it's a fork. It's a *guple* at home. At school, it's a fork."

Even in the melting pot, it's a challenge to fit in. One way to be accepted was to be part of a crowd or gang, which were very common in our neighborhood. Some were violent and criminal, but the boys' group was more of an exclusive social club.

Mo's crowd was called the Ibex and he became its president. One of the members of his crowd also belonged to a Ravens gang and that allowed Mo's gang to walk on Ravens' turf without any harm and they could walk in the Ibex's. The Ibex had a tune that they whistled if any of them were in trouble and everyone answered that call if they heard it. The words of the tune meant, "I need you, but I can't see you," in Spanish.

Mo acted like a tough guy. But being tough doesn't always count. He almost lost his left arm to blood poisoning. From a splinter, no less. He got it jumping over a fence in the neighborhood. The doctors wanted to take the arm off, but I wouldn't let them. I had learned a lot while in the hospital for three years. I told them to drain Mo's arm, another alternative. It was risky, the doctors told us, but I told them to go ahead. It worked.

Mo was brave during the procedure. We never let him in on the worst-case scenarios, but he had to be fearful because of the pain he was in. I expected him to break down and cry, but he never did. Hannah and I did, though. When alone, we sobbed in each other's arms like babies while discussing our options. Watching your child in a hospital bed, suffering, it's very humbling. It was our job to protect him. We gave him freedom and then things like this happen and you're helpless.

145

Being in the hospital, Mo lost a lot of school. He was a good student. This was the term that he had an opportunity to make the "Rapids." Instead of taking three years to complete junior high, he could complete it in two. We were afraid he wouldn't make it into the accelerated track because of all the school lost. But he did. He had the potential to be a top student, but he got cocky, maybe as a result of his gang involvement. Overly confident in his smarts, he stopped working at it, stopped doing his homework and studying. His grades slipped and he was more like an average student than a high achiever. Either way, he was much brighter than I ever was as a result of the opportunities I never had.

I still had to worry about my own health. Every six months I would go for checkups. The New York Jewish Federation paid the doctors I saw. One day in 1938 my doctor said to me, "You look pretty good. For four years nothing has happened, so I think you can go back to work as long as it's not too demanding."

I returned to the office of the trolley company where I had worked before. They wanted to give me a job, but not in the office, not doing light work. Since I had been a motorman before, they wanted me to drive a bus.

When I told the doctor, he shot back, "Don't you dare. You can't do that. It's very hard work. You can't drive a bus. You'll kill yourself." At that time, the buses didn't have power steering, power brakes. When driving a bus, you had to put your shoulder into it.

I went to the office and said the doctor wouldn't let me drive a bus. My boss told me, "That's the only job that's open right now."

Four years gone by during which I couldn't work and when I try to find work... Something had to give. I borrowed to open a store, a cleaning and tailoring shop on the same block we lived.

Hannah knew how to sew. I knew a little and the rest I figured I'd learn. Hannah's brother, Sid, was a tailor. He promised me over the years to teach me and this was my opportunity to take him up on the offer.

We opened the Trinity Avenue store in 1938. Mo was ten years old and in sixth grade. His school, P.S. 51, James K. Spaulding Jr. High School was across the street, as was Sid and Doris's apartment.

We paid $30 rent a month for the space. It was on the first floor of an old high-rise apartment building, which also housed a small five-and-dime store. The area attracted a seedy clientele that we had to constantly discourage from loitering outside our shop.

We had a sewing machine. I bought a pressing machine, and *voilà*, we were in the tailoring business. We assumed we would prosper just because we were cheaper than our competition a few blocks away. They charged a quarter to make a hem or cuffs on a pair of pants. We only charged a dime.

Hannah couldn't bring herself to take advantage. "How can I charge so much for a job that takes me only a few minutes to do?"

If someone brought back a suit we cleaned, I often pressed it for free. Turns out we both were poor businesspeople. We didn't know any better.

It often took six weeks for customers to pick up their suits. And when they did come to pick it up, they'd say they couldn't pay, but needed the suit. We allowed a lot of people to pay on credit and had to trust them to come back. Most of them didn't. The last customer brought us some drapes to clean. When the owner came for them, it was the same story.

"I can't give it to you if you don't pay for it," I said, standing my ground at the counter as Hannah worked on a sewing project, the hum of the machine entrancing her. When she stopped to reposition the material, she heard the conversation and quickly retreated to the back of the shop in fear.

147

"At least you have to give me back my cost," I said, forcefully.

"Well, I haven't even got that!" His face was turning red, his fists clenching.

"Then you can't get the drapes. It's as simple as that."

He held my glare for a minute, debating his next move, his arms stiff at his side now too. *Was he going to hit me?* He turned to leave, spouting Yiddish curses on his way, something about salt in my eyes and pepper in my nose. "I'll be back!"

Wouldn't you know we received a summons to return the drapes or face legal action? We returned them, but were never paid. That was the last straw. The store had to close.

Again, we appealed to the Jewish Federation. They couldn't help us when Hannah and I were working. But now that we had closed the store, they considered our case. "I have to work," I pleaded. "I have to do something. Please... I have a family to support."

22 PARTY CRASHER

It was the middle of 1938. After several months on a waiting list, the Federation took me into their Chesed Workshop, a vocational rehabilitation service in the Bronx. The Chesed, or Chesed Health and Rehabilitation Services, which took its name from its philosophy of Jewish mercy, began about 25 years earlier to care for Jewish tuberculosis patients like myself. It was among the oldest workshops in the nation for rehabilitating the chronically ill. The program was supported by private donations, not the government. Without such assistance, TB patients had to work long hours in crowded and unsanitary conditions that perpetuated their health problems and led to relapses.

The sewing plant or garment factory that I worked in made hospital gowns and nurse caps (blue on one side and red on the other) for hospitals around the country and uniforms (pants, shirts, skirts and aprons) for major hotels and restaurants such as Horn & Hardart.

Each order was for several thousand uniforms at a time. I began as a stock boy, packing and loading boxes of uniforms for sale.

Getting into the Chesed was by no means a cinch. Only people with TB, heart disorders or mental disorders were hired. You had to be referred by a hospital, clinic, doctor or social worker. These were men and women who were out of circulation for a while, sometimes a couple of years without being able to hold down a job. If you didn't come in with a skill you could still perform, you were trained so you could make a living after being discharged.

Patients began by working one hour a day and then gradually worked their way up to eight hours a day. You'd work three hours in the morning with an hour nap and then you could continue working in the afternoon. Doctors and nurses monitored your progress and determined how long you could work. It had been like ten years since the family had any money. Our income had been dropping since 1929. Times were bad for other people, but we were also struggling with my health problems. Through it all, Hannah was a pillar of steel. She had picked up a job as seamstress in a factory making wedding gowns and other dresses.

As soon as I went into the Chesed, though, she stopped working. I was making more than she was, and more than we were getting from home relief from the city.

I worked my way up from the stock room to the sewing machines. There, I could practice my trade: tailoring. A little bit I knew, a little bit I faked. But I let myself be taught. I watched and I saw, and I was learning fast.

Some of the other workers were jealous of my progress. I tried to tell them I had previous experience; I already had the skills and that's why I was advancing at a faster rate than them. "I learned how to sew and press before I came to the Chesed, working with my wife, repairing suits and pants at our tailor shop." It didn't matter. To them, it was just unfair, and sometimes I'd hear them whispering behind my back.

Usually it takes about one-and-a-half to two years until you get up to eight hours, but I was in pretty good shape. The bosses saw what I was doing, that I was dedicated and wanted to work. I started working three-hour days and a month or two later they gave me an hour more. Come nine months, I was on eight hours. I became a regular worker.

I was no longer considered a patient. They made me an assistant foreman, part of the training personnel. It meant a steady job teaching patients how to use sewing machines.

The Chesed actually started with a clerical specialty, which expanded, improved machinery and hired more workers. The bureau provided businesses with such services as mimeographing, offset printing, addressing, stuffing and mailing and later IBM card punching and sorting. They had a printing press, printing names on envelopes for schools, all kinds of reports and books.

From there, the Chesed developed other departments: carpentry, electrical, data processing, jewelry, and watch repair. The mechanical division made tools and assembled electronic wiring and automatic controllers for heating systems. It also made an electronic device for submarines.

We were still close with Sid and he offered to draw on his experience in the clothing industry to help us find a bargain. Sid, Doris, Hannah, Mo and I went on a junket to the stores on Prospect Avenue. We found a light-blue gabardine suit. Shop owners would try to entice shoppers by promising all sorts of bargains. It was considered good luck to make the first sale of the day, which meant we were able to haggle for a bargain by getting an early start.

Mo's bar mitzvah at the synagogue on Forest Avenue, where I served as a secretary, was quite an emotional event for us. Our oldest became a man in the eyes of Judaism. Not only the culmination of his Jewish education, but also a tribute to the hardships our people had faced throughout history and even at this time in Europe.

The service was spectacular. Our large family from New York and Canada surrounded us, congregants we knew well as regulars, and Mo's friends from Jewish social events, including the Federation-sponsored boys summer camp in the mountains he and Hershel attended every year.

We served those deli sandwiches in a party after services. While small and intimate, it was a celebration worth every penny just to *kvell* about Mo's accomplishment and to see the children having such a good time.

The kids were older now and Hannah went back to work at the dress factory. We moved from our three-bedroom apartment. We were still a bit crunched. I took Deborah with me to look for rooms. We found a nice apartment on Eaton Avenue, which was not too far from my workplace. And we fell in love with it. We didn't know we would need the extra room for another reason. Late in 1943, Hannah told me that we would be having another baby.

Oh my. One would have thought we were done having babies. It had been 12 years since we had a baby in the house. There was nearly a riot in the house the day we all found out. The biggest objection from the kids was from Hershel. "You need it like a *loch in kop*," he said, slapping his forehead.

"You're going to take care of a baby now? You're already 40 years old. And who's going to take care of us?" He directed his anger at Hannah.

In 1944 we had another girl, Sheryl, named for Hannah's mother. She arrived on Mo's 16th birthday, ruining his plans for a Sweet 16.

From that birthday on, his celebration was overshadowed by what he considered his sister's bad timing. For many years, Sheryl captured everyone's attention and he barely felt noticed on his special day.

We reminded him each year, "You are supposed to be happy. She's a sort of gift to you, don't you think?" He didn't see it that way. She was another mouth to feed – and he was helping pay for the food as part of an already stretched budget – another noisy infant, another *shmutzy* diaper to smell, and another responsibility.

For us, it was the perfect balance: two girls, two boys. Mo would be out of the house soon. He was recruited to work for the Air Force in Rome, N.Y. Mo's big joke was that we traded a big eater for a little one.

A year-and-a-half later we had yet another little baby. No matter what we did; no matter how much we did to avoid it. All of a sudden, BOOM, Hannah was saying, "I'm pregnant."

"What are you, *meshugeneh*? There must be a mistake! It's impossible! You're getting too old. I'm getting too old." I had a slight hesitation. I didn't even remember sleeping with her. Guess the few-and-far-between times we slept together were quite powerful. Who would have believed we would be fertile soon after having another child?

Mo was the one who asked me this time why his mother was having babies all the time. "What's going on? Are you going to have another family?"

I replied, "With a new daughter and all the rest of you preparing to leave home, Sheryl needs someone to grow up with and play with. Mama decided to have one more so that Sheryl wouldn't be lonely."

The older children originally fought the idea before realizing it could be fun having a baby in the house. They got to play with the baby and Hannah did all the rest. Deborah probably had more fun with the babies than the boys, though. She was 14 and could already be counted on to babysit. Mo and Hershel had a room down a long hallway, a distance from where Sheryl and Eliza slept with Hannah and me. Deborah's room was next door to ours.

With a larger family, it meant we had to work harder and smarter. That would have been much easier if my health would have held up. I was working a little too much in the shop, only taking one day off a week. By then, I had become a foreman, and we even saved a bit.

We were not the type of family that spent lavishly on ourselves. We ate well, but never any steak. Dinner could be as basic as potatoes or rice, or a bowl of vegetable soup and bread with butter. Every Friday night we had soup and boiled chicken.

Mo gave his whole paycheck to Hannah each week, and she gave him back what she determined he needed to get back and forth to work, buy lunches and go to the movies or out to dinner on Sunday nights with a date.

Mo's first serious crush was a Puerto Rican girl, a dark beauty with bright green eyes and silky black hair that touched her *tukhes*. Her name was Noreen, but she went by Rena.

Mo and Rena became high-school sweethearts. It had something to do with the way she looked at him, always straight in the eyes, with the confidence of a very mature woman. Yet, she was only a girl, a year younger than he was.

When they met, Mo told Rena that they were going to get married. She thought he was nuts, but she played along with his prophecy. "Okay, so we'll have three children. Our first-born will be a doctor, our middle child a lawyer, and our daughter, the baby, will be a social worker. How does that all sound to you?" It was playful banter and they reveled in it.

Around Passover 1944, Mo asked if he could invite Rena to the *seder* so we could meet her. We were quite impressed. She came from a good Jewish family. Her plans included going to college and becoming a nurse. In our mind, she was driven and would make a fine wife for Mo.

Graduating a year early from high school, Mo left home to work at an airfield in Rome, N.Y., about 300 miles away. He was hired as a junior mechanic, but when he arrived, he was downgraded to general mechanics helper, responsible for preparing aircraft engines for shipment overseas as replacements. His job was to help "pickle," oil or lubricate the aircraft to prevent it from rusting or corroding during shipment overseas.

Mo was gone until the end of August when he got in trouble with the C.O. there. In the middle of the summer, a division was closed and he was given 200 women to supervise. Mo was angry because he wasn't making much more than some of the women. And he wouldn't have the ladies climbing all about the aircraft in skirts, so he sent them home one day to get slacks like the men. Called before the C.O. for his actions, he addressed his concerns.

"You're just a smart-assed kid. Go back to work and do your job," the C.O. said, pointing to the door.

"No, I will not just pretend I don't know any better. If I don't get a raise, I'll quit!"

"Then I'll have you drafted as soon as you quit."

Mo laughed. "Just try. I'm only 16."

He wasn't drafted, but the incident cost him a future as a mechanic. A military man through and through, Mo found his way back into the service. It was a deep-seated interest that stemmed from his experience at a semi-military vocational school during high school. He went to an engine shop for six months and learned about airplane engines. On his 18th birthday in 1946, he was the first guy on the line at the enlistment office. He had gotten there around five o'clock in the morning. We didn't know until later.

When he came home, he told Rena first. "I'm leaving in two days' time. I just joined the Army." Basic training was in Fort McClellan,

Alabama. She was heartbroken. He promised that when he returned, they would be married.

Then he told us. We were furious that he hadn't come to discuss the Army idea with us before rushing into something so dangerous. He probably knew we wouldn't have been very supportive. We would've tried to talk him out of it. A year earlier he wanted to go into the Navy and I wouldn't sign for him. So, he went and did this. With a parent's signature, you could get in the Navy at 17, but you had to be 18 to get into the Army – and no permission was required.

PART 3

23 THE RECOVERY

I've faced war several times and each time I've managed to escape military service. When I came to America I was classified as 3A, considered an alien, non-resident. Despite that, I could have been drafted if I didn't have so many children. Two of my sons, however, *chose* to serve. After he finished high school, Hershel followed Mo into the military, the Navy. I didn't want him to go for the usual reasons – he could die or be injured – and because Hannah needed his help paying the bills and caring for the younger children. But he was as headstrong as a few others in the family. I raised independent thinkers. He simply did what he wanted.

The children of immigrants, Mo and Hershel were proud to fight for this country. I reminded them often how much their commitment meant to me, how we had come full circle. "I might not be a true American, but you boys are. Just don't forget your foreign roots or what Mama and I went through to get you to this point."

While in the service in Europe, Mo was very conscious of his ancestry. He kept with him a list of 32 relatives Hannah and I gave him hoping he would encounter or learn about them. He was constantly hunting for them, but never located any until one found him, ending a similar exhaustive quest to return a remnant of my past. He met Herman, my younger brother, who had something for me that I thought was lost forever.

Mo was stationed in in Karlsruhe, Germany. One day he received a phone call from the airfield. "There is a man at the base looking for you. This guy says he's your uncle."

When Mo returned to base, Herman was there. Mo said that from the air he took a picture of the man and could have sworn Herman was me. It was Pesach 1947. Herman had a *bintelle,* a package of food with him so he wouldn't have to eat *traif* during the holiday. Mo had access to plenty of boxes of military food, but Herman wouldn't accept any of it because it wasn't kosher, let alone kosher for Passover.

But Herman had something to give Mo. Even now the lump forms in my throat as I think about how something that precious came into my brother's possession and was salvaged at the end of the war. My friend from Jacovo, Avrum, returned home bragging to his friends about this watch he traded for his own, practically worthless timepiece with the *schnook* who didn't know the difference. Herman wasn't among the group of boys who listened to the braggart, but he heard the story second hand. Inquiring further, he determined it was his grandmother's watch and the *schnook* was his brother. After checking with Bubbie she told him how she gave it to me. Herman convinced the boy to give up the watch in exchange for a bag of chocolates, which were far more precious to the young than jewelry.

Herman wrapped the watch in a soft cotton swatch and kept it under his bed for years. When the family got wind that the Nazis were forcing Jews from their homes, he quickly buried the watch below our home, under a trick floorboard only the family knew existed. The Nazis might wreck homes and lives, but Herman pledged, they weren't getting Bubbie's watch.

When he returned to the site after the war, he didn't find a soul he knew, but he *did* find the watch. The Nazis weren't that smart, after all. Bubbie's watch remained undamaged and undisturbed, although, just like the hearts of millions the Nazis massacred, it, too, had stopped ticking. Herman wouldn't have believed it himself had he not been there. Without taking any more chances that it might be lost again, he stitched it into the lining of his coat for safekeeping hoping he would someday find me. Why he wanted to return it to me when I was so careless all those years ago to flee with the family's earnings and carelessly give the watch away, I didn't know. Why was he so willing to forgive and forget? "Because that's the way it is with family," he would tell me later. "It's black and white. You are family, regardless of what you do and say. Bubbie intended the watch to be yours and so it should be." It still would be many years before I would express my appreciation in person. At this point, it was changing hands once again, to Mo's safekeeping.

Many of our relatives, Mo learned from Herman, died in the Auschwitz concentration camps including my siblings: Mina, Moshe and Shlomo. Nine of Shlomo's ten children were also killed.

After the Nazis hauled away her husband, Mina decided it was too difficult to support her six children. Two daughters were put in the care of their aunt in Seged, a larger city. They survived and settled later in Israel.

The torment this period in Europe brought us when Mo told us was unbelievable. We heard of the 6 million men, women and children who died in the death camps of Germany, Poland and elsewhere in Europe through news report in the Jewish papers and buried in the pages of The New York Times. We read various reports and saw a few newsreels taken by sneaky filmmakers starting in 1939 of what the Nazis were doing in Europe to the Jews. But who would have believed it was true?

My two sisters, a brother and I, here in America, tried to bring over my mother and other siblings. We wrote to them a few times. But they didn't want to come. They were earning a good living there before things got bad for them. Why should they come over here, where people were struggling to make ends meet in the '30s? "How can we convince them what we see is going on?" I'd ask Hannah. "This Hitler *noodnik*, surely good people won't listen to his *mishigas*," she would respond. If they had an inkling of the fate that would befall the Jews, they might have fled before the situation escalated. But no one knew. How could it be believed that such atrocities would take place, that human beings could be so evil to others? It's unfathomable.

I can't put words to the anguish I went through upon hearing report after report about what came to be known as the Shoah, the Holocaust. The "what ifs" were endless and wracked my existence for months upon months. Couldn't I have done more? Shouldn't I have returned to drag them with me? Should I have stayed? If I had stayed, I would have met the same demise, no doubt. Ultimately, I'd face the same trite questions as other survivors: Why them and not me? Why didn't God intervene? Or anyone else? It was just beyond comprehension, the persecution they endured, that which we escaped by leaving when we had the chance, before Europe was hit by an earthquake of hatred and insanity. We were all left helpless and speechless. There were no words to soothe. No consolation one could seek from family or spirituality to understand, to accept and certainly not to forgive and forget. We would forever mourn, even more, I imagine, than if they had died naturally or even from a disease.

From the depths of despair emerged Herman.

After Herman's short visit with Mo, he returned to a Jewish DP camp in Pocking, Germany, and Mo resumed his duties. Parting, Mo promised that he would try to visit Herman in the DP camp. He was true to his word. Mo asked for a leave of absence, which was granted.

Base supervisors were very sympathetic because they had never known anyone who had survived the Holocaust. In fact, the time Mo took off was never officially recorded, so he didn't lose any accrued leave time.

He had one of the pilots fly him to Munich and from there he took a train to the camp. Herman met Mo at the gate of the camp and they walked together. As they passed by, people stared at the uniformed stranger. One man, speaking to those nearby, said in Yiddish, *"Kenst zen buy de nuz oz er iz yid.* You can see by his nose, he's a Jew." To this, Mo shot back, *"Tsu rikhtik.* You are right." His recognition of the language certainly threw the man making the remark off-guard.

Herman gave Mo a tour of the camp, ending with the barracks-like building where Herman lived. His was one of the many blocks of these stark, corrugated tin shells filled with rows of cots separated by thin metal walls. Hidden under the makeshift beds or aside them were carpetbags packed with clothes and other possessions. The potent smell of disinfectant powder pervaded the air. To keep warm, a number of men were gathered around a solitary hissing electric heater, rubbing their hands and laughing as they shared stories of the Old Country. Compared to the concentration camps, their accommodations were quite comfortable, and no one complained about overcrowding.

Mo also met Aaron, one of Shlomo's children. He was living with Herman and Shaydel in Pocking. Aaron was actually the one who started the trail of events that put Herman and Mo together. After the war, Aaron returned to what was left of his home in Jacovo and found papers with an address of his aunt in New York. He wrote the address in pen inside the sleeve of his jacket. Then he sent a letter to his aunt, my sister, Sophie, telling her that they were all right and where they were staying. Sophie referred the news to me and I, in turn, wrote Herman how to find Mo and vice versa.

Millions of Jews were displaced by the war from their homes, from their towns, from their former lives. In DP camps they could find shelter, food, medical care, schooling for the children, assistance locating new homes overseas.

We were told later that Herman's first wife, Freida, was murdered in Auschwitz with their four children. After the war, Herman remarried Shayndel. She was a little neighborhood girl of five when Herman and Freida were married. Their families lived in the same apartment building in Munkach. There were five apartments, each with two rooms and a kitchen. They shared a courtyard, entered by a big wrought-iron gate. Shayndel later babysat the couple's first child. Herman and Freida became so fond of the little neighbor, that they even took her with them when they returned to Jacovo to visit family. On the trip, the cherry trees were close enough to the wagon to snatch handfuls of the sweet fruit for everyone to enjoy. All before the Nazis stormed in.

Herman told us later how the guards in the labor camps beat him for doing things he knew would garner an extra serving of stale bread. One night some 3,000 men were marched from Yugoslavia to Germany. Anyone who fell to the ground in exhaustion was shot. In the morning, 300 men were left alive.

After arriving in the cattle cars to Auschwitz, Shayndel held her breath as the weak, ill, pregnant, old, and very young were separated and taken away, never to be seen again. Those remaining were shaved and stripped of clothing. At 18, she stood naked with the others in front of male soldiers, her dignity and modesty robbed from her like everything else.

Prisoners received a plain gray dress and a belt. If you wore out your shoes, you were given wooden ones. No stockings, bra or panties to protect against the morning chill. At night, they slept 13 in a wooden bunk without blankets.

They were forced to line up twice a day and stand for hours to be counted. Every six weeks, when you were taken for a shower, you wondered if clean water or poisonous gas would spray, Shayndel said. Her job was dangerous too. She cleaned spent armament shells with an acidic bath for many hours a day.

Shayndel was ready to end her life before the Nazis got a chance. A friend who received a sweater in return for favors to a particular Jewish guard, agreed to share it with Shayndel. "Here, take it. We'll share it. When you're on work detail, I'll pass it to you, and when you're done, you can give it back." When Shayndel was ultimately discovered accepting the sweater during one such swap, she was punished with another head shaving. The degradation of losing her beauty once more was too much, and she attempted suicide by throwing herself on the electric fence surrounding the camp. The fences were on 23 hours per day with one hour for recharging, which was when Shayndel had thrown herself on the fence.

Holocaust survivors, Herman and Shayndel, met each other while roaming the streets of Munkach looking for relatives and friends. In the summer of 1944, some 25,000 Jews were sent from Munkach to Auschwitz. Only a few hundred of those survived, according to Shayndel's calculations. If they returned to their former homes, they found them stripped to the bare walls by their neighbors. These would have been the same people who lined the streets to hurl stones, to spit and call the Jews nasty names as they were hauled away by the Nazis.

Searching for a reason to live upon their return, Herman and Shayndel found solace in each other's embrace. The warmth of familiarity. The shared struggle. The horrors of their experiences. Their union allowed them to defy fate, to bridge the gap between hope and despair.

When the Russians took over the area, the couple knew it was time to leave. Some drunken Slovaks who wanted to send Herman and the other men back to Munkach caught them at the border. A quick-thinking Herman offered quite a few packs of cigarettes to a guard as a weeping Shayndel begged at the soldier's feet to allow them safe passage. "I could shoot you right now, you know. Go! I'm feeling generous. Go! Run kikes run!" They did, and the bullets flew. A few of the men in their group fell, but Shayndel and Herman didn't look back. They made their way to Pocking.

The town was in the southeast corner of Germany near the country's border with Czechoslovakia and Austria. Their son, Saul, was about five months old when Mo found the family. He had been born in the DP camp in December 1946. Somehow the couple also landed in the same DP camp as Aaron. The Nazis had wiped out his whole family. He didn't talk too much about it. He was 21 at that time, two years older than Mo, but much older in terms of the hardships he had suffered the past few years. Mo took in many of their stories. Although often heavy and tragic, they still had hope in the future and what has abroad.

Herman and Shayndel wanted to know about America and about Mo's life in the army. Mo brought items such as cigarettes and chocolate that he could use to barter for more important things like vegetables and meat. One time he brought contained peaches. "How do you pronounce it?" asked Shayndel.

"Pee-ches," he said, breaking up the syllables.

Again, she asked him to repeat it and again, he told her, "Peaches."

To this, she became flushed with embarrassment. Herman explained that it sounded like the root Czech word for vagina, *pochva*. They all had a good laugh over that one.

For dinner during Mo's visit, Aaron donned a long yellow raincoat to kill a chicken. He grabbed the bird's neck and twirled it until it snapped off and he was standing with the head in his hand. The chicken, sans head, was running around and spraying blood all over, and the raincoat protected Aaron's clothes from the spewing blood.

There were two rooms in the barracks, one for Aaron and one for Shayndel and Herman. They slept on cots. The United Nations' relief service gave them food, along with the Hebrew Immigrant Aid Society (HIAS), which helped Jews come to America. Following their visit, Mo took Herman to HIAS in Munich. There was a line of Jews looking to get papers to come to the United States. Mo started to walk up to the front and Herman informed him that they would have to wait at the end of the line. Mo explained that when you're in uniform, you have certain liberties. They passed a thousand people in line, maybe more, and he took him all the way to the front of the line and told them, "You take care of him," motioning to his uncle. Everyone in line was angry, but it seemed to be a thrill for Herman.

He completed applications for the remaining family. Before they could get immigration papers, we had to sign for them that they would not be a burden on the US. My sister, Sophie, and I agreed to put them up in our homes until they could get on their feet in America.

24 POST-WAR WEDDING

While Mo was on duty in Auschwitz, Polish DPs, who were forced laborers in Germany, were being returned to their homeland against their will. They didn't want to go back. They were being fed by the Americans at the DP camps and eating better than they had in years; they weren't in a rush to leave. But they couldn't stay in Germany because its people didn't have enough to eat themselves. The economy was poor. So, the American soldiers took them back at gunpoint to Poland, where they dumped them.

On another trip to Auschwitz, the soldiers took a trainload of UNRRA supplies back to Poland. It took them 15 days. During that trip, the Russians arrested Mo twice. The soldiers had stopped in the town of Pilsen, Czechoslovakia. Their train was going to be sidetracked because it was heading east and another was coming west. It was a single track. During the six-hour wait on the track, they took turns going into town. Half of them went into town and saw this big factory. They saw a man walking to some showers. Since they hadn't had showers in a few days, they just stripped down and took showers. When they got out of the showers all their clothes were gone and Russians with guns awaited them. They marched them through town naked and put them in jail. A lieutenant in charge of their whole outfit came to get them out. The Russians returned their clothes, guns, ammunition and cameras, minus the film that had been removed for some reason.

The second time Mo was arrested was in Auschwitz. The soldiers had been eating ten-in-one rations: the box of food could feed ten GIs for one day or one GI for ten days. A few of the men caught sight of some chickens. Up for a challenge, they made a trail of the crackers that went behind a freight car. When the chicken came around the corner eating the trail, a soldier hit the chicken over the head with a piece of wood and killed it.

The woman who owned the chicken saw them and screamed out the window. The Russians chased Mo and another guy, George, until they were caught in a blind alley. George was an Ozark moonshiner. He would have fought the Russians if Mo hadn't stopped him. "You crazy bastard," Mo said when George readied his rifle and began jumping around like a boxer, jabbing at the air.

One of the Russians had a burp gun, a machine gun with round barrels that shoot 3,000 rounds a minute. Mo talked him into dropping his rifle if the two gave up. They were taken to jail and then to court. The judge spoke only Polish. To pay for the chickens, they agreed to give the woman a pack of cigarettes. One pack was worth $10 in trade there or two bottles of *tzuika*, a popular plum brandy, which was actually moonshine made mostly from beetroot or sweetcorn. The woman allowed them to keep the chicken and threw in a jar of stewed cherries.

Mo was still in Germany when he learned about me being sick again and requiring medical care. He asked Hannah if she wanted him to get a hardship discharge and come home. She told him no. The Jewish Federation, providing assistance again, informed her that if her son lived at home, their aid would stop and he would have to support the family. It was more important for her to continue receiving Federation support along with the monthly allotment Mo sent home. Each month, he mailed half his pay to Rena and half to us. He kept $20 a month to live on, supplemented by black market profits from cigarettes, chocolate, coffee and sugar.

When Mo came home on a short furlough, he visited the store of a relative of Rena's and bought her an engagement watch, just as I told him I had once hoped to do with Bubbie's watch when proposing to Hannah. He couldn't afford a diamond ring at the time, either, though he had given her a friendship ring with a tiny pearl a year earlier when they were at our house for dinner before he left for overseas. She was embarrassed receiving it in front of everyone and too reserved to thank him properly in front of everyone, other than a peck on the cheek.

Alone after dinner, having taken a walk in a nearby park, she couldn't keep her hands off of him. They agreed not to go "all the way" until after they were married, but they got pretty intimate that night under the stars with the sign of commitment newly planted on Rena's finger. Groping and feeling and massaging and making out would have to be enough at this point. They were going to wait, they both resolved, begrudgingly as the sexual tension grew between them.

They told us the story a few weeks later, when they came to the apartment with Rena's parents, Lawrence and Sheila. "The children want to get married." It was surprising to us. I wasn't prepared for such excitement in the family, the planning of a wedding. They were engaged and had a party at Rena's house, which we attended. It was there that we got to know our future in-laws.

Mo left to go overseas and when he returned and visited me, he told me that he and Rena were making plans to get married. I was violently against it, not because of Rena. We had grown to enjoy her company. The timing was just off. I thought they were too young and I had hoped Mo would work and help support the family until we were in good financial shape. "Sorry to spoil your plans Dad," Mo snapped. He was getting married and no one was going to stop him. Just like when he joined the Army, he didn't ask for permission.

It didn't take three months; we took them into a little shul and they had a little wedding.

They stayed with the in-laws for a couple of weeks. Then they found an apartment in the West Bronx.

When we went to the wedding and I think we had $15 to our name and I took it along. I figured I might need to buy something. It was a good thing I did.

Some of our relatives brought children, who weren't invited. I really didn't think twice about it. As long as they were well behaved, what did I care? As the parents of the bride, I assumed Mo's in-laws would pick up the tab. Wrong. They came over to my table in the synagogue social hall while we were eating our chicken dinner, and confronted me. "Tell your family that I'm not paying for the kids!" Startled and confused, I nearly spit out the chicken chunk I had in my mouth. What? I eyed the children suspiciously. Did they eat more than normal? Were they misbehaving? Someone step out of line?

"This is the first I'm hearing about this," I stammered, not fully composed. I wiped my mouth and rose from my seat to their level. "What do you want me to do? I wasn't going to tell them to go home. They're family."

"Well, there seems to be a big misunderstanding," Rena's father scolded, his wife at his side, her lips and eyebrows tightening in anger.

"I'm sorry. I can't pay for them." All hell broke loose with his voice rising even further and mine doing the same in response while our family was looking on in disbelief. So, I grabbed him by the arm and led him outside in the hall and I did what I had to do to keep the peace.

Rena and Mo were thankfully oblivious to the goings on at the time, busy greeting guests on the other side of the room, but they heard about it forever more afterwards. What could I do? I left my last dollar there and came home with nothing.

We generally got along with others. But our relationship with Rena's family was never the same after that.

25 TEST CASE

The war may have ended, but my health battles raged on. I was sick again in 1947. This third bout was the worst one. *How long can I go on like this? How much can a body take?*

It was back to Montefore Hospital. Like in 1932 with Deborah, I had another little baby to leave at home – Eliza. It didn't matter; I had to go.

The doctors didn't have much of a cure for me now, but medicine had come a little further than in 1932.

I had a little more security. The Chesed took care of Hannah. When she came to visit, she brought the little girls, taking the train from the Bronx. They sat outside the hospital in the park and I stood outside on my balcony and looked down on them. Sometimes I was able to go down to see them. Even if I couldn't, it was enough that she came every Sunday.

I was there a couple of months. The doctors determined I needed an operation. My lung was pretty well damaged. It was split in half basically. They said I had a big hole. I was hemorrhaging a little.

"Listen, you're a fighter," my doctor reassured me. "You've got a better chance than most."

"I've got little babies at home," I informed them. "I've got to get well and go home and take care of my children."

God helped me and he listened to my prayers and to Hannah's too, I guess. Either that or I was really intended to be more immortal than a cat with nine lives.

I opted for the operation on my lung. It was miserable. They sort of took out half the ribs and squeezed together the lungs to close the gap, so it could heal. The operation can't be done at one time. I actually had two operations. Nobody can hold up on the table more than four hours because they have to chop seven ribs. They did four the first time and then three the second time.

I sailed through the first operation, which involved removing a lung and shortening some ribs to reach the other lung. But four weeks after the operation, I became sick. The doctors decided to wait another week to see if I got better. I didn't. I needed a second operation to remove a lesion on the remaining lung. It nearly did me in because something went wrong. They didn't have the proper medication and it couldn't be found anywhere. The doctors didn't give me much hope of surviving more than a few months. Since I didn't have much hope of recovering, they offered me a new, experimental drug called streptomycin. The way the doctors pitched it to me, I didn't have anything to lose. My situation was dire – so I agreed.

I was considered something of a guinea pig for the drug in the United States, testing the effectiveness of streptomycin for TB. Every day I had to appear before an audience of doctors and medical technicians at Montefore. Sitting up on stage of this auditorium in the hospital, a panel of doctors and other medical personnel asked me all kinds of questions: How did you feel before and after the shots? Do you sleep well? Do you have an appetite?

I had a serious infection in the lung. With so many tubes draining and replenishing fluid in and out of my body, I must have looked like some sort of alien creature trying to walk around. I was a sick man, very, very sick.

My body was basically full of the poison, the new drug the doctor gave me. The drug didn't go to the heart or brain, but my face was full of white puss, same with my neck and mouth. They kept giving me the drug. My hair fell out. I couldn't talk. My voice was nearly gone and so was my hearing. Little by little I was losing my senses. On top of that, they ran out of the drug because it was just after the war and they didn't produce enough. Most of it went to soldiers at the Army and Navy.

I was sick for five days. "We can't do anything. We don't have the medication," the doctors said. "We'll continue to try to get some."

"If that's the case," I said, "I want to go home." They wouldn't let me because I was full of tubes. "I'm going to walk out myself," I threatened. I wouldn't go back to bed. No fever, but there was a horrible taste in my mouth from the drug. It kept getting worse and worse. I reiterated my plea.

Eventually, they conceded. I was allowed to go home. They took out all the tubes except one. This little bottle remained attached to me to catch the drainage. I was sent home with a six-hour pass. They didn't want to let me go home by train, but I did. I walked up four flights of steps to the subway. Took the pass and came home.

It was a weekday. Hannah was home with the children. After six hours I had to go back; it was the same night. The nurses did what they were supposed to do, put me back in bed. Two or three days later I was very sick and I couldn't get off the bed. They couldn't wake me. They gave me four or five blood transfusions within 24 or 36 hours.

This was what I call my third wrestling match with death. The first time it happened I didn't think anything of it. I was confident I would pull through. Young and cocky, you think you're invincible. When it happened the second time, I knew I had persevered the first time, so this time shouldn't be any different. But this time, I started thinking about how hard I had to fight. I had three grown kids and two babies, and I knew a lot more about the disease. It took me three years to recover from the first hospital stay and a little over a year the second time.

The doctors had pretty much given up on me. I was unconscious in a coma. It was slightly different from the 1925 episode. Still asleep, I walked and wandered in the dark, in my dream, crossing fields and rivers, trying to get out and not knowing how to get to the highway.

I went one way, another way, a third way, but everything was dark, and I couldn't see how to get there. The only thing I could see was light up in the air. A little baby came to me and she said, "Come. Hold onto my hand, come."

"Where are we going?"

"Well, you don't want to stay here. We have to go out where it's light. It's too dark over here."

She led me out from the dark. "Come with me Daddy. We have to go home." My little Eliza rescued me, and I *did* come home to the family. Thank God.

It's not easy to talk about it. (I can barely do it now without choking up). And I made up my mind then that if I lived through this, I would devote myself more to my family, be kinder to them and really appreciate them.

That I came through this time was nothing short of a miracle. I don't know, God's help, I guess was what did it and having Hannah as my co-pilot, so to speak. She was there for me as she was the first two times.

Before I left Montefore, there was a very big meeting. Many doctors were there from all over. They had 50 or 60 doctors in the auditorium. They presented my case to the staff, to the doctors, and to the surgeons. One guy got up, the chief from the hospital, and announced at the end, "Who can say that we don't cure people at Montefore Hospital? Who will ever say it again? Never. Don't believe it." He received a standing ovation, the din of applause echoing through some nearby halls, and the meeting was adjourned, doctors scuttling away.

Unlike when I was there earlier, Montefore had a bad name at this time. When anyone got sick and went into Montefore, forget it. It was a one-way ticket. I walked out alive after two operations. Many people had operations. There were two good surgeons, but the chances of full recovery were slim. At first, they gave patients a 50-50 chance of recovery and then the ratio was reduced because the operations were new in those days and only a few doctors knew how to perform them. But they learned, little by little. They practiced on me, and a few other people. I knew quite a few boys who were in the hospital with me and who were gone even before I had my second operation.

After the operations, they sent me to the sanatorium in Bedford Hills to recuperate again for a couple of months. They took me back, despite my bad behavior the last time. Figuring I had learned my lesson about getting along with others, they gave me a second chance. I gained ten pounds there having lost double after the operations.

When I came home in February 1948, it was just in time for Deborah's 16th birthday the following month. I was supposed to stay at the hospital another couple of weeks, but I pleaded with the doctors. They took sympathy on me and let me go home and we celebrated my release and Deborah's young adulthood. Sheryl was a little girl. Eliza was still only a baby.

I remained very conscious of my susceptibility to illness – only having one lung – and to exposing others to whatever I might catch. That's why I never again slept with Hannah. Plus, every time we were under the covers together, we had another baby and after five babies, I had all I could handle. I wasn't the same man I had been before anyway. I didn't have quite the same *koyekh*.

Luckily, I was home, though, and I had the strength to keep going to support that brood.

The Chesed took me back and I worked my way up in the shop, climbing the ladder. My health had interrupted me, but I was back here again, fighting and surviving.

"We are never losers," Hannah would tell the children, hoping they would follow our example. "Somehow we survive. We always come out on top." I have to agree with her.

Part of my recuperation involved taking a vacation. The Chesed gave me two weeks a year for this purpose. Having saved up a little and determining ourselves rich, we went to the country, to Tivoli, on the Hudson River. It was '49 or '50. I recall running to the trains, nearly busting my chops because we were late. We hardly even knew where we were going, somewhere near Poughkeepsie. Eliza and Sheryl were running after us carrying a bag or a bundle.

Arriving in Tivoli by train, we were met by the owners of the bungalows in a station wagon with fake wooden sides. They took us to what would become our private hideaway, and offered to bring us wherever we wanted whenever we wanted. A long path through tall grass and over a set of railroad tracks led to the river, where we could fish.

The children and I would take Hannah's leftover *shlishkahs*, boiled potato dough the consistency of pasta, as our worms. The fish didn't seem to mind our human food. The *shlishkahs* were starting to go bad at that point or we would have eaten them ourselves.

It was only the four of us there most times. Working back in the city, Hershel and Deborah came to visit, but they couldn't stay long. We tried to return every year.

With Hershel and Deborah working a little, we made a living. We weren't fancy, but we had a few luxuries. On Fridays, when I came home from work, I'd pick up two chickens from the butcher.

As a general rule, when I picked up chicken it was because Hannah didn't have the time, with working and taking care of the children. Her selection process was quite an art form. She would go to the chicken market and feel the backside of the live chickens. To this day, I'm not sure what she was feeling for: how fatty it was, how beefy, tender? Don't know.

Anyway, she felt many chickens before she decided. We all had a good time joking about the practice of feeling backsides. "Juicy indeed, quite juicy... I'd say this one has some good meat on it. Let me see..." as I pretended to take a bite. The kids would run around trying to pinch each other's tushies after that, usually until they were too tired from laughing so much, or someone got hurt.

It's actually serious business, *kashering* a chicken. Quite complex, in fact. The local *shochet* cuts the throat of the chicken and puts it in a pot upside down for the blood to drain. Jews are not supposed to consume blood. When the chicken is dead, someone takes the chicken and plucks the *pinchus*, feathers from it. Then it's cut up and sold.

We'd have to drag that smelly chicken up two flights of stairs to the third floor of our apartment building. Thank God I was well enough, it wasn't a problem. When you've got your health, stairs are accomplishments, not hurdles.

When we'd get home, Hannah would turn on the gas burner on the stove and burn the pinfeathers off the skin. Then she soaked the meat in cold water for a half-hour before salting, rinsing and cooking.

Hannah, coming from the Old Country like me, didn't believe in waste. Money was just too tight to discard food. The *schmaltz* was gathered for future use. The skin was eaten along with the *greebenes*, the greasy chicken skin remnants left in the pan after the chicken was removed. If we had had dogs, she might have fed the bones to them.

Along with the chicken, we'd have cakes and rolls, 3 for a nickel, 15 or 20 cents for a pound of strawberry shortcake. Or Hannah bought lemon meringue pie or *rugalach*. Sweets weren't as expensive as other extras, so we could afford them.

That doesn't mean the children were demanding. They knew if they asked for something we couldn't afford, it wouldn't accomplish anything to fuss about it. They really didn't know if we had a dime or a dollar. In comparison to others, we might even have been considered prosperous because the children never had patches on their clothes or holes in their shoes. I could always fix those anyway. The children never went hungry and they probably believed the entire world lived like they did, that rich people were only in movies because they didn't know anyone like that in our neighborhoods.

Having a seamstress and tailor for parents, our children were sure to be neatly dressed for school and Shabbos. Dresses for girls, suits for boys. Their shoes were shiny. They had their play clothes and their nicer clothes. If anything were torn, we'd sew it up. No children of ours would be ragamuffins.

In the winter, for instance, Sheryl and Eliza had camel-colored coats with fake fur at the collar and wrist, and matching hats.

Sometimes we'd hear a complaint. Eliza would whine periodically, "How come I have to wear Sheryl's hand-me-downs? All the other girls at school have new dresses."

"Maybe the other girls don't have beautiful dresses sitting in a closet that are just as nice as something new in the store." Another of Hannah's favorite responses was, "If you don't like it, just wait until you are older and you'll get a job and then you can buy as many dresses as you want with your own money."

The protest generally didn't last long. In terms of new clothes, they were few and far between and even then, if the children were particular about brand or style, Hannah would answer, "I'll sew a label on it" and that was the end of that discussion.

My children, like most, didn't comprehend how good they had it. When I grew up, I didn't always have shoes to wear. Shoes were more expensive than other clothes. One pair of shoes would be handed down three times. All summer we ran around barefooted in town. At other times during the year, we just couldn't afford shoes. Only on Friday nights did we have to wear shoes. They didn't necessarily fit properly, but luckily, we only had to wear them a few hours. Once a year, on Passover, everyone had something new to wear: a shirt, a tie, a cap, a pair of slacks, a jacket, and a pair of shoes.

Otherwise, it was too expensive to buy new clothes and my mother, like my wife, made most of ours by hand or had a tailor friend make them at a discounted rate. She bought materials that she liked or sent my father to buy some. The tailor would use that to make us clothes for school. Short pants, long pants, a jacket for shul.

Children learn to appreciate more when they have their own families to support, as was the case for Mo.

We had a married son now. I thought for sure when I got home from the hospital, the older kids would help us more. They were too busy.

Deborah and Hershel were active in the dating circuit, bringing home boys and girls for us to meet. The house was constantly full. Hannah was always busy cooking and baking.

Our youngest girls were growing up little by little. Pretty soon Sheryl and Eliza started school.

Hershel was in the Navy Reserves then. He worked all week and Saturday as a handyman, mainly plumbing jobs. Then, on Sunday, I took him to the Reserves. It was on Jamaica Bay at the southern end of Brooklyn.

We hoped our children were happy. I think we created for them a calm environment, a warm, loving, patient atmosphere, something I didn't have in my youth. We tried not to raise our voices. I'd come home from work and play soothing Jewish cantorial music. The children would bounce in from school to the smells of fresh-baked goods. We didn't have to say, "I love you." The words could not have captured the emotions expressed daily through a quick peck and embrace, my occasional *tukhes zetz*, and more importantly, words of reassurance and comfort.

Life couldn't have been more fulfilled when Mo had his first child, Harry, exactly nine months after the wedding. Cutting it close, like us. Must be inherited. At least they waited 'til the official 'I do' though.

Harry was our first grandson, a spitting image of Mo with such light blond hair you'd think it was white. It was quite something to have a grandson and to watch your son – who just yesterday, it seemed, was a boy himself – become a father. He was a little stronger in the discipline department than I ever was, but I was impressed with his parenting nevertheless. Nice to see our children making progress. Like many men, he enjoyed getting a rise out of the gentler sex on occasion. He often wrestled with Harry to the child's delight, throwing him into the air to the panic of Rena and Hannah. "Ah, it's good for him," Mo would say as Harry squealed with sheer joy. Up and down Harry would go as the women yelled at Mo, their fears about the child falling and having to be rushed to the hospital for stitches.

26   THE UNSUNG HEROES

To support his family, Mo was working his way up the ranks of a New York company that printed major newspapers and magazines.

He started there as a flyboy, gathering torn paper from the floor. Once these big boxes of paper shreds were full, he'd empty them into balers. When the magazines came off the press, he put them in neat bundles before stacking them on skids for shipment. Flyboys also cleaned the presses when they were running and served as gophers for the pressmen.

After achieving junior pressman status, his Army service interrupted the job. He was supposed to get his seniority back when he returned, according to the G.I. Bill of Rights. But he didn't, so he sued the company. Other veterans later joined the case, which he won, forcing the union to redo its seniority list.

Non-union flyboys who heard about Mo's vet case, filed a separate suit, claiming non-union workers shouldn't be paid differently than union members. Non-union flyboys – Mo was still considered one – were being paid 50 percent of pressmen's wages instead of the 60 percent union workers were receiving. The suit garnered $110,000 for the non-union workers, which they divided between them.

Meanwhile, Mo saw an ad in a trade magazine about a new plant being built in Philly that was looking for workers. Timing is everything. He and Rena never intended to stay long in New York anyway. It wasn't where they wanted to raise their family.

Mo asked the New York union for a recommendation to transfer to its Philly counterpart. He received a glowing report, and the job. Typically, it would have taken him about 20 years to become a pressman. But he was able to bypass that with the new job and earn 50 percent more than he was making in New York. How could he turn it down? The New York union and the company were glad to get rid of him and he was happy to make more.

In Philly, Mo had little competition in his job. Within a year, he was a pressman in charge, meaning he was the head pressman on the crew that ran the press for that shift. He also was a union shop steward and a member of the negotiating committee during collective bargaining negotiations. Promotions continued over time, including full-time foreman and later, pressroom superintendent.

We looked for every opportunity to visit Mo and spend time with our grandson.

Come Sunday morning, 6 or 7 o'clock, we'd cross the Kosciuszko Bridge and the George Washington Bridge and enter Philadelphia.

In 1953, a second child, a girl, was born to Mo and Rena. Her name was Lydia. Mark followed her in birth three years later.

We were in the country, our summer getaway, when Mark was born.

The family continued to grow. Hershel got himself a girl, Bobbie, in 1953. He introduced her to us for the first time in Tivoli. Bobbie was pretty and smart enough, a strong woman with a good head on her shoulders. She was a bank teller in New York. But she was somehow not right for my Hershel. Here I was meddling in his business after experiencing that from the other end of my family. I was a parent now and certainly felt I had earned the right to guide. If not me, who?

It was *Yiddishkeit* that Bobbie lacked, a commitment to Judaism that is passed down over generations, through holiday celebrations and attendance in Hebrew school and family gatherings.

I spoke to Hershel about my concerns, and I remember, like it was yesterday, the argument that ensued. "Are you sure you're not jumping into something because of Lois?" Hershel was on the rebound from a girl he had been crazy about. We were in love with her too. When he went into the Navy, she married someone else. Hershel only got madder about the comparison of the two women. "She is not the kind of girl that you would want," I said of Bobbie, sitting Hershel down for a serious discussion on the matter, hoping to change his mind before it was too late. "Her parents didn't bring her up the way we brought you up." I quickly reviewed the divisions that exist between different levels of Judaism, us being more observant, and how important it was for our faith to continue after all our people had been through. What could happen if we continued to chip away at the beliefs we held dear.

He held his stance. "I'm not marrying the parents. I'm marrying the girl. And you should be happy she's Jewish at all."

"Fine." I tried. It's all I could do.

He was on his own.

Another rebel, my son. They got married and moved to an apartment in Hackensack, New Jersey. A son, Barry, arrived in 1954 and two years later, Lisa was born. We had two places to go now, New Jersey and Philadelphia.

Meanwhile, Deborah, in her early twenties, was running around with boys. I had to take her here and there. She brought some boyfriends home I approved and others I didn't. A few took advantage of her, leading her on and then not calling her for long stretches. I had to step in sometimes and break it up because she was miserable. One of them, I threw out of the house. He needed to be thrown out. I wanted the best for my children. If she couldn't get it, I believe I had the responsibility to step in. She shouldn't be with just any *schmo*.

The next guy was Jerry, also kind of a *schmo*, but she liked him. He was a psychologist or psychiatrist or something like that, analyzing people's thoughts and dreams and trying to help them feel better about themselves. Who knew of such things? The younger people understood such things. My generation just considered people with problems *meshuga* and you lived with it. There were no cures for that. We just accepted that that's just how some people were.

Deborah and Jerry got engaged. He gave her a ring.

They went searching for rooms because they didn't want to get married and live with their folks. Deborah found in the papers an advertisement for two bedrooms in the West Bronx. Deborah and I went to see it. Who did we find there? One of her old boyfriends. Awkward. His name was Peter. He had loved her very much.

Seeing Deborah and the ring, Peter was beside himself, peppering her with questions about her seriousness with this new guy and warning her about the perils of marriage. Still, he had a soft spot for her. "I'm going to vacate the apartment. If you want it, you can have it." He gave her a deal. "Only because it's you," he said, still flirty. "Otherwise, I'm going to play hard ball on the price."

A few minutes later, his wife showed up with her mother and they started a scene with him, screaming about him settling for such a low price. And here I stood with Deborah. They quieted down when Jerry arrived.

Deborah showed him the apartment and they went off to discuss it privately. They talked for a long time in the corner, out of earshot.

But I could tell they were arguing and Deborah was visibly upset by whatever Jerry was saying.

As he rushed out, I heard him scold, "Why are you rushing me? Why are you rushing me to get married?"

I don't know if Deborah was either disappointed or embarrassed.

He took his car and went home. "Take me to his house," Deborah insisted. I complied. "Wait for me downstairs in the car." She went upstairs and about 15 minutes later she came down and said, "It's all over."

"What's the matter, why?"

"I gave him back the ring. I don't want him no more."

I was glad I could be there for her in this moment after missing so much of her childhood.

The same week she went to a Jewish singles party and met Arthur. She brought him home after the party, and you could tell they were smitten.

You'd think they'd known each other before, how quickly they fell in love. I didn't dare comment. She had been through too much. Besides, I remembered what I had been through with Hershel. I held my tongue even when I learned about Arthur's profession. He was an unemployed chiropractor trying to make a living doing what many viewed as an experimental or unconventional form of medicine.

I don't know what they lived on, but they got married the summer of 1956. We did it, so could they.

They lived with his parents for quite a number of weeks in Philly until they could afford to move out. Not only did they leave the nest, they left the city, settling in Ellenville, New York, close to where we used to vacation.

Their financial stability was a concern, but I really just wanted Deborah to be happy. I'm not sure she was. She wanted her own way, but life doesn't work like that. Arthur adored her, though; he worshipped the ground she walked on.

Who was I to talk about Arthur's problems? We were nearly broke again when we made their wedding. I couldn't even afford to go to the country as I had done every year. Deborah convinced Arthur to lend us $300 from what they collected at the wedding.

"My father needs it worse than we do," she told him. "He'll pay us back, don't worry. Just think how we'll regret it if he gets sick again and we didn't try to help him to rest up when we had the chance. You don't know how much he loves that place in the country."

They were insistent on me taking the money and we had just drained all our savings for their wedding. I could have borrowed from someone or somewhere else. Every year, I took from my shop to go to the bungalow, whether I needed to or not. If I didn't need it, I put it in the bank and I socked it away. That was all gone now, though.

When I look back at it, considering my condition, it was worth borrowing from the children and doing without in other areas.

Of course, I paid him back. I was working six days a week, including Saturday after Shabbos. Then on Sunday, we'd run to Ellenville to Deborah, to Hershel in Jersey, or Mo in Philly. That's how it should be. Children get married; you have some place to go to visit.

A year after the wedding, Little Helen arrived to Deborah and Arthur, a beautiful girl, the spitting image of her mother. I think she reinforced their love. We all went to the country in the summer.

Arthur thought he was some sort of *makher,* a big shot, confident he was going to make a lot this time in the Big Apple. He had his hands in many different get-rich-quick schemes. He just wasn't very lucky. When he ran a car wash, it was as if he were trying to sell umbrellas in a drought and then, when the rainy season started, he'd already thrown in the towel and was out of the business.

Seeing how he struggled, I tried to help him when he took over a franchise that published an advertising circular. I stood on street corners with a box full of the free papers and handed them out to anyone who passed by. Some handed them back on the spot. Others took them a few blocks and tossed them. I'd always check the trashcans and retrieve them if they weren't all messed up.

My wild child, Eliza, was like the horses she loved to ride: sometimes difficult to tame, free-spirited, restless, and uninhibited. Sheryl was just the opposite. She was calm, conservative, introspective, a lover of art and literature. The two sisters, while close in age – only two years apart – couldn't be more different. It made for quite a few conflicts between them, one challenging the other's actions and viewpoints.

While pulling them apart from vicious hair pulling, arm biting and otherwise hostile wrestling matches, Hannah often would curse them. "I hope you have daughters who act just like you two someday and you'll see what this is like." Prophetic as she was, her words rang true. Many years later, Sheryl, would feel the déjà vu as she separated her own two daughters from such catfights.

We lived on Eaton Avenue from the mid-40s to the late-50s on the third floor of the five-story building.

The front room, with its large queen bed, was mine. Hannah and I slept in separate rooms by this point. In my youth I wondered how this practice started. Did older couples just give up on sex because it just got too difficult with aching bones or too disgusting with all the sagging skin or did both parties just need their room to stretch? For us, it was some of that and also to get a good night's rest as a result of the snoring battles that ensued periodically. If we felt particularly energetic enough for lovemaking, Hannah could stay in my bed or drag herself to her own room afterwards, which she shared with Eliza.

189

I had a clear view of the two-story Orthodox shul across the street looking out the windows of my bedroom, the brightest in the home, *luftig*, with its cool breeze blowing through in the summer. We specifically positioned two overstuffed chairs by those windows so Hannah and I could watch the children playing bottle caps and stickball below while we chatted about family matters and the day's events. The Pelham Bay subway line stopped down the block and we could hear the trains overhead and observe the people as they descended the stairs from the station onto our street.

Leaning out those windows we could yell to the children to welcome them home or retrieve them for dinner. Screaming for relatives and friends from windows and fire escapes was a common practice among neighbors.

There was a small alley that separated each apartment building as well as the houses in which one family lived on the first floor and another on the second. The children enjoyed climbing on the stone lion statues that marked the entrance to these homes. From our living room, we looked down on their rooftops and the alleyway. The living room, while smaller than our sitting room and not as airy, was a center of activity with its TV, radio and record player.

Our apartment retained a musty smell from the items left by the previous owners, including an old captain's chest they found in the master bedroom filled with clothes and worthless European coins the kids referred to as treasures, otherwise considered junk. Sheryl and Eliza spent hours making up stories based on the adventures they imagined the former tenants encountered.

If that wasn't enough fun, they could always play with the pull-chain toilet, despite our threats that they'd have to pay for the wasted water.

Yet another favorite childhood pastime was rigging the dumbwaiter in the kitchen. You opened the door to this contraption, pulled the ropes to get the platform to your apartment, put your garbage on it and pulled the cord to send it down to the basement. There, the super collected the garbage to put in cans. Sometimes the kids would pull pranks, putting toy animals, specifically reptiles or bugs, on the dumbwaiter and we'd open it up and get a scare because it was supposed to be empty.

Hannah didn't always have a sense of humor about it when she was the one to put out the garbage. After gasping in fright, she'd regain her composure long enough to holler, "Who was the wise guy who put the plastic alligator in the dumbwaiter? If I find out, I tell you, you won't be laughing anymore." To that, she'd walk off spouting Yiddish obscenities only I could understand.

We tried to keep the place clean, but those apartments attract all kinds of pests – mostly roaches and mice. Every once in a while, I would put a mouse trap in the living room and inevitably the girls would be the first to discover and report with vivid detail and excitement how a mouse had been caught.

I almost ended up like those mice one Wednesday afternoon in March of 1958. It was like any other workday at the Chesed. Outside, the cool weather was giving in to the warmth of spring. Foliage was starting to thaw out from a harsh winter beating, and you could see the transformation from shades of brown to the hues of the sun.

It was getting close to quitting time at the Boone Street plant (2:25 p.m.). I was helping to train newer workers when a short, stocky Asian man, in his late thirties – someone I recognized had worked until a few days ago as a machine operator in the packaging department – waltzed into the plant to pick up his paycheck for part-time work. Seemingly unsatisfied with his payment, he tore up the check and began yelling with a strong accent, "Nobody likes me. I'm going back to China." He walked over to his old workspace, presumably to get his belongings, abruptly stopped, pulled out a .32-caliber revolver and began firing at people and equipment. It all happened so fast. Women were screaming and diving for cover under workbenches and heavy machinery. About 200 of us were working there at the time.

When the gunman stopped to reload – as he did three times – I realized one of my co-workers, an older man in his seventies had been killed and another man, a 50-year-old Italian man, was wounded pretty badly. A security guard, hearing the ruckus, ordered the gunman to drop his weapon, but instead, the two traded shots until the guard fell to the ground, moaning, grabbing his bloody arm.

His gun was beyond his reach and I knew if I grabbed it, the gunman would surely shoot me.

Regardless, I flew into action. I still don't know how I summoned courage in the face of pending mortality, but I was able to talk the man into handing over his gun. All I remember is standing up and walking towards him until he was about six feet from me.

"You don't want to hurt anybody else." I remember saying, "These people are trying to learn a trade just like you were. Maybe we can talk about this with the boss... Why don't you give me the gun?"

At first, he just stood there, looking at me, gun raised, still pointing it in the direction of the security guard. Then, possibly as shocked as I was about my audacity, he turned the weapon toward me. I figured I was a goner. After yelling at me in what I assume was Chinese, he must have come to his senses. He surveyed the scene and then dropped down on one knee and began to sob uncontrollably and then slid his gun toward my feet. This gave my co-workers the chance to force him to the ground and hold him there until police arrived. A bookkeeper had managed to slip outside and flag down a passing radio car, and two patrolmen raced into the building. The gunman was still bawling when he was cuffed and taken to the police car.

Turns out the man had been fired for tardiness several months earlier, and when he couldn't find another job to support his family, he went berserk, ranting, raving and punching walls and then crying. His wife had him locked up in a mental institution. Somehow, he escaped and found his way back to the plant to seek revenge. Some of these people at the Chesed, after all, were former psychiatric patients, mainly schizophrenics, who came from state mental hospitals.

The local newspapers dubbed me a hero. Truth was, I practically wet my pants when confronting him.

When I got home and told Hannah and the kids what had happened, we all sat huddled in the living room, bawling until we made ourselves sick.

27 COVERED IN BLOOD

I had a few problems in the early-60s. Again, I was told not to overexert myself. The only ones left at home with us were the girls. They were in high school. Tired of Eaton Avenue, they encouraged us to move to a bigger house, a better location. We lived pretty comfortably, I thought. But they wanted something better to woo boyfriends. I wanted something better too, a change, so I went along.

Still, I didn't know how we were going to be able to afford a new apartment so soon after a new car. I had traded in my green Buick for a Ford Fairlane 500 and was quite a big shot with that car, and now we were looking for rooms too.

In 1964, upscale high-rise apartments were being built near where we lived, on the other side of Bruckner Boulevard in the Bronx, on Morrison Avenue. Military barracks were torn down to make room for these high-rises.

The girls said they would help. They'd work and we'd all help pay for it. They basically paid rent for their room with its twin beds. I really wanted something new for once, a new apartment. This one had an elevator to our apartment on the 11th floor, the top. No more walking up three flights of stairs, which was especially hard on Hannah's legs. We took it.

You move into a new apartment, you've got to have new furniture, right? The girls want to bring in boys. Who are we to stand in their way? You've got nice furniture; they're going to bring home nice boys. We went to Saks and we bought the best, a blond chest, dresser and nightstand for the girls and Italian provincial for the living room. Hannah and I had differences of opinion about what we should buy. "The furniture we had on Eaton Avenue would have been just fine," she'd say. "It was beautiful. Why can't we just use what we have?" Instead, she reluctantly agreed with my decision.

"Hannah, don't be afraid to splurge once in a while? Can't we enjoy our lives for once? Why do we always have to do without? Let's just try, and see how good it feels?"

For me, it felt fantastic. For her, maybe not so much. She went along, as usual.

We made ourselves a nice little home. There was a galley kitchen off the dining area. It even had a terrace or balcony, entered by a glass sliding door from the dining room. A terrace. It made you feel like a millionaire! And the 11th floor, looking over east Bronx, the Triborough and Throgs Neck bridges. Gee-whiz, it was fine living. I was in seventh heaven. Hannah too. We loved it.

At night, you could look out the picture window and see the streetlights lining the bridge. It was a magnificent view.

It was in a bad neighborhood, though. There were many apartments vacant in the area and so they were opened up to low-income and subsidized housing. Some of the buildings became desecrated by graffiti and run down. Trash, bugs, noise, loud music. We had guards and guard dogs, but it was still unsafe at times.

Also, it was harder for us to get around, especially for Hannah. There was a commuter bus that could take us to the train station on

Westchester Avenue or we could walk up and over the Bruckner Expressway. Every night Hannah came home lugging a shopping bag. She walked from Westchester Avenue all the way across Bruckner Boulevard. A lot of *schlepping* and it was hard on her legs.

We had a bit of a scare when Eliza told us a black man who lived in the building was following her. He rode the same bus on her schedule. She eluded him by leaving earlier and coming home later. Then he'd leave her notes asking why she was avoiding him. Must have been scared off after I cornered him. I found him loitering in the lobby. "You either back off or I'm calling the cops, you hear me?"

"I'm not doing anything man. What did I do?"

"WHATEVER YOU'RE DOING IS FRIGHTENING MY DAUGHTER! YOU NEED TO FIND SOMEONE ELSE TO BOTHER, SOMEONE YOUR OWN AGE MAYBE! YOU SHOULD BE ASHAMED OF YOURSELF, A GROWN MAN SNIFFING AROUND A YOUNG GIRL! JUST STAY FAR AWAY FROM HER OR YOU'LL FIND YOURSELF IN THE SLAMMER. FORGET WHAT I'LL DO TO YOU FIRST IF I SEE YOU SO MUCH AS GO NEAR HER AGAIN! *FARSHTAIST*?"

With that, I punched my fist into the wall. Left a mark too, not only in the plaster. My knuckles hurt for days. Here we were in this new apartment and already we were concerned for our safety. The new place was good luck for Sheryl though. We had been there a few months when she found a serious beau. She was going with Ronnie, and it was pretty steady through high school. In their senior year, Ronnie moved to Yonkers. He got a Corvair and he'd take Sheryl to his house. His parents took them to Chinese or Italian restaurants, a fact Sheryl never shared with us, as she knew we wouldn't have approved of the *traif*.

During the summer, he got them free passes to Freedomland amusement park in the upper Bronx, where he worked. We thought for sure Sheryl would marry the guy, and we'd have one left at home. It didn't turn out that way. Ronnie went off to Cornell, and Sheryl went to work as a bookkeeper. She visited him at Cornell, going for a weekend and sometimes bringing Eliza along. While Sheryl was still committed to Ronnie, he had been influenced by the immoralities of college life. She tried to keep up with him, drawing out a covert wild side when she was with him. But he grew tired of her and she grew tired of his irresponsibility, so she resolved herself to dating boys of her own age, who could take her to nightclubs.

Then Stewart came along. Sheryl became a bookkeeper for his father's office supply business. She was one of a dozen workers, but one of the few unmarried Jewish women. Manny Kahn had his eye on Sheryl for some time as a prospective wife for his son, who he feared would never settle down despite his good looks and high intelligence.

At 27 – eight years older than Sheryl – he had served in the Navy for four years and then graduated from a New York junior college with an engineering degree and was designing planes for a large aerospace company. He was trying desperately to save enough to move out of the house and have his own space, and he was almost there.

In his free time, he was either reading science fiction and adventure novels or drawing comic-book figures.

"Would you like to go out with my son?" Mr. Kahn cornered Sheryl one day, when they passed in the hallway outside the office. She had just returned from the bathroom and he was waiting for the elevator. "He's handsome, and I'm not just saying that because he's my son. He's a bit of a bookworm, I'll admit, but he's doing very well at his job. I'd say he's a good catch."

A little introspective with great financial prospects for the future, was how his father described him.

She resisted, hemming and hawing about already dating someone, without being too specific. What she was really thinking: *Nearly 30 and his father has to set him up on dates? Must be something seriously wrong with him.*

She was off the hook for now. But Mr. Kahn persisted. He stopped her on several occasions in the coming months to inquire again about the possibility of dating his son.

"Your job isn't on the line or anything," he said, his tone light and comical. "I just think you'd make a nice pair. Don't worry; it'll be our little secret. No one has to know you're going out with the boss's son. And if it doesn't work out, so be it. You will have met my son and we'll pretend nothing ever happened."

The thought hadn't really crossed her mind about the secrecy involved with dating the boss's son or about losing her job over this. She was sort of naive that way. And now she was feeling guilty about declining. Either way, she figured, she was stuck. *If she doesn't go out with him, the boss is disappointed, and if it's a bad date, the boss will still be upset. Definitely between a rock and a hard place.*

Unable to keep lying about having a boyfriend that no one ever saw, she caved in and accepted the invitation. *Just one date. It'll be over in a few hours and she could always ask the guy to drive her home early, complaining of feeling ill or some other complication. She'd deal with his father whatever the consequence. She'd hold him to his word.*

When she met Stewart, she was quite surprised to find him attractive with dark hair, blue-green eyes and large protruding arm muscles. Shouldn't have been a shock as his father was also tall and debonair. As his father described, Stewart was also quite reserved. There was something mysterious about him too in the way he kept to himself and said more with expressions than with words. He'd smile at her and then become serious again and quiet. Hearing him speak about his father in a vindictive way scared Sheryl a little, but also enhanced the bad-boy image he was painting for himself – a little danger that was quite intriguing to her.

Quite the gentleman, he always wore a suit on their dates. He held doors for her and helped her to her seat. He also appeared to have a lot of money to spare on her, taking her to restaurants with white linen tablecloths, such as in Manhattan's Astor Hotel, where waiters take your napkin off the table and set it on your lap. She had grown accustomed to dates taking her to greasy burger or pizza joints, or for ice cream, so this four-star treatment was a very exciting change.

Over a dinner of lobster with tiny cups of melted butter for dipping – a delicacy for Sheryl since she only had a few opportunities for such *traif* – they learned of their common interest in the arts, such as theater, opera and classical music. One of the more memorable dates, he picked her up in his green Chrysler Newport and whisked her away to the Broadway show, *Oliver*, where he had tickets in the third row. He even tipped the *maître d'* who escorted them to their seats. Whenever she had gone to the theater or opera in the past, she sat in the last row on the balcony.

She brought him home. He seemed a nice boy on the surface: polite, quiet. I had nothing against him per se. There was just something mysterious about him I couldn't put my finger on. He rubbed me the wrong way, though. Maybe it was how standoffish he was, how tightlipped, like he was hiding something. I learned from Sheryl about his family. How meticulous they were, their house being spotless down to its plush white carpet, and demanding of perfection from him as the oldest of two children. They weren't as observant of Jewish tradition as we were, but Sheryl described Stewart as a voracious reader of books on Judaism and Torah, which was very pleasing to me.

Regardless of my opinion, she saw in him what I didn't – maybe a responsible provider in addition to his good looks – and apparently had pried him out of his shell from the time spent together.

There might have been a better boy for her, I thought at the time, a better husband. Something just wasn't quite on the up and up with this one. Who am I to judge?

He caught a great girl. I just prayed he was worthy of her. She married him. Okay. He worked hard to support her. I did hear that he had quite a temper, but he never raised his hand to her.

When Stewart was ready to start a family, she was too. They had three children, two girls and then a boy – a beautiful family.

That left Eliza. I called her my shiny pebbles child. She liked to bring me shiny pebbles. A sort of fascination she had with them. Never really understood, nor why she snuck out of bed at night as a youngster and we'd find her in the morning under the dining room table or in the coat closet fast asleep. She later explained she wanted to be closer to us and hear what adults talk about when they think children are asleep. It didn't matter that Hannah and I spoke in Yiddish, Eliza picked up a few words and deciphered most of what we were saying. She was especially interested in learning about the family in Europe and elsewhere in America. Didn't know what else she might have been exposed to this way; too late to take it back, to protect her.

Her nightly ritual ended when, just hours after having her tonsils removed, she had a reaction to the nuts Hannah had set out on the table in preparation for her special *rugalach*. Eliza reached up from under the table and grabbed a handful and returned to bed unnoticed. Later that evening, she woke Hannah.

"I need a tissue Mama. My nose is running."

Hannah turned on the light.

"Blood!" she shrieked, flipping the covers off to reveal deep stains. "The whole bed is covered in blood!"

The house was awakened in panic as Hannah called for me. I woke and charged into the room to find her sopping up Eliza. Her face was a gooey mess. It took us a few minutes to determine where all the blood was coming from – her nose and mouth.

"Quick Hannah, wrap her in her blanket and take her to the car," I commanded. "I'll be right there."

Here we were back again at the hospital so soon after being there earlier in the day for the tonsil surgery. The nuts caused her to hemorrhage and now she had to stay there several days to recover. When we'd visit, she'd ask why we had abandoned her, why she couldn't come home. "Am I in trouble? Why can't you take me home? All the other children here are going home."

"I promise to be a good girl. I won't hide any more. Please, please don't leave me here."

Not sure why, on one hand, she clung to us so, and on the other, she was in such a rush to be an adult, to learn what adults discuss privately.

When she was all grown up, she too wanted to go her own way. We knew we had to let her, but at certain times we just couldn't stand the idea of not having children at home any more. She had a boyfriend whose family had a home in the New Jersey countryside with a horse, and they wanted to go riding together. We *schlepped* there to bring her – a two-hour drive – and then drove home.

Without her, it was so lonely in the big apartment. We asked ourselves, "Why do we need such a big place?" Friday night, instead of coming home, Eliza called. "I'm going to ride horses." She wasn't coming home that weekend. It was a clear sign to us; she too would be on her own soon.

It was 1966. I was close to 62 years old. The doctor I visited weekly said, "You're working too hard. You should just retire already."

He had given me pills for my heart to take in case I needed them. I had worked every day for 28 years at the Chesed and now I had reached retirement age, and the timing was right.

"Where am I going to retire? How?"

"Go away." *Do doctors only know how to prescribe rest as the cure-all to everything? Seems so.* "Go away from New York and save some of your health. Relax. Stay close to water. It's very calming." Still, I didn't think of me, nor of Hannah. She adjusted well enough to changes. But how would the kids survive without us close by? They were adults now. You'd think I wouldn't treat them like children any more, dependent on us. I wanted to believe they still needed us. They didn't. Even Eliza, 20 then, was making plans to move into a studio apartment in Forest Hills despite Hannah's concerns about living alone in the city. We didn't push it. Time to let go, even of our baby.

28 TWO YEARS TO LIVE
FALL 1966

New Jersey

Something came along. Hannah's sister-in-law, Sadie, lived in Mays Landing, N.J., on a chicken farm. It was about two hours away from our home in New York. I always wanted to return to a farm. We used to like to go out there to visit. On one such visit, we scoped out the area as a retirement spot and Sadie sort of hinted that she was going to buy a bigger farm out there and raise her chickens and sell their eggs. I was helping her sort eggs in the chicken coop when she mentioned it. "Maybe if you retired," she bellowed over the drone of the chicken cackling, "you could manage this bigger place, help out on the farm. I'll give you a nice percentage of the profits." I looked around and imagined myself as farmer again like I had done so many years ago in Europe.

To me it sounded pretty positive, but what did I really know about this woman? She acted like a shrewd businesswoman and I took the bait. We signed the paperwork and handed over our investment. She moved to the bigger farm, taking her chicken houses and chickens with her and leaving us with her old property. We never got our cut.

I didn't care for the way she did it, but I didn't want to take anything from her. She worked hard. She earned what she got over the years, and she deserves every penny. It was my fault for trusting. As it turned out, despite what seemed like a bad business deal, it was a great retirement spot for us. The house on the property was much like the bungalows we stayed in while vacationing in upstate New York, very rustic and primitively comfortable. There were also a vegetable garden and fruit trees for me to tend, which I enjoyed.

When I retired, I received a small pension from the Chesed. I had a little nest egg and was pretty healthy. The more I worked on what remained of the farm Sadie left, the more I knew it was mine. Family and friends criticized us for leaving New York – why move to a place so far away from everyone? But it was our place. I made it look beautiful. I painted it, remodeled it, put in a stove for heat. We planted flowers and more fruit trees. Even got a German shepherd puppy from a litter born to the family dog in a neighboring farm. Sheryl and her husband came to visit and decided to get one too from the same litter. We called ours Princess, and they named theirs Queenie. The dogs once got into a fight and Sheryl, trying to separate them, nearly lost two of her fingers. First calamity while we were there. Not the last, or most serious.

For six and a half years we were happy there. Hannah came to like it, although she remained quite lonely for relatives and the familiar. To ease her pain, whenever she desired, we returned to New York to visit. She knew the fresh air away from the city was good for me, but she also was concerned about being stranded if I became sick. She didn't know how to drive. We'd be in trouble, she knew, if we had an emergency and the children weren't there, at the time.

That major crisis came in 1967. In my life, it seems, I can't get too complacent. Just when everything is going well and I'm comfortable, happiness trembles within me and BAM! The bottom falls out and I have to start again at the bottom, rebuild, recover. I don't blame anyone. I'm not bitter. It's just my lot, I guess, and I accepted it and am wary of taking happiness for granted. It was bound to change on a dime. So was it with our lives in New Jersey. Tragedy strikes when you least expect it.

Arthur, Deborah's husband, was the first to tell us about Hershel. He had leukemia. There were no warning signs. He tried to participate in a blood drive at his office, but during preliminary screenings there, he was directed to see a doctor.

Because of Arthur's medical background, he was able to get Hershel into Sloan-Kettering's cancer research program in Manhattan. There were many tests and treatments: chemo, radiation, surgery, even experimental therapies and drugs. He was like a human guinea pig being stuck with needles and rigged up to different contraptions. Nothing really took. His was a chronic case for which there is seldom a cure, we were told. The prognosis wasn't promising.

We would visit him during the months he was at the hospital. When the doctors exhausted all their treatments and concluded they couldn't do any more for him, they sent him home bald and drawn with a thousand pills for pain and a prescription for rest. Oh, and the death notice: *Two years to live.* When I first heard it, I must have repeated it 50 times, alternating between tears and shaking my head in disbelief. "This can't be. My children can't go before me. I'm the one who is supposed to go. I'm the one on borrowed time." I woke up every night for days after that trying to decipher between reality and what I hoped was just a bad dream. *Two years. Two years to do everything you wanted to do in the 30 or 40 years you expected to still have left.*

Knowing that your son has only two years to live gives you a harsh dose of reality. The other children advised us to continue doing what we were doing, not to come rushing back to New York.

How can I continue doing what I'm doing if my son is dying? Impossible. Nothing would be the same again. As might be expected, I questioned God's motives. *Why couldn't he take me first? Me. Why couldn't he have taken me back when I was hanging on by a thread, standing at death's door anyway, and spare my child now? Why take my son before me, an old man. Why uproot this young man who had yet to reach middle age?* Barry and Lisa were still teenagers, a time in which they really needed guidance and discipline.

The news hit everyone hard. The timing – as if it could ever be right – was totally unfortunate. Barry was to become a bar mitzvah only days after the prognosis. They considered postponing the big event, but decided against it. Life goes on and all that *mishigas*. Talk about growing up in a hurry, being forced to become a man – not only in the religious sense. He was expected to assume more family responsibilities, to contribute what he earned working part-time after school at a music store. Instead of stepping up to the plate and helping to pay bills, Barry got in with the wrong crowd and spent his money recklessly.

We tried to help, to set him on a better path. I stayed with him after school while his mother was at the hospital to ensure that he did his homework. On Shabbos, I dragged him along to synagogue. One summer, he stayed with us on the farm, hoping a new environment would do him some good. It was all futile. Away from family, he returned to his unhealthy patterns. He was much tougher than his father ever was.

Meanwhile, Hershel came to us to rest periodically for a day or so, and we did what we could to keep him comfortable, well fed and relaxed. When we first contemplated moving to the farm, he would scream and holler. "I don't want you to go because it's a lonely world over there. It's not for you." Now he didn't know what to do first – fish at the dock, read in the garden or stroll down the dirt roads. So much fun. He probably thought we spent too much. Didn't matter. It was mine and I hadn't owned something like that before.

In the end, Hershel lived four more years – not two – and died at the age of 42. It was September 7, 1971 – just days before Rosh Hashanah.

Winter 1971, New York

After that, Hannah and I decided to move back to New York. Perhaps the family would be happier if held together. We had often been going back between the farm and New York anyway to visit Hershel, and we wanted to be close to a hospital in case I got sick again. It happened once or twice before while we were there and that scared her. What would she do if I ended up in the hospital?

Hannah couldn't drive and felt stranded on the farm. In New York, she had plenty of transportation options. For us, it was also important to watch Barry, who remained so wild. We could have stayed on the farm longer and enjoyed the tranquility of our retirement. It was time to be with family again.

We moved back. Not into an apartment though. We bought a beautiful house a few doors down and across the street from Deborah in Queens. Plenty of privacy, plenty of room.

Arthur used to tell me "Dad, this is the best investment you can ever make." It was our first house, a nice little two-bedroom with a basement and space for a little garden for me to tend. My refuge within a concrete jungle of a city.

We hosted many family celebrations in that house. While those who lived closer came to visit more often, we looked forward to the larger gatherings at Passover. Everyone knew they could join us and we'd have a full spread, chairs lining both sides of several tables strung together from the dining room to the living room. It was always a challenge to find a matching *Haggadah* for each of us, sometimes as many as 20 in all. We accumulated quite a few of the books over the years as the family grew, so it wasn't a problem, and most didn't mind sharing.

A few Passovers stand out. When Eliza brought our grandson, Andy, for his first *seder*. You see, us leaving Eliza in New York all those years earlier allowed her to express her individuality. We certainly didn't intend her to marry a non-Jew, but we learned to accept this for the sake of her happiness. Coincidentally, their child was born on Hannah's birthday. The girls, my grown daughters, chatted with Eliza as she nursed the baby in an upstairs bedroom that Passover, while Mo played magic games with the other *kinderlach* in the foyer while waiting for the *seder* to begin.

Mama and the girls cooked for hours in preparation for the evening meal. Grinding potatoes and onions for the potato kugel, broiling chicken and brisket, baking mandel bread and honey cake. *Oh*, the sweet smells that wafted through the air as we all anticipated dinnertime. The moans and pangs of hunger, though, weren't enough to keep me from singing the melodies we practically knew by heart – with a little harmony from Sheryl as a soprano to my alto – and reciting every bit of the *seder* as was our tradition. The old ways were too often discarded these days and I wasn't going to have that at my own table. When it was finally time to eat, we were truly famished. A little bitterness to withstand, considering the slavery of our ancestors in the Passover story.

Another Passover I treasured was when Lisa's boyfriend and future husband, Uri, lent his authentic Israeli accent and ingrained understanding of Hebrew to our *seder* ritual. Those were the days.

We stayed a while in that home in Queens before we realized a house might not have been the best place for us at that point in our lives.

Hannah began to have difficulty with her legs, and walking the stairs posed a problem. In an apartment, she had elevators. She also had gained quite a bit of weight over the years. It didn't bother me; I always saw her as a voluptuous beauty. I never cared for the Twiggy types. But the extra weight was heavy on her legs, especially when she'd stand on them for hours cooking and baking.

Whenever she returned from shopping, she complained about her legs hurting.

The first time she had trouble, we took her to Bronx-Lebanon Hospital. Here we go in and out of hospitals and back and forth to doctors again – this time not for me though.

The doctors prescribed special shoes with thick rubber soles. When we went to the store, she refused to try them on. "They're ugly and I'm not going to wear ugly shoes all the time," she protested, arms folded in defiance. "They're awful. I don't care how good they are for my feet. I'd rather have sore feet than wear disgusting shoes. I may be old, but I still have some standards. You used to be a shoemaker. Make me a nicer pair."

I didn't remember how anymore and even if I did, but I certainly couldn't make something designed specifically for her foot problems.

She was like a stubborn child, swearing never to wear them. Because she didn't, her problems persisted.

There might not have been so much misery and trouble if Hannah were a better patient. "You can be so bullheaded sometimes, Hannah! You know that? If you just did what the doctors told you, you'd be better by now. But no, you'd rather be in pain." *Not that I was so different.*

Afraid to go to an eye doctor, she nearly lost her eye when a bug flew into it and scratched it. While the eye was sore, she wore a patch on it until it healed.

Every summer, we went to a doctor to examine her leg, take X-rays. The blood wasn't circulating properly through her veins and that made the leg itch. She scratched them up and made them bleed. Creams and vitamins didn't help.

Each doctor we saw had a different method of treatment. One suggested packing the leg in ice to freeze away the problem. Another thought she might have a type of arthritis and opted to do an experimental surgery in which surgeons go through your stomach to take out one of the extra bones you have in your back. The surgery was six hours and it didn't work. She was in her early 80s then.

No wonder she was afraid of going to hospitals after this.

When Barry got married in June 1986, she fell down a few times. That was the last time she walked without assistance. She was 82 and I was 81. We were getting old, but I really felt like we had more time.

Not being able to walk definitely put a damper on our plans for the future. I know we were fighting against our mortality, but we still had dreams. We wanted to go to Florida, but didn't go. We wanted to go to Israel and postponed that trip, too. Actually, I was afraid to go to Israel because I wasn't a US citizen yet, and I didn't know if they would let me return if I left. (The dream would later be fulfilled; we visited Israel three times).

Selling the house across the street from Deborah, we moved a few blocks away, renting an apartment across the street from our shul to allow us to walk there, and closer to stores we frequented. It wasn't too bad, except for the woman who lived above us who stomped around her apartment at all hours of the night when she couldn't sleep, which kept us up. And yet, we got used to it or accepted it because, in the back of our minds, we knew we'd change one of these days, that this was only a temporary stop.

Spring 1985, Philadelphia

We didn't believe in divorce, but we didn't believe in intermarriage either. Eliza and her husband couldn't work it out and split up. Just like that. They didn't need our permission, I know. You move on. What other choice do you have? Now Eliza was living alone in Philadelphia and raising Andy by herself. Caught in the middle of the divorce, Andy was nearing bar mitzvah age. His father wasn't around and Eliza was traveling a lot. Yet they wanted Andy to have a strong Jewish upbringing. They needed us, and what parent wouldn't want to be needed? Philadelphia put us closer to Mo, too, and his family. We had fond memories of Philly, having visited when we lived in Mays Landing, and Philly had good doctors and medical services for the elderly.

Hannah was the happiest person in the world when we moved. Not because of our new house or because we were moving around the corner from Eliza. She mentioned many a time after that how she wanted to live away from the city, how it wasn't the proper place to grow old. "Now we will live our old age in peace and quiet, without a lot of traffic, and running around." She smiled then, a broad grin that revealed her every wrinkle, her fake teeth. She was content.

And I felt the same because when she was happy, I was happy. We could even walk to shul like we did in New York.

Just like when we moved into that first house in the Big Apple, things were good for a while, but within about six months they turned sour again. It was not meant to be.

You'd think we'd be smarter than to buy another multi-leveled house. Hannah couldn't move far without a walker. We had to build a bathroom on the main floor with a wide doorway that she could pass through with her walker. We built a chair lift to take her to the bedroom.

For a woman who was used to doing everything for everyone else, it was very frustrating not to be able to do anything for anyone, including herself. She frightened away a number of cleaning ladies, complaining they didn't do the job as well as she would have.

Not being able to stand long enough to cook, she turned to Eliza and our other children who came to visit and took turns preparing meals that could be kept in the freezer and be heated up as needed.

In the last four years, I can tell you, it was not what I wanted it to be, what Hannah wanted it to be. We went through a lot. Hannah is my rock of Gibraltar. She will go through pain; she will not complain, even when I felt healthy and she didn't. Even when it hurts, she manages. And God keeps her here with us, for me, for the family.

Something happened to us and we had to just weather the changes. We had become dependent on others. It was the very worst thing and I wasn't really ready to face it. She had to go through all that suffering, and I know that life was never going to be the same for her, for me, for the family. What can anybody say when a thing like this happens? What?

I think about how Hannah compares to my mother. Their character, their nature, eerily similar. Subconsciously maybe, I sought my mother's likeness in women. Sigmund Freud – coincidentally from the same area as Hannah – would probably have something to say about that. Were they all strong, bold, liberated? Perhaps. Hannah, definitely.

In the beginning, I had certain problems with Hannah, probably like all married couples have. She had her ways, especially when it came to the children. But we grew to understand each other's differences and either appreciate or put up with them.

Just like my mother did with my father, if the children did something wrong, the minute I came home from work, Hannah provoked the children, "Should I tell him?" They didn't like her for that. Sometimes they hated it. I know the feeling because my mother did the same thing, report me to my father and have to relive the incident and apologize and beg forgiveness from yet another adult.

The two women had another thing in common. Neither of them was well educated. Girls weren't really required to have much in the way of brains in the Old Country. Both women, though, wanted their children to have an education. I tried to teach the children. Hannah couldn't. She also didn't have enough time or patience to teach them. I even tried teaching Hannah a little – English, Judaism. I read to her from the Yiddish *Forverts*, but also the New York Post. Otherwise, all she could do was look at the pictures and the advertisements and try to decide from those, the direction the world was heading.

Sheryl and Eliza saved enough from working at different jobs during high school to pay for a few years of college for the children.

Hannah and I didn't go to college. Besides studying Hebrew and Judaism over the years through our synagogues, the biggest study session we had was to become citizens. It was probably one of the biggest achievements in my life, besides coming to America, meeting Hannah and having my five children. In 1979, we had started the process to become citizens. Hannah had a green card and papers from Canada. I didn't have a visa or other immigration papers when I landed in Canada and no papers when I crossed the border into the United States. Through Eliza's law firm, we had gotten temporary papers that allowed us to go with our grandson, Benjamin, Sheryl's son, to Israel for his bar mitzvah in 1983. But we still weren't legally Americans yet.

I wanted to be a citizen so badly that I drilled Hannah constantly before the test to prepare her. "Who was the president? The vice president? Who was the first president of the US?" When the question came about who was the governor of New York, Hannah was nervous and answered Perry Como, the singer. She meant Mario Cuomo. But we did it. We became citizens – together. After the ceremony, we went back to lunch at Deborah's. It was a memorable day, back in 1985. I wanted so much to be a citizen and I was one now after more than a half-century – 60 years – in this country already. To me, I was already a citizen, but this made it official. I suppose it's what a convert to Judaism must feel. You want it, but you have to study hard and jump through many hoops to prove you are worthy of the honor, and then, maybe, just maybe, you'll be accepted. It's something you feel in your blood. And even then, somehow, you wonder whether anyone can see through you to know – without the foreign tongue to give it away – you're not the genuine article, but an outsider who wants to be in. It may have been one of the reasons I was so determined not to let our differences be a deterrent to living peacefully among our neighbors.

Consider the Jehovah Witnesses who appeared periodically on our doorstep. The children may have giggled at these strangers, dressed in white robes. I related to them, not in their attempt to convert, but in the strength of their convictions. Whenever the opportunity presented itself, I'd invite them in for mutual education about our alternative beliefs. We'd sit in the kitchen over Hannah's sponge cake and hot tea as long as they agreed to my rules. "I'll let you talk about your organization and religion if you give me equal time to tell you about mine." They didn't shy away from the challenge, and neither did I. When I finished speaking, we resolved to disagree. It certainly wasn't the result they were looking for – figuratively scratched their heads as they retreated – and we never saw the same group twice. A waste of time? A test of patience? Maybe for others. The melting pot of America extends this right to speak my mind and hold strong to my religious beliefs, and I take those privileges seriously as they are not so readily available elsewhere.

When Sheryl and Deborah took me to the Liberty Bell in Philadelphia years later, I had the same appreciation. I could hardly walk then or even breathe easily. Because of my condition, the girls were granted permission for us to move to the front of the line. There, I brought fingers to lips and reached out the kissed fingertips to touch the prominent crack in the bell as if it was the Wailing Wall or Torah, which you aren't technically supposed to touch with bare hands. At that point, a guard, apparently on alert for such wayward activity, practically flew over to scold me for the intrusion. "Did you read the signs, sir? Do you think these ropes are here for no reason?"

He motioned to the myriad of notices warning visitors to stay back and the rope cordoning off the bell. "I'm afraid we can't allow people to touch the bell or it might damage the historic integrity of the relic."

"I'm an old man. What do I know from such rules? Besides, I'm an historical relic myself. If you only knew how difficult it was to even get to this country... You don't know about freedom like I know about freedom." Of course, I hadn't read the postings. I was too busy focusing on the significance of the moment. A few Yiddish curse words and he shook his head in confusion, as the girls, through restrained giggles, convinced the officer that they would set me straight. In my mind, a rebellion worthy of the reprimand. So much for American freedom.

29 CHOCOLATE SIDE DOWN

We have *yahrtzeit* today for Hershel. It's been 18 years since his death. Ironic how 18, in Hebrew, is *chai,* life, and yet we are marking death. Not just any death, but the death of a son way before his time. We still live and he's long gone. I can hardly say this without choking on my words. I'm all *ferklempt.* What we felt then... it never goes away. Oh, if only that guy could see how his family has developed, his children married, a 3-year-old granddaughter now.

Just like we did in 1971, when he died, we have to go on for the sake of the family.

I'm certainly not the man I used to be. My mind doesn't work right. It wanders.

This beat-up old heart of mine probably has done what it was asked to do. It held out. Nothing more, nothing less than I deserve. I don't know what I expected at the end of my days.

All in all, it's been pretty exciting. Those days, you can't replace them. May not have accomplished everything I thought I would. Maybe I would have become a *chazzan* or traveled more. Perhaps I would have moved to Israel or taught Torah to children. I could have owned a fruit and vegetable stand.

If I could do it all over again, I'd certainly change a few things. I'd have left for America the first time I had a chance instead of losing my nerve. Depended less on my family. Picked a different roommate, a cleaner one. Avoided the trolley accident. Stepped up quicker when I saw that gunman was taking aim. Definitely been more up-front with Hannah and my children.

Okay, maybe I still have time to remedy that last part.

Under the circumstances, I am pretty well off. When I get up in the morning, when I go to sleep, I tell the Almighty what I think, how grateful I am to be alive, and to have my family. I still fight with Him; question why bad things happen to good people and the like. For as long as I can remember, I've been questioning. My father, may he rest in peace, used to say: "Who are you to ask God questions? Who are you to expect any answers?" Still not worthy of a response, and yet, I hold out for hope.

God and I understand each other, I think. He doesn't talk back to me directly, but I get this overwhelming message in my mind in talking it over with myself: "Just do what you have to do as best as you know how." In a way then, I guess He **is** speaking to me.

If there's something I've learned, it's that some days start out badly and don't get any better. Other days are quite momentous and you have to hold tight to those. Be thankful for every day you experience love and blessings because you never know when your faith will be tested again.

A couple of days ago, I knew I was heading for another rough patch. It was kind of funny when it happened. Either that, or pathetic. Eliza brought me a birthday cake. I was turning 85. We had a little birthday party and she took home the rest of the cake. On the way out, she dropped its chocolate side down. Why couldn't it fall the other way and we could have salvaged some of it. It had to fall so that it's a total loss? That's how things were going for the last couple of months.

In early 1990, everyone thought I was a goner. The children decided – not easily – we needed nursing home care. They settled on Manor Crest, not far from Eliza. Disheartened by this lack of independence, I was given a sedative, an antidepressant that caused me to hallucinate. Apparently, I imagined my youngest child, Eliza, as my grandmother, for whom she was named. Eliza had come to help Hannah deal with me when I started hallucinating and babbling nonsense. "Take me home Bubbie," I greeted Eliza. "It's Shabbos. Take me home."

I was transported from Manor Crest's rehab center to Philadelphia General. Eliza was allowed to ride in the ambulance because the doctor noticed the relationship and told her that it would help me recover. Later that night, after Eliza had gone home, a nurse from General called to tell her to return to my side, that I probably wouldn't make it. "You'll want to be here," the nurse said. Visiting hours were over, but my personal nurse, more like a protective mother to her patients, told Eliza how to sneak into the hospital and up the back stairs. Eliza could sleep in the unoccupied bed in my room. If anyone checked my room, she said, they would assume another patient was asleep in the second bed.

She did it. Upon arriving, she was greeted by my comatose whimpering: "I'm not ready. This is not fair. Hannah is not ready. Not this time." After trying to comfort me, Eliza climbed in the extra bed and fell asleep. In the morning, I sat up and demanded, "Where's my breakfast?"

I guess I was okay. Then it was Hannah's turn to be bedridden. In December 1990, she had fallen off the bed at the nursing home because it was too high, and broke her hip. She had only been at the home for like a month when she was taken to the same hospital at which I was treated, and underwent an operation.

Hannah was not allowed back to the nursing home because she had to be on medication and a feeding tube. Eliza requested that the feeding tube be removed after Hannah repeatedly pulled it out. The hospital tried several things to get her to eat, including an implant, but she still wouldn't. Her veins were so sore, intravenous didn't even work. The feeding tube was the only way to sustain her.

The medical staff strapped her down and reinstalled the tube, causing her to squirm and moan. "I don't want to live like this," Hannah, barely audible, told Eliza. "This is no life." She didn't speak much after that.

Eliza again requested the feeding tubes be removed, replaced with saline, so Hannah didn't have to be tied down and I could be with her.

Those final times together in the hospital, hand-in-hand were unreal, like the slow-motion hallucinations I had from certain medications. Everything we had been through. I always believed she would be there to watch me go. It's how it should have been, years earlier when I was very sick and on borrowed time. This was almost too much to bear, watching her slip away and leaving me here, alone, a mere shadow of what I used to be. I couldn't even grieve. Could this really be happening – to her, to us? Had we really reached the end of our lives and we wouldn't be together anymore? We had been together so long. One would think we were always meant to be that way. Was this to be our ever after, right here, right now?

So, I sat there during one of our last visits, reviewing what our lives had been. How she got in my blood when I was in the hospital and I called for her and knew then that she was the one to go through life with. How we raised five children and lost one. How we grew old together.

Her hands were cold now, even as I held them in mine. They never really warmed in my grasp. She was barely breathing, taking short, labored puffs of air. I surveyed her face, so ashen. Her hair, once the shade of a setting sun before it hits the horizon, now silver, held back in a gold clip as Eliza fixed it on her last visit. Periodically, while she lay there, she'd writhe in pain, semi-consciously, and I'd brace for further complications.

Despite the look on her face as she suffered, I could see the younger, healthier woman she once was. She was old now – no doubt. But she was still beautiful to me. Lying in slumber, I saw a strong, voluptuous girl who, when touched for the first time, sent a shock of static electricity through my fingers and into my veins. I can see our reaction, our mutual embarrassment at the sensation. And yet, it was that spark that ignited our bond.

As I was contemplating what my days were like with her and what it would be like without her, she opened her eyes, saw me sitting there cradling her tender, vein-branched hands, with head bowed in prayer. And she whispered to me about an afterlife in which we'd be together again. She reminded me to tell the children about her previous marriage so that they didn't have to hear it first from others in the family. Also, to ensure Mo that we were very much in love when we conceived him, in case he figures out it was out-of-wedlock.

Then it was my turn. I shared with her the trolley accident and how I had supported a second family along with my own. I couldn't begin to stop the tears from flowing as I dug up the past and lay it before us. It was too much for her and she drifted off again after something that sounded like "give." I keep praying it was "forgive."

I don't know if she heard me acknowledge her request to tell the children everything. It was the last time we spoke, the last time she said anything other than to wail in pain.

Certainly, I would honor her wishes. What else could I do? I wanted to leave with her, to jump out the window and be with her then. But she had different plans. She left me with a mission to accomplish – for her – and now it was for me, too. If it wasn't for that, I couldn't see where there was anything worth sticking around for.

Who needs me anymore? I'm an old man tucked away in a nursing home. Hardly anyone comes and visits any more, except a few true faithfuls who live in the area or make what seems an obligatory trip as if they were clocking into work.

Even right before we moved into the nursing home, I realized the station one reaches when you're the matriarch or patriarch of a family. During family gatherings, Hannah and I would get tucked in a corner in a comfortable couch or set under an umbrella during outdoor events with food and drink. One by one the children, leading the grandchildren and great-grandchildren would file by us out of respect, exchanging trite pleasantries. How are you feeling? Can I get you anything? Have you seen the new baby?

They'd stand or sit for short spells, point and laugh at other activities around us, and then excuse themselves to rejoin the festivities; unless a history project was being pursued in school in which our experience was needed or someone had a question about family history or certain relatives in our past, we became part of the furniture – antiques at that.

The morning of Hannah's passing, January 31, 1991, my grandson, Barry, and his wife, Jodi, picked me up from Manor Crest and drove me to the hospital for what had become my daily visit. Family members took turns accompanying me.

Of all of them, Barry was probably the most ostentatious. He had something to prove and I allowed him his eccentricities, considering he grew up without a father and turned to me to fill that void. I accepted the paternal role wholeheartedly. It wasn't an easy responsibility when it came to Barry, but I knew what to expect by now. With scraggly beard and mustache, his chest hair and a heavy gold chain exposed through an unbuttoned t-shirt and black leather jacket, Barry exuded a confident defiance.

"You all right, Grandpa? Everything working okay?" Barry was clearly amused with himself. He helped me on with my coat before escorting me to his latest conquest, a red Ford Mustang convertible.

"What do you think? Pretty nice wheels, huh?"

"Ach, what do you need such a fancy sports car for anyway? Who are you trying to impress?" I said, Jodi sliding into the back seat as Barry helped me lower myself into the front.

"It's just a nice car, Grandpa. Top of the line."

"What do I know? Use it in *gut* health, that's all I can say."

When we arrived at the hospital, we heard someone screaming at the top of her lungs. The woman we heard hollering was Hannah's roommate.

Barry, cutting an intimidating figure with his coarse façade, went over to the nurses' station and asked the nurses, a bit aggressively, if one or the other woman in the room could be moved.

"I'm sorry sir, but you'll have to wait," said a large, elderly nurse, sporting a supervisor's badge, standing up from her files and pushing past the younger nurses at the desk to calm an agitated Barry. "There are no beds available and we can't move anyone just yet. But as soon as a room becomes available..."

"That's just not going to be good enough!" Barry said, interrupting the nurse mid-sentence. "My grandmother is in pain and she shouldn't have to go through this! She hasn't slept all night because this woman has been screaming!" Barry yelled at the nurse, forcing the other nurses to get up and rally around in case of further incident.

"Please sir, lower your voice." One of the younger nurses approached. "Should I call security?" She motioned to the phone.

Barry turned and trudged back to the room, still yelling down the hall about inferior service and lawsuits. When he returned to Hannah's room, after she reiterated her dying wishes to me a few weeks earlier that I tie up loose ends with the family and meet her in heaven when I was ready, she began complaining of chest pains, moaning that it hurt when she breathed.

"Oy... oy... oy vey iz mir... oy... please... oy..." She was begging, pleading, as she clutched above her breast, clutching her skin.

Barry stormed back over to the nurses' station and again barked at the nurse he had challenged before, spitting his words. "She's having trouble breathing now and is saying she's having chest pains! Don't you people give a shit? A woman needs a doctor here, dammit!"

The nurse rudely responded that there were no doctors in the hospital because it was Saturday. Upon hearing this, Barry, known to have the same temper as other Fox men, flew off the handle, grabbing the nurse by her blouse and practically lifting her off the ground with his grip.

She was standing across the counter from him, but he reached over and grabbed her anyway. He lost it. "You're full of shit! I'm not a fucking moron. This is a hospital. I don't believe there's not a doctor. You better find one or I'm going to rip your nose off your face. Just try me." He let go of her blouse and began walking away. He was going to look for a doctor himself when he saw an Asian woman in scrubs rushing toward him. She wore a stethoscope around her neck, unlike the other nurses on the floor. Barry cornered her. "Could you please look at my grandmother? She is complaining it is hard for her to breathe and she is feeling chest pains."

Barry, Jodi and I stayed in the room as the doctor examined Hannah, and the next thing we knew, we were all thrown out. The doctor went somewhere and a heart monitor was rolled in, along with several other machines. Barry called Mo at his home and Eliza at hers and let them know that Hannah was having a heart attack. She was rushed to the cardiac-care unit and was in a coma. Mo and Eliza never made it to the hospital in time to see her alive. She died January 31 of heart failure. Can you believe that? A failed heart? A broken heart?

I was there. I watched her slip away, taking much of who I was with her as she left. I stayed for a long time near her, asking the others to leave, so I could study her for the last time, telling her what she meant to me, knowing she would never answer. The room inside was as chilly as the air out. Snow was falling again. I touched her hand and it, too, was without her usual warmth. I caressed it with my lips, heavily moistened by tears, which filled my mouth with saltiness, and caused her hand to slip from my grasp. I wiped the tears from my face with the back of my hand and kissed her on the forehead. A long kiss as if my lips were glued to her skin. Then, I too left.

I was in a sleepy fog for quite a while after that. Whole days would pass when I could not shake myself out of it. At Eliza's home for the seven-day *shiva*, our huge family and dear friends came to say, and not be able to say without hesitation, reservations, what Hannah had meant to them. I nodded my head, dutifully, as they greeted me, their hung heads in their own despair or understanding of mine. I sat on the hard chairs of a family in mourning. I ripped my jacket, as is the custom. What does one care for clothes at a time like this? I wasn't really there. The people were a mere blur, shadows passing me, eating from the spread donated by our old *shul* and friends.

Does everyone who's lost someone feel like this, this medicated feeling like I had when I was in the hospital before? I could see it, too, in my children's drained, tear-streaked faces, as they sat beside me, taking turns holding my hand.

Whenever I wasn't at Eliza's house, I was in bed at Manor Crest. Here I could escape to my subconscious, where Hannah and I were happy, young lovers, rather than facing whatever was left for me, the business she wanted fulfilled. Hannah. She was gone. I was alone now. Alone. The nurses gave me sedatives to calm me because I was moaning too loudly in my dreams. The medication kept me groggy, but that state felt much safer for me now. How could I be anything now without my Hannah? How does one go on when something like this happens? I certainly didn't know.

The children would come and visit and try to comfort me. Actually, we'd comfort each other, if you can even find that when someone you loved so much and for so long is to be forever absent. I didn't have the energy to speak for long. Most of the time we just alternated crying about her death and laughing at some of our memories of her, including the games she played or the delicacies she prepared for us.

"Maybe it'd be therapeutic to say what you're feeling right now Daddy," Eliza suggested during one such visit. She was fascinated not with pebbles nowadays but with self-help philosophies. "You know, Dad, talk it through into the tape recorder. I left you a new pack of tapes, remember? You started on it a while back, when Mom... uh... fell." She was all tears, *ferklempt*, as she reached for the nightstand drawer handle and showed me the stack. "It might do you some good to get it out."

What did I know from such *narrischkeit*, a contraption, this box that records your voice and plays it back? The things they invent nowadays. First radios, then televisions. And now these small recording devices. Eliza said it would be good to leave something for the grandchildren, that they were constantly asking about the stories for history projects.

"Mom would have liked that, don't you think, Dad? Anything for the *kinderlach*."

"Yes, I suppose so," I said, wearily. "I'll try. It's very confusing with all these buttons. I had trouble when I tried it last time. The machine jammed up on me or something. It just stopped after a while. I don't know what happened."

"It probably just needed a new tape Dad. That's it. The tape stopped because it was full and needed to be turned over." She chuckled, shaking her head.

"Don't laugh. It's not funny. So, I'm a little *farblonjet?* So what! Just tell me again. I just press here, right? Nothing else?"

"That's it, Daddy. It's not that complicated. Just put the tape in here like this and push here, see? Just like I showed you before. I'll check that you're doing it right when I come back if you'd like."

"Fine, fine."

With that, she kissed my forehead. "Okay, Daddy. I'll be here tomorrow. Try to move around a little today."

"All right." I nodded.

When she disappeared, I sat up in the bed and turned toward the icy window. The tree limbs were covered in snow and beyond that all I saw was misty gray. I pulled open the drawer near my bed and retrieved the black Panasonic recorder. Flipping open its compartment cover, I inserted a fresh tape and waited for it to click into the slot, like she showed me. I closed the cover, pressed the button and began speaking, holding the box a few inches from my lips.

"I've been asked on many occasions, by my children and grandchildren, to record my life history..."

30 THE AFTERLIFE

Jews believe in a yearlong mourning period, ending with the recognition of the *yahrtzeit*. According to another Jewish tradition, the wife is charged with preparing the home and meal for her husband's arrival as Shabbos begins.

As Eliza recounted it to the family when she handed out copies of the tapes, Sam stopped talking and recording on Hannah's *yahrtzeit*, January 31, 1992, a year to the date of his wife's passing. It was a Friday night, the beginning of Shabbos. He was 86 and he was starting to leave. After glancing at his gold watch, the one he'd been carrying since it was returned to him from his brother from Nazi Europe, he stared out the window, eyes agape at a cloudless sky.

Eliza, who was there nearly to the end of Hannah's life, too, sensed that he was drifting. His Shiny Pebbles Child whispered in his ear: "You know what day it is today, Daddy, don't you? She's waiting for you. She knows. She's got everything ready. It's just a matter of when you decide."

He turned to Eliza with eyes open wide and broke his silence, wailing, "Hannah! Hannah!" With that, he squeezed Eliza's hand so tight it hurt.

She told him again, "She knows, she's waiting for you." Then she kissed him goodbye and said she'd see him later.

He was still mumbling, "Hannah, Hannah, Hannah," when she left.

That evening, Friday night, as the sun cast its final iridescent glow of the week, signaling the start of Shabbos, he was gone.

GLOSSARY

Ainekel: grandson

Alter cocker: old person

Araynkumen: come in

Bisl: little

Bubbie: grandmother

Bubelah: an endearment toward a young child; literally, little grandmother

Bupkes: nothing

Challah: egg bread used for Sabbath and holiday blessings

Chazerei: sugary sweets

Chazzan: cantor, song leader

Cheder: school

Chesed: kindness

Chuppah: wedding canopy under which the bride and groom stand in a Jewish wedding

Chutzpah: gall, audacity, brazenness, daring, boldness

Dreck: garbage, throwaway

Farblonjet: completely lost, wandering aimlessly, confused, mixed up

Farshtaist: understand

Feesela: foot

Ferdray: worry

Ferklempt: choked up, overcome with emotion

Farshtinkener: stinking

Forshpeiz: appetizer

Forverts: Yiddish newspaper, The Jewish Daily Forward, or The Forward

Gantse megillah: whole complicated story or big production

Gay gezunt: go in health

Glezel tay: glass of tea

Gornisht: Nothing

Gottenyu: dear God, oh Lord

Goy/goyim: non-Jew(s)

Greebenes: chicken skin cracklings, what's left after cooked, see *schmaltz*

Grundbesitzer: having a large property

Gut zets: good smack

Haggadah: text recounting the Exodus from Egypt story during the Passover seder

Iz duss meyn, ya: This is mine, right?

Kashering: making something kosher

Kibitzing: casually chatting

Kinderlach: children

Kishkes: guts, intestines, innards

Knish: filling, typically potato, covered with dough and baked or fried.

Kosher: food that complies with strict set of dietary rules in Judaism

Koyekh: strength

Kugel/Lukshen kugel: thick noodle casserole

Kvell: bursting with pride, happiness

Kvetch: complain

Loch in kop: hole in the head

Luftig: airy, breezy

Luftmensch: impractical contemplative person

Makher: important person

Meshuga: crazy

Meshugener: crazy person

Mishigas: craziness

Mishpachah: family

Mitzvah: good deed, literally commandment

Moyl: mouth

Naches: good luck

Narrischkeit: foolishness, nonsense

Nu: So? Well?

Nudniks: pestering, nagging or irritating person

Oneg: the meal after a Sabbath service or special occasion

Oy: oh, woe, often *oy vey,* see *vey iz mir*

Patsh: pat, spank

Pinchus: feathers

Pisher: inexperienced, unimportant person

Putz: stupid person, fool, jerk

Schlep: drag

Schmaltz: chicken fat, grease

Schmattes: rags, ragged piece of cloth or worn clothing

Schmo: a stupid or ordinary person

Schnapps: alcohol such as brandy, gin or liqueur

Schnook: a stupid, easily victimized person

Seder: festive Passover dinner

Shabbat/Shabbos: Jewish Sabbath

Shammes: Caretaker in a synagogue

Shicker: drunk

Shlemiel: bumbling, foolish, incompetent person. See *shmendrick*

Shlishkahs: potato-based small dumpling

Shmendrick: bumbling, foolish or incompetent person. See *shlemiel*

Shochet: slaughterer, butcher

Shmutzy: dirty

Shtetl: small Jewish town or village in eastern Europe

Shul: synagogue

Shvitzing: sweating

Simcha: celebration

Tallis: prayer shawl

Tatelah: little boy

Tchotchke: small decorative object, trinket

Tefillin: phylacteries, black leather boxes containing Hebrew parchment scrolls with Torah verses secured to the forehead and wrapped around the arms by religious Jews in morning prayers.

Traif: not kosher

Tsuris: worries, troubles

Tukhes: backside, derriere

Tzuika: plum brandy

Vey iz mir: woe is me, often *oy vey iz mir*

Villenkolonie: a large villa colony, district

Vos is dos: what is this

Ya, gain tzu hoiza: Yes, going home

Yahrtzeit: anniversary of a death, a time for mourning

Yenta: busybody or matchmaker

Zaftig: having a full, rounded figure, plump or curvaceous, big breasted

Zayde: grandfather

Zets: smack, hit as reprimand

Zol zein: let it be, that's all

ABOUT THE AUTHOR

Hands of Gold capitalizes on award-winning author Roni Robbins'
35 years as a published writer. Currently an editor/writer for
Medscape/WebMD after serving as associate editor of the Atlanta
Jewish Times/The Times of Israel, she has a seasoned history as a
staff reporter for daily and weekly newspapers and as a freelancer for
national, regional and online publications.

Robbins' freelance articles have appeared in The Huffington Post,
Forbes, the New York Daily News, Adweek, WebMD and
Healthline. She wrote for the Mother Nature Network; The
Forward; FromTheGrapevine; and Hadassah magazine, among
others. Robbins was also a staff writer for Florida Today/USA Today,
The Birmingham News and the Atlanta Business
Chronicle/American City Business Journals.

In addition to major CEOs and politicians, she has interviewed such celebrities as Wolf Blitzer, Andy Gibb, Hank Aaron and Usher.

In 2009, *Hands of Gold* was a quarterfinalist for historical fiction in the Amazon Breakthrough Novel Award contest.

In 2022 it was Finalist in the American Fiction Awards, Family Saga.

In 2023 *Hands of Gold* was a Winner in the International Book Awards, Fiction - Multicultural.

Robbins also won three Simon Rockower Awards for Jewish journalism from the American Jewish Press Association, including an investigative piece about Jewish seniors who feel "Out of Touch" in nursing homes. Other prestigious news-writing awards come from The State Bar of Georgia, the Alabama Associated Press and the South Carolina Press Association.

Hands of Gold is her first novel.

www.ronirobbins.com

AMSTERDAM PUBLISHERS
HOLOCAUST LIBRARY

The series **Holocaust Survivor Memoirs World War II** consists of the following autobiographies of survivors:

Outcry. Holocaust Memoirs, by Manny Steinberg

Hank Brodt Holocaust Memoirs. A Candle and a Promise, by Deborah Donnelly

The Dead Years. Holocaust Memoirs, by Joseph Schupack

Rescued from the Ashes. The Diary of Leokadia Schmidt, Survivor of the Warsaw Ghetto, by Leokadia Schmidt

My Lvov. Holocaust Memoir of a twelve-year-old Girl, by Janina Hescheles

Remembering Ravensbrück. From Holocaust to Healing, by Natalie Hess

Wolf. A Story of Hate, by Zeev Scheinwald with Ella Scheinwald

Save my Children. An Astonishing Tale of Survival and its Unlikely Hero, by Leon Kleiner with Edwin Stepp

Holocaust Memoirs of a Bergen-Belsen Survivor & Classmate of Anne Frank, by Nanette Blitz Konig

Defiant German - Defiant Jew. A Holocaust Memoir from inside the Third Reich, by Walter Leopold with Les Leopold

In a Land of Forest and Darkness. The Holocaust Story of two Jewish Partisans, by Sara Lustigman Omelinski

Holocaust Memories. Annihilation and Survival in Slovakia, by Paul Davidovits

From Auschwitz with Love. The Inspiring Memoir of Two Sisters' Survival, Devotion and Triumph Told by Manci Grunberger Beran & Ruth Grunberger Mermelstein, by Daniel Seymour

Remetz. Resistance Fighter and Survivor of the Warsaw Ghetto, by Jan Yohay Remetz

My March Through Hell. A Young Girl's Terrifying Journey to Survival, by Halina Kleiner with Edwin Stepp

Roman's Journey, by Roman Halter

Beyond Borders. Escaping the Holocaust and Fighting the Nazis. 1938-1948, by Rudi Haymann

The Engineers. A memoir of survival through World War II in Poland and Hungary, by Henry Reiss

Memoirs by Elmar Rivosh, Sculptor (1906-1967). Riga Ghetto and Beyond, by Elmar Rivosh

The series **Holocaust Survivor True Stories** consists of the following biographies:

Among the Reeds. The true story of how a family survived the Holocaust, by Tammy Bottner

A Holocaust Memoir of Love & Resilience. Mama's Survival from Lithuania to America, by Ettie Zilber

Living among the Dead. My Grandmother's Holocaust Survival Story of Love and Strength, by Adena Bernstein Astrowsky

Heart Songs. A Holocaust Memoir, by Barbara Gilford

Shoes of the Shoah. The Tomorrow of Yesterday, by Dorothy Pierce

Hidden in Berlin. A Holocaust Memoir, by Evelyn Joseph Grossman

Separated Together. The Incredible True WWII Story of Soulmates Stranded an Ocean Apart, by Kenneth P. Price, Ph.D.

The Man Across the River. The incredible story of one man's will to survive the Holocaust, by Zvi Wiesenfeld

If Anyone Calls, Tell Them I Died. A Memoir, by Emanuel (Manu) Rosen

The House on Thrömerstrasse. A Story of Rebirth and Renewal in the Wake of the Holocaust, by Ron Vincent

Dancing with my Father. His hidden past. Her quest for truth. How Nazi Vienna shaped a family's identity, by Jo Sorochinsky

The Story Keeper. Weaving the Threads of Time and Memory - A Memoir, by Fred Feldman

Krisia's Silence. The Girl who was not on Schindler's List, by Ronny Hein

Defying Death on the Danube. A Holocaust Survival Story, by Debbie J. Callahan with Henry Stern

A Doorway to Heroism. A decorated German-Jewish Soldier who became an American Hero, by Rabbi W. Jack Romberg

The Shoemaker's Son. The Life of a Holocaust Resister, by Laura Beth Bakst

The Redhead of Auschwitz. A True Story, by Nechama Birnbaum

Land of Many Bridges. My Father's Story, by Bela Ruth Samuel Tenenholtz

Creating Beauty from the Abyss. The Amazing Story of Sam Herciger, Auschwitz Survivor and Artist, by Lesley Ann Richardson

On Sunny Days We Sang. A Holocaust Story of Survival and Resilience, by Jeannette Grunhaus de Gelman

Painful Joy. A Holocaust Family Memoir, by Max J. Friedman

I Give You My Heart. A True Story of Courage and Survival, by Wendy Holden

In the Time of Madmen, by Mark A. Prelas

Monsters and Miracles. Horror, Heroes and the Holocaust, by Ira Wesley Kitmacher

Flower of Vlora. Growing up Jewish in Communist Albania, by Anna Kohen

Aftermath: Coming of Age on Three Continents. A Memoir, by Annette Libeskind Berkovits

Not a real Enemy. The True Story of a Hungarian Jewish Man's Fight for Freedom, by Robert Wolf

Zaidy's War. Four Armies, Three Continents, Two Brothers. One Man's Impossible Story of Endurance, by Martin Bodek

The Glassmaker's Son. Looking for the World my Father left behind in Nazi Germany, by Peter Kupfer

The Apprentice of Buchenwald. The True Story of the Teenage Boy Who Sabotaged Hitler's War Machine, by Oren Schneider

Good for a Single Journey, by Helen Joyce

Burying the Ghosts. She escaped Nazi Germany only to have her life torn apart by the woman she saved from the camps: her mother, by Sonia Case

American Wolf. From Nazi Refugee to American Spy. A True Story, by Audrey Birnbaum

Bipolar Refugee. A Saga of Survival and Resilience, by Peter Wiesner

Before the Beginning and After the End, by Hymie Anisman

Malka Owsiany recounts, by Mark Turkow (editor)

I Will Give Them an Everlasting Name. Jacksonville's Stories of the Holocaust, by Samuel P. Cox

The series **Jewish Children in the Holocaust** consists of the following autobiographies of Jewish children hidden during WWII in the Netherlands:

Searching for Home. The Impact of WWII on a Hidden Child, by Joseph Gosler

See You Tonight and Promise to be a Good Boy! War memories, by Salo Muller

Sounds from Silence. Reflections of a Child Holocaust Survivor, Psychiatrist and Teacher, by Robert Krell

Sabine's Odyssey. A Hidden Child and her Dutch Rescuers, by Agnes Schipper

The Journey of a Hidden Child, by Harry Pila and Robin Black

The series **New Jewish Fiction** consists of the following novels, written by Jewish authors. All novels are set in the time during or after the Holocaust.

The Corset Maker. A Novel, by Annette Libeskind Berkovits

Escaping the Whale. The Holocaust is over. But is it ever over for the next generation? by Ruth Rotkowitz

When the Music Stopped. Willy Rosen's Holocaust, by Casey Hayes

Hands of Gold. One Man's Quest to Find the Silver Lining in Misfortune, by Roni Robbins

The Girl Who Counted Numbers. A Novel, by Roslyn Bernstein

There was a garden in Nuremberg. A Novel, by Navina Michal Clemerson

The Butterfly and the Axe, by Omer Bartov

To Live Another Day. A Novel, Elizabeth Rosenberg

A Worthy Life. Based on a True Story, by Dahlia Moore

The series **Holocaust Heritage** consists of the following memoirs by 2G:

The Cello Still Sings. A Generational Story of the Holocaust and of the Transformative Power of Music, by Janet Horvath

The Fire and the Bonfire. A Journey into Memory, by Ardyn Halter

The Silk Factory: Finding Threads of My Family's True Holocaust Story, by Michael Hickins

Hidden in Plain Sight: A Journey into Memory and Place, by Julie Brill

The series **Holocaust Books for Young Adults** consists of the
following novels, based on true stories:

The Boy behind the Door. How Salomon Kool Escaped the Nazis. Inspired
by a True Story, by David Tabatsky

Running for Shelter. A True Story, by Suzette Sheft

The Precious Few. An Inspirational Saga of Courage based on True Stories,
by David Twain with Art Twain

The series **WWII Historical Fiction** consists of the following novels, some of which are based on true stories:

Mendelevski's Box. A Heartwarming and Heartbreaking Jewish Survivor's Story, by Roger Swindells

A Quiet Genocide. The Untold Holocaust of Disabled Children in WWII Germany, by Glenn Bryant

The Knife-Edge Path, by Patrick T. Leahy

Brave Face. The Inspiring WWII Memoir of a Dutch/German Child, by I. Caroline Crocker and Meta A. Evenbly

When We Had Wings. The Gripping Story of an Orphan in Janusz Korczak's Orphanage. A Historical Novel, by Tami Shem-Tov

Jacob's Courage. Romance and Survival amidst the Horrors of War, by Charles S. Weinblatt

Join the AP Review Team

Reviews are very important in a world dominated by the social media. Feedback for Holocaust books is more than just a customer review; it also shows the relevance and importance of such books in today's society.

Please go over to the AmsterdamPublishers.com website (top of page) if you want to join the *AP review team,* showing **at least one review on Amazon** for one of our books. You will get updates about new releases and will get the chance to read and review.

Printed in the USA
CPSIA information can be obtained
at www.ICGtesting.com
LVHW040149221123
764347LV00062B/1113/J